# LATIN MOON
# IN MANHATTAN

# Books by Jaime Manrique

FICTION
*El cadáver de papá*
*Columbian Gold*
*Latin Moon in Manhattan*
*Twilight at the Equator*

POETRY
*Los adoradores de la luna*
*Scarecrow* (chapbook)
*My Night with Federico García Lorca*
*Tarzan, My Body, Christopher Columbus*

CRITICISM
*Notas de cine: Confesiones de un crítico amateur*

MEMOIR
*Eminent Maricones: Arenas, Lorca, Puig, and Me*

# LATIN MOON
# IN MANHATTAN

A Novel

JAIME MANRIQUE

The University of Wisconsin Press

The University of Wisconsin Press
1930 Monroe Street
Madison, Wisconsin 53711

www.wisc.edu/wisconsinpress/

3 Henrietta Street
London WC2E 8LU, England

5     4     3     2     1

Printed in the United States of America

Library of Congress Cataloging-in-Publication Data
Manrique Ardila, Jaime, 1949–
Latin moon in Manhattan : a novel / Jaime Manrique
p.      cm.
ISBN 0-299-18754-3 (paper)
1. New York (N.Y.)—Fiction. 2. Hispanic Americans—Fiction.
3. Manhattan (New York, N.Y.)—Fiction. I. Title.
PS3563.A573 L38      2003
813'.54—dc21      2002075666

# Acknowledgments

My thanks to The Virginia Center for the Creative Arts for a residency in which this novel evolved into its final shape; to Laura Segal for helping me translate the tango lyrics and, most importantly, for the gift of Mr. O'Donnell; to Bill Sullivan for his unflagging enthusiasm; to the Ash Wednesday group, where I first workshopped the manuscript; and, most respectfully, to Helen O'Donnell, in memoriam.

For Tom and Elaine Colchie

# LATIN MOON
# IN MANHATTAN

# PART ONE

AND IT WAS A LONG, LONE
SHADOW.

José Asunción Silva

# 1

# Little Colombia, Jackson Heights

After it leaves Manhattan, the number seven train becomes an elevated, and crosses a landscape of abandoned railroad tracks, dilapidated buildings and, later, a conglomerate of ugly factories that blow serpentine plumes of gaudy poisonous smoke. As the train journeys deeper into Queens, the Manhattan skyscrapers in the distance resemble monuments of an enchanted place—ancient Baghdad, or even the Land of Oz. The sun, setting behind the towers of the World Trade Center, burnishes the sky with a warm orange glow and the windows of the towers look like gold-leafed entrances to huge hives bursting with honey.

Riding the number seven train to Jackson Heights, I thought of our immigration to the United States eighteen years ago. But "immigration" is too big a word to describe what happened. Let's just say we moved from Bogotá, Colombia, to Jackson Heights, Queens—from one cocaine capital to another, the main difference being that the former sits ten thousand feet up in the Andes, while the latter is a mere twenty-minute train ride from Manhattan.

I finished high school and college in Queens and it wasn't until years later, when I settled in Times Square, that I finally felt I was living in a foreign country. What I had observed through the years was that while Queens became more prosperous and upscale, the city of New York more and more resembled a third world capital; there was a wide—and ever widening—gap between rich and poor, and the streets teemed with crazies, junkies, homeless people, street urchins, hustlers, hookers, and pickpockets, just like in Bogotá. Since I had arrived in America, the human traffic on the number seven train had also changed; there were still a few blacks going to Queens, but now the Asians were just as numerous as the South Americans. The nicely dressed, well-scrubbed people riding in my car looked like solid, hard-working, law-abiding Republicans. That, plus the lack of graffiti, made the Queens-bound trains different from the Brooklyn and Bronx lines.

I was so engrossed in my observations that I almost missed my stop. Ninetieth Street, with its garish shops, vegetable and root stands, and South American eateries—everything in a small, Lilliputian scale—looks unreal, like a movie set. All the signs are in Spanish, and the pedestrians talk in the various regional accents of Colombia.

I walked under the elevated, and turned right at Eighty-seventh Street. I began to metamorphose; the closer I got to my mother's house, the more Colombian I became. Intense cravings for foods that were unavailable to me in the city—such as *ajiaco, arepa de huevo, morcillas, chicharrones*—awoke in me. The tree-shaded street was getting dark and, although this was hardly the country, I felt light-years away from the overheated cement of Forty-second Street. I passed pretty two-story houses with attics and gabled roofs, cypresses on their lawns, rose gardens in bloom, and sidewalks spattered with dog shit. It was hard to believe that just a few blocks away there was a world of drugs and crime in which coke-crazed Colombians iced each other in the most vicious, post-modern ways.

My mother's house was in darkness, except for the light above the side entrance that led to the kitchen. This was the house that Victor, my mother's present husband, gave her as a wedding present. Victor, a Sicilian who worked all his life for the mob and Queens politicians, had supported my mother nicely by running numbers until he developed Alzheimer's disease and was put in an institution. Now my mother lives alone, except for the periods when my nephew Eugene runs away from my sister's apartment.

I climbed the steps to the landing outside the kitchen and was about to open the door—which my mother still left open after all these years—when I felt something rubbing against my ankles. It was Puss, one of Mother's cats. Since her cats were not allowed inside the house, I sat on the steps to play with him. Puss was old and had lost a lot of his thick, tawny coat, but his tail was still beautiful and soft, like an ostrich feather.

"Hi, Puss. How're you doing, you old cat? Where is Me-shu?" I said, looking around for Mother's other cat, who was shy. Although Puss had lived all his life outside—maybe because of it—he craved human affection. He purred and purred, lying at my feet, while I scratched him behind the ears. He was wearing the flea collar I had given him a couple of months ago, but he had fleas, and his hair was so matted in places that he looked like a Rastafarian.

It was dark now, and the pertinacious mosquitoes were determined to get their evening meal. I got up, and as I turned the doorknob, I could hear Simón Bolívar screeching inside, "Who is it?" I tensed up; I intensely dislike my mother's parrot. Turning on the kitchen light, I saw to my relief that Simón Bolívar was caged. "Hello, hello, hello," he shrieked stupidly.

"Hi, Simón," I acknowledged him so he would shut up.

On the kitchen table Mother had left me a note: "I went to play bingo. Will be back late. Your dinner is on the stove. Love, Mother."

I was hungry so I uncovered the pans: Mother had cooked tongue stew, coconut rice with raisins, and fried ripe plantains. Everything was still warm. Serving myself, I sat down to eat. I picked up *El Espectador,* a Bogotá newspaper Mother bought every day, and began to peruse the headlines. Although I no longer feel very connected to Colombian life, I still read the newspapers and magazines Mother buys because, invariably, the first question I'm always asked by people I meet is, "How are things in Colombia?" Consequently, even though I'm an American citizen now, I keep abreast of the latest developments in the war against drugs and guerrilla insurgency down home.

There was a pitcher full of *peto* on the table, a Colombian corn drink; I poured myself a glass and started sipping it, tasting the cinnamon and nutmeg with which my mother peppered the drink.

Suddenly Simón Bolívar said in Spanish, "Long live the Liberal party!" He sat on his perch, staring at me uncannily with his bright yellow eyes.

"Shut up," I said, and threatened to fling the remnants of my *peto* at him. This created pandemonium. Thinking he was about to get a bath, Simón started flapping his brightly colored wings.

At my grandmother's death, my mother had inherited two ancestral avocado trees and a parrot. Simón had thus immigrated to the States ten years ago and I used to tease my mother that he was the only Colombian in Jackson Heights with a green card.

Imitating Flaubert's Felicité, my mother fell in love with the parrot. Some years back, in early spring, she placed his cage out in the backyard to give the bird some sun, and somehow Simón Bolívar managed to escape. Mother was sure he had been stolen, though why anyone would have wanted to steal such an obstreperous animal is beyond my understanding. Mother cried and cried and stopped eating and when these measures didn't bring Simón back, she built a shrine to San Martín de Porres in her living room and prayed to the Peruvian saint for the return of her parrot. Months later, a storm awakened her late at night. She claims she saw light streaming through the curtains of her bedroom window. She knew San Martín had answered her prayer, and when she opened the windows she found Simón Bolívar seeking shelter from the rain in the cypress tree. Since that time, Mother has declared him a holy parrot who has been to heaven and back. It was hard for me to believe that this was God's envoy as he sat on his perch screaming the sickeningly hackneyed words of some Julio Iglesias song.

I looked away, ignoring his nonsense. I had lost my appetite; it was too warm in the kitchen to eat. I set aside the newspaper. Simón Bolívar had quieted down, but suddenly I heard him screech, "Who's there?" I heard noises outside. The doorknob turned, the door opened, and a pair of huge decomposing Reeboks burst into the kitchen.

"Sammy, dude, what's happening?" my nephew Gene greeted me.

"Hi, Gene," I replied.

Gene sat at the table, lit a Marlboro and started whiffling clouds of smoke. He was seventeen and already six foot two, with the face of a baby Gulliver. Gene glanced suspiciously at the food on my plate. "Is that tongue?" He indicated the stew on my plate, making a face.

"It's better than hamburger, which is probably all you eat."

"Look, Sammy, I'm an American, not a Colombian, and Americans don't eat tongue."

"That just shows what a hick you are. In French cuisine tongue is considered a great delicacy."

"Oh, yeah? But we're in America not in France."

"We're in Jackson Heights, Colombia," I said.

"But don't let me spoil your chow," he added magnanimously. "It's cool with me, man. If you want to eat tongue, go right ahead."

"I've had enough. So you're living here now?"

"I guess so. School's out."

"Are you getting along with Wilbrajan?"

"Oh yeah, everything's cool."

"Is she working?"

"She's singing tangos at the Rose Saigon. The Japanese love tangos."

"But Saigon is not in Japan."

Gene shrugged. "What do I know; I just finished the tenth grade. I like to come here to keep grandma company. She's lonely, and she's getting old."

Guiltily, I said, "That's really nice of you."

"She nags like hell, though."

"You know what the French say: 'If you can't send them the devil, send them an old woman.' "

Gene smiled. "You're so mean."

I got up to turn on the air conditioner.

"Better not," Gene warned. "Grandma doesn't like it on unless it's above one hundred degrees. She's pretty nuts about conserving energy."

"You want to go outside and sit in the garden?"

As we were getting ready to leave the kitchen, Simón Bolívar, pissed off that were leaving him behind, started a racket.

"Shut up, asshole," Gene ordered him.

"Asshole, asshole, asshole," Simón Bolívar echoed as we stepped outside.

"Maybe I should leave the door open and let the cats in. I'm sure they'd love him for dinner. What do you think?" I asked, grinning.

"The cats are scared shitless of him. That parrot could scare a Colombian pusher away. He's the meanest mother I know."

We walked to the back of the house where Mother had her vegetable and flower gardens and sat down on the wooden chairs next to the barbecue grill. Above us was a patch of open sky. The night was clear and cool, and we could see a spattering of stars and a crescent moon. Pointing to the sky, I said, "That's the North Star over there, see it? If you ever get lost at sea just follow it and you'll reach land."

"You know the weirdest shit," Gene snorted. "Thanks for the tip, but I hate the sea. All that activity makes me crazy." There was a pause, which Gene broke by saying, "I haven't seen you in a long time. What's up?"

"Everything's okay," I said, not wanting to sound too pessimistic in front of a teenager. "I've been thinking about going back to school to finish my Ph.D."

Gene chortled. "Sammy, you have more degrees than a thermometer. Why don't you finish your book? That'd make you feel better." He referred to my Christopher Columbus epic, which I had been writing for some years.

"I haven't written anything new in some time. You know, one day it occurred to me that I couldn't go on writing it until I saw one of the caravels in which Columbus traveled."

"What's that?"

"You know, one of the ships he sailed to the New World in. There's a replica of one in the Barcelona harbor and somehow I feel I have to go see it before I can finish the poem," I concluded.

"And when are you going?"

"Soon," I said cryptically.

"Sammy, why don't you write something good?"

I bristled at his criticism. "What do you mean 'something good?' I want to write a great epic poem."

"That's what I mean. When was the last time there was a best-seller epic poem? Write something like . . . like . . . a story about teenagers. In English. You know, I could help you with it. What you have to do is write something that English teachers like so that they recommend it to the students. I'll guarantee you it'll make a million bucks."

"You write the teenager story, okay, and I'll write whatever I want to write."

"No need to get sore, man. I'm not gonna write anything. I just want to be an actor."

"Like Rocky Rambo, I suppose."

"Fuck no. Like Marlon Brando. Man, he's neat as shit. Did you see him in *The Wild One*? You haven't? I've seen it thirty-seven times. The way he rides that motorcycle all dressed up in black leather and chains. He's so cool, so radical—a real bad dude. He's awesome," Gene sighed, his face glowing in the dark. "I'm gonna buy me a motorcycle," he vowed.

"I wish you wouldn't; motorcycles are extremely dangerous. People get killed on those things all the time."

"You're so uncool; you don't know anything. More people get killed going to the post office, at least here in Jackson Heights."

"Who's giving you the money to buy a motorcycle?"

"I got a summer job. I'm going to save all the money I make, and in the fall I'll buy it."

"What kind of a job?"

"Making . . . deliveries . . . here in Queens. Hey, you want to get high?" Gene pulled a fat joint from his pack of Marlboros.

"I quit smoking," I said. Recently I had come to the sudden realization that it was because of drugs and alcohol that I had dropped out of graduate school and the reason why in the past ten years I had accomplished so little.

Gene lit the joint and inhaled deeply. "You want to smoke this," he said melodramatically, holding the smoke in his lungs. "This is great Colombian shit; this kind of thing never hits the streets of Manhattan. The Colombians smoke it all as soon as it comes in."

"Well, a puff won't do me any harm, I suppose."

Gene was right; this was great pot. It was like pouring hot water in a glass full of ice—I melted right away. Yet the sense of guilt gnawed at my conscience. I said, "Gene, I hope you're not into heavy drugs."

"No, man. Rusty and the Boners—you've got to meet them sometime; they're my best friends—do all kinds of shit. I just smoke pot, and drink beer on the weekends and do a line of coke once in a while."

I was horrified. "Gene, I didn't start doing anything until I was twenty-one."

"Yeah, well, that was a long time ago, right? You're old, Sammy; you know that."

"If you're lucky, some day you'll be my age," I said, pissed off, as if I were putting a curse on him. "Promise me you'll never do crack."

"You think I'm fucking crazy? I don't wanna get fucked up; I wanna be a famous actor."

Let's hope his thespian instincts will win out in the long run, I thought. We finished smoking the joint; I felt as if I were tripping.

"What are you doing tonight?" Gene asked.

"Nothing; just hanging out. Want to go see a movie?"

"Maybe tomorrow. I'm going to a party. Want to come along?"

"What's the occasion?" I asked, although I had no intention of going to a party with a bunch of drug-addicted teenagers.

"You know, girls, beer. We smoke jays and listen to Sinead O'Connor." Gene stood up. "Okay, Sammy, I've got to go. I promised the Boners I'd be there by now."

"What kind of name is that—the Boners?"

"They're twins. You have to meet them. They're real sleaze balls, but I know you'll like them. They're cool and neat as hell. They've done so many drugs they're all skin and bones. The Boners, you got it now?"

"I got it."

"If you get bored, just go by the Rose Saigon. Mom goes on around midnight. Okay, catch you later."

"Have a nice time and don't get too wasted," I said, feeling old. Gene disappeared into the darkness, and I was left by myself, pleasantly stoned. I thought about uncles and nephews, and, specifically, I thought about my Uncle Hernán, whom I worshiped in my adolescence. Twelve years before, he had died in a plane accident. In the sixties, he became mixed up with radical politics in Colombia and fled to Venezuela when the military got on his case. There, he go a job working in the diamond mines near Ciudad Bolívar. One Christmas, he was on his way to visit my grandparents when a bomb went off in the plane, blowing it to pieces and all that they could find of him was his arm.

The last time I had seen Uncle Hernán I was around Gene's age. That was the year my mother came to New York to see about settling here. She had dismantled our home in Bogotá and my sister and I were sent to stay with our maternal grandparents in the country. Uncle Hernán was twenty-two then, the youngest of my uncles. Although I had many cousins, he felt a special kinship for me. Every day after lunch he'd pack his rifle and I my fishing gear and we'd ride to Las Marías, my grandfather's farm a few miles outside of town. Uncle Hernán taught me to ride horses, burros and mules, to lasso cows and milk them, to fish and swim in the ponds of the Magdalena and César rivers. He read books about Marxism and the Cuban and Russian revolutions and was passionate about radical politics. Yet hunting was his favorite occupation. Every afternoon, he'd hunt ducks and other birds, and each night after supper he'd drive the jeep down to the savannah, where enormous termite colonies loomed, spectral and lunar in the darkness. There he'd hunt deer, tigers, armadillos, and wild boar.

My male cousins made fun of how clumsy I was at all the country activities for boys, but Uncle Hernán was patient. Sometimes, he'd take a break from tracking prey and, finding a shady tree on the plain, he'd read to me about Lenin or Trotsky. But that December, I had turned sixteen, and he informed me that the time had come for me to visit the town's whorehouse. The particular afternoon I remember so vividly, he had been looking for game without success and we had wandered far away from the farmhouse, arriving at the foothills of the Sierra Nevada. It was getting late, and in the mountains it was much cooler than in the town. The brooks and streams we waded through were cold and clear, and their sandy beds glittered with gold. In my grandfather's youth, this had been a gold-mining region and there was still gold to be found, but not in quantities sufficient to exploit commercially. The hills we ascended were paved with the palest green grass; the mango and ciruela trees, upon which fed flocks of parrots, macaws, and parakeets, and bands of boisterous monkeys, were now below us in the plain surrounding the river. Occasionally we ran into stray cows and menacing bulls and shy wild horses, but Uncle Hernán seemed pretty sure of the direction in which we were heading.

I was beginning to get tired of carrying his heavy rifle, as I always did, but I felt it would be unmanly to complain. Now we had an unobstructed view of the snowy peaks of the Sierra Nevada as they caught the reflection of the setting sun. The world was growing still, hushed. We started descending into an open *potrero* of verdant pastures with high hills on all sides fencing it in. At its center was a shallow pond where scores of burros were drinking and playing in the water. Above them, rainbow-colored dragonflies darted about. The burros seemed young, but tame and friendly. Uncle Hernán approached them cautiously, talking to them in low, silky tones, patting their backs and stroking their long ears. *"Burra, burrita,"* he said, separating two of them and patting their behinds until they had wandered meters away from the rest of the herd. Then Uncle Hernán stood behind one of the burras and lifted her tail, putting his fingers inside her vulva. He motioned me to do the same with the other donkey which stood still, expectantly. When I lifted her tail, little white gnats flew into the saffron light of sunset. It was smelly down there. The rims of the vulva were pinkish and ivory, and the tips of my fingers felt warm and gluey. A few inches inside the vagina a flexible but resistant membrane stopped my fingers from exploring further. Even though the animal seemed to enjoy it, I was afraid of pursuing this activity. I saw Uncle Hernán unzip his pants. With his huge dick sticking out, he approached me. Not understanding what was happening, I was seized with terror and started to shake. He motioned for me to move aside, and penetrated the burra once, twice, rocking back and forth. The burra stamped one of her hind hoofs on the ground and grunted, as if she were pleased. Uncle Hernán grinned. "Okay, Sammy, she's all yours: a virgin no more."

He hurried over to the other burra, which had stood motionless, waiting for him, and penetrated her. I imitated his bumping motions and was about to get an erection when several male burros with their black, baseball-bat-sized members, began circling the herd at a gallop and braying hysterically. I was afraid that they were angry and were getting ready to attack us. My cock kept falling out of the enormous vagina. Soon, Uncle Hernán was in a frenzy, eyes closed, his buttocks pushing in and out, in and out; he moaned and cried in pleasure when he finished. Then he rested his head on the burra's rump and embraced her around her haunches. He remained that way, panting, until he stepped backward and collapsed on the grass, his penis limp but still large, his pants tangled around his boots. I walked over to the burra he had just fucked, and what seemed like large quantities of semen oozed out of her vagina. Becoming aroused, I put my hard cock inside her.

A car door slamming brought me back to reality. Mother was back home from her bingo game.

*"Buenas noches, mi amor,"* Mother called out to her friend as the car pulled away.

# 2

## Volver

I had locked up Mr. O'Donnell in the bathroom by mistake. At first, he sat behind the door, patiently waiting for me to realize it. As time passed, he became anxious and started scratching the door and pacing the room restlessly. Getting frantic, he jumped from the bathtub to the sink, and, losing his balance, fell into the toilet, which automatically flushed. Tail first, Mr. O'Donnell began to disappear. . . . I woke up panting, the palms of my hands clammy. I sat in bed. It was true I was worried about my cat, Mr. O'Donnell, but I was sure the nightmare had been caused by my mother's Colombian cuisine.

A gentle breeze blew through the white lace curtains and through them I caught a glimpse of a sunny day and a cloudless sky. After many months in Manhattan where I had only seen concrete and glass, the deep green branches of the tree by my window had a soothing effect on me.

Although I had left home over ten years ago, nothing had changed in my room. The old Janis Joplin poster hung over my desk, the colors faded, Janis looking more ghostly than ever. The black Olivetti typewriter I had brought with me from Colombia now prehistoric. No new books had been added to the bookshelves, but the volumes were dustless and neatly arranged. Becoming nostalgic for my adolescence, I longed to be sick, to surrender to an asthma attack and to have the course of my life stopped. I longed for the freedom I had experienced during those times: no school, no duties, long stays in bed reading *Crime and Punishment, Wuthering Heights,* and other morbid books, and having my mother make baby pigeon soup for me and feed me spoonfuls of hot, buttery carrots and potatoes puree.

I could have stayed in bed indulging myself with these reveries, but the smells of *arepas, chicharrones* and *tostones* traveled up from the kitchen, their potent aromas luring me like a siren's song. I had decided to visit my friend Bobby. Perhaps this was the main reason for my trip to Queens this weekend. Bobby was deteriorating very fast and he was dying. I got out of bed, showered and shaved before going downstairs to meet my mother.

In the kitchen, a Spanish radio station was playing a Gardel program. I could hear my mother, singing along with Gardel, the lyrics of *"Yira, Yira":*

> When luck is rotten
> Laughing and laughing
> While you lie in the streets.
> When you're down in the gutter
> Lost, in despair;
> When you've lost even hope
> And you're drinking the dregs,
> When your last cent is gone
> And you're looking for crumbs
> To keep you alive
> The world couldn't care less.
> Yira, yira.

It wasn't exactly the most cheerful music to listen to first thing in the morning, and Simón Bolívar, who was particularly excited by Mother's tango renditions, squealed along, *"Yira, yira, yira, yira."* On the other hand, it was better to listen to such existential angst in the morning. I could see how listening to these tangos late at night could drive one to suicide. My mother and Gardel were reaching a crescendo:

> Even if life breaks you up
> And the pain doesn't end
> Don't wait for a handout, or a favor,
> or friends.

"Sammy," Mother cried, stopping her singing. "Did you sleep well?" she added in Spanish, rushing over to kiss me. "I've been making your breakfast."

There was enough food on the table for a baseball team. "How are you, Mother?" I asked, sitting at the table and pouring myself a cup of chocolate. The pile of *arepas* in a straw basket was warm and tender.

"I'm as good as could be expected, considering everything. How's Mr. MacDonald?" she asked.

It was nice of her to inquire after my cat, but it mortified me that after many years she hadn't taken the trouble to get his name correctly. "His name is Mr. O'Donnell. He's the same, I guess."

"No wonder he's sick, cooped up in that apartment all the time. Look at my cats, they've lived all their lives outside and they're as healthy as can be."

"Mother," I said calmly, concentrating on my breathing, trying to muster a serenity I never had when we conversed. "First, I cannot let him out in Manhattan; he'd be killed in a minute. Second, he has an enlarged heart, and that's a congenital condition." As I finished saying this, I realized the absurdity of trying to explain anything rationally to a Colombian.

"Anyway, it's unnatural to love a cat that way," Mother said, baiting me. "That's what happens to men when they don't get married and have a family."

I felt like saying, Oh yeah? And why is it more *natural* to love a stupid parrot? But I held back. I didn't want to get upset before breakfast. Besides, I had been in her presence barely five minutes and had the rest of the weekend to fight.

She placed a tray of pork *chicharrones* on the table. "It's been fifty years since Gardel died," she said dreamily, changing the subject, "but for my money he sings better every day."

I cut open an *arepa* and buttered it. "Ummm, it's delicious," I commented, since I didn't feel like discussing Gardel. Half-closing her eyes, Mother hummed to herself the last bars of *"Yira, Yira."*

Waiting for the song to end, I picked up one of the *chicharrones* and bit off a juicy piece of pork meat. As I chewed, I studied my mother who was sitting next to me, her legs crossed. Even this early in the morning she wore a ton of jewelry, Colombian style: her wedding band, her heart-shaped emerald ring, gold bracelets, a gold chain with an emerald and diamond crucifix, plus her diamond earrings. I wondered if she ever took these things off. As usual, her auburn hair was made up and lacquered, her fingernails manicured and painted a transparent pink. She wore a Mexican cotton blouse with short sleeves, khaki bermudas, and open-toed blue cotton slippers. She had turned seventy in the spring, but with the years she had grown svelte. It bothered me that I got a kick out of how nice she still looked.

Mother selected a *chicharrón* and took a dainty bite. Her wonderfully lustrous maple sugar skin was smooth, unwrinkled, and the only places her age showed were on the back of her hands, and her neck and thighs, where her flesh sagged a bit. When she married Victor, over ten years ago, mother had the bags under her eyes removed and this procedure had considerably enlarged her marvelous hazel eyes so that at first she looked spooked, as if she had just seen a ghost. But with the passage of time, the eyes became more natural-looking and attractive. The Gardel program came to an end and Mother got up to turn off the radio. Then she got a pitcher of *guanabana* juice out of the refrigerator and poured me a glassful. I realized these gargantuan breakfasts Mother subjected me to were a continuation of my grandparents' breakfast table, where meat, fish, wild game, *suero,* butter and cheese, breads, *arepas,* and *empanadas,* fried plantains and *yucca,* papaya, mango, pineapple juice, coffee, chocolate, and *kumis* were the fare.

I was finishing my first cup of deliciously brewed Colombian coffee, when the phone rang.

"You'd better get it; it's for you," Mother informed me.

"*Lorito real, lorito real,*" Simón Bolívar twaddled, excited by the phone.

"It's Carmen Elvira," Mother went on. "I told her you'd be up by eleven and to call you then."

"Why is Carmen Elvira calling me?"

"She wants to invite you to become a member of their literary society, The Colombian Parnassus. Please, Santiago, don't humiliate me. She's one of my best friends. So please accept her invitation. It's a great honor."

The phone kept ringing and Simón Bolívar continued screaming his nonsense and flapping his wings.

"Please, Santiago, it will be the last thing I'll ever ask of you. She knows you're here. If you don't pick up, she'll come over."

"This is blackmail," I protested, picking up the receiver. "Hello," I said with great trepidation.

"*Hola, Sammy. Es Carmen Elvira.*"

"Hello, Carmen Elvira. How are you?"

"Fine, thank you, honey, and you?" she said in her polite *cachaco* manner. "I'm calling to give you great news; you're being invited to become a member of The Colombian Parnassus. *Enhorabuena!* Congratulations," she added in English.

I couldn't feign surprise, or happiness for that matter. But I saw Mother getting up and approaching me, so I said, "Thank you very much; I'm honored." Mother smiled at me.

"I thought you'd be. Anyway, we plan to induct you this afternoon. We're meeting at Olga's home around 12:30, American time. You know where she lives, don't you?"

"Yes," I said grimly.

"Well, *cariño,* it's been a real pleasure talking to you. Say hello to Lucy," she said, referring to my mother.

"Thank you very much. I will."

After I hung up, Mother rushed over and kissed me on both cheeks. Taking advantage of the proximity, Simón Bolívar bit me on the shoulder.

"Ouch," I complained. "Mother, he bit me."

"God, you're sensitive," she said. "He pecked you affectionately, that's all."

"Jesus, Mother!" I burst out. "What have you made me do? And the gall of that woman! She expects me to show up at 12:30 and I just found out about it. What if I had made plans?" Feeling all sorts of emotions welling up, I picked up an *arepa* and started gobbling it down.

"What plans? People in Queens don't make plans. And don't stuff yourself. They're making a delicious lunch just for you. So, please, Sammy, please be a gentleman and eat everything they serve you. Show them I've taught you some manners."

"I refuse to eat iguana stew!"

"I don't know when you became such a squeamish gringo; you used to love iguana eggs, and you ate plenty of iguana when you visited your grandparents in the country."

"I never ate iguana," I protested. "I loathe iguana eggs. They smell worse than a skunk's fart."

"Iguana stew," Mother said sadistically, "and rattlesnake *sancocho,* and barbecued sloth, and alligator tail fricasse. You ate all those things. And monkey brains soufflé."

"I'm going to puke if you don't stop."

Simón Bolívar leaped off my mother's shoulder onto the table and scurried toward me. I hopped off my seat. "Get that fucking bird away from me before I wring his neck!"

"Don't you dare use that language in front of me, Santiago! And don't talk about him like that. He understands you. He speaks."

"He doesn't speak; he imitates sounds."

"He's bilingual," Mother said. Looking dejected she stood up. "Come here, Simón. He wants you in prison. Come here, my darling," she purred, offering him her wrist. "What's going to happen to you after I'm gone?" Tenderly she stroked his feathers. "I only pray to God that when my time's up, he'll take you with me. Who's going to take care of you after I'm gone, my love?"

I shuddered. I knew that parrots lived to be a hundred years or more, so in all likelihood he'd outlive my mother and, with my luck, probably me too. "Mother, cut it out," I begged her. "Put that bird in his cage. You know he hates me and is going to bite me first chance he gets."

"*Lorito real, lorito real,*" the cunning parrot protested, looking like an innocent.

When the parrot was safely behind bars, I sat down to the table to finish my *guanabana* juice.

"It would be nice if you went to the nursing home to see Victor," Mother said, referring to my stepfather. "I told him you were coming this weekend, and you know he likes you very much. He'd be so happy to see you."

"I don't know. It's so depressing. The last time I was there he didn't recognize me at all."

"I think the doctors are wrong," she said. "Just because he can't talk doesn't mean he doesn't know who we are. I see how his eyes light up when I visit him and tell him stories. And you should feel grateful to Victor. It was he who put you through college. I couldn't have done it on my own."

"I know that, Mother, and I like him a lot, but what's the point? He's a vegetable; I'm going to skip visiting him this time. I have other plans."

"Like what?" she asked, displeased.

"I want to visit Bobby."

Mother stared at me. I realized that Bobby too was a vegetable. On my last visit, he hadn't recognized me either.

"I visit him at least once a week."

"That's very nice of you, Mother."

"It could happen in my own family, too, so I'm getting prepared. But it breaks my heart, Santiago. You know I've loved Bobby since the two of you met in Colegio Americano in Barranquilla. He always called me his second mother. By the way, Leticia finally came."

"When?"

"About a week ago. I guess all those letters I wrote her worked. Did you know she refuses to touch him? She won't even go into his room. She stands by the door, with her hands behind her back, and talks to him as if he were a baby, but she won't touch him with a ten-foot pole."

"What a hideous woman; that's horrible."

"I tried to explain to her that AIDS can't be caught by casual contact. To show her, I sat on Bobby's bed and combed his hair and arranged his pillows. Santiago," Mother said beseechingly, "why don't you get married? Why don't you marry Claudia? She's always been in love with you. I know. Paulina told me so. And she's rich," Mother threw in to tempt me.

Although Mother knows perfectly well what my sexual preference is, ever since Bobby had come down with AIDS she started an insane campaign to try to get me married to my childhood friend Claudia Urrutia, hoping perhaps I'd be spared Bobby's fate.

Deciding to ignore the marriage talk, I said, "Sure, I'd be rich like them if I were in the drug trade."

Mother made an angry face. "They're not in the drug business. How can you say that about Paulina? She's my best friend; she's practically my sister," she said, sincerely outraged.

"Mother, come off it. How can you be so naïve? Okay, so they're not in the drug trade. Then how did they make all those millions?"

"Working, of course. How else?"

"I never heard of anyone in that family working. Besides, nobody makes that kind of dough working. They own mansions all over the world, and planes and yachts and Mercedes Benzes and . . ."

"Are you saying Paulina and Claudia are in the mafia? Is that what you're saying?"

"Maybe they aren't personally," I relented. "But all the men in the family sure are. Everyone in Jackson Heights—except you, of course—knows that."

"Claudia is an architect, Santiago. She went to jail."

"Yale, Mother," I corrected her for the millionth time. "Anyway, she's never practiced, and she lives like a queen. . . ."

"She loves you, and that ought to be enough for you."

"Mother, Claudia is a . . ." dyke, I was going to add, but I knew this would just make matters worse. "I think she's nuts."

"Well, she's a little odd."

"A little odd, ha! That's got to be the understatement of the millennium. Is that what you call a girl who rides a motorcycle and wears a helmet all the time? She'd be the perfect wife for Gene," I chuckled. "He'd love to get a hold of her motorcycles."

"You and your sister are going to kill me," Mother said pathetically. "Maybe God is punishing me for having been such a bad mother. But Santiago, you're intelligent and you should know better." She paused, in pain, looking like a Greek tragedienne. "You won't marry, and your sister goes through men like through a box of Kleenex. And that poor boy, your nephew. What's going to happen to him after I'm gone?"

And don't forget Simón Bolívar, I was going to say but refrained myself. I started to shake, so I got up. I had to get away from that kitchen as soon as possible.

Mother got up and approached me. "Where are you going? Isn't it too early to leave now?"

I backed away. "I want to go for a walk; I want to see the roses in bloom," I lied.

"Make sure you go by Romelda's house. Her yellow roses this year are divine."

"Okay, I will."

"Don't be too late for dinner. Don't have any snacks after lunch and spoil your appetite. I'm making your favorite tonight."

"What's that?"

"Pigs feet and chick peas."

"Oh, great."

"Sammy," mother began sweetly, "if you don't have plans for tonight, why don't you take Claudia to the Saigon Rose to hear Wilbrajan."

"I hadn't thought about it."

"Well, think about it. I would love to go too; that is, if you don't mind."

"I got to go, Mother. I'll see you later," I said, and left the kitchen.

It was a lovely summer day. I put on my sunglasses and stood still, taking a whiff of the crisp, balmy air. Suddenly, in a flash, I saw myself as a child, walking with my mother along the beach at Puerto Colombia, digging for coquinas. Even here in Queens, the air smelled strongly of that ocean, because it wasn't New York's Atlantic I smelled, but Barranquilla's Caribbean: salty, dry, scorching, charged with the scent of honeysuckle. I descended the steps to the driveway and started walking toward the street. Feeling ornery yet amused, I said to myself, "I can't believe my luck. Here I am, on my way to becoming an immortal."

# 3

## Colombian Queens

I had known Carmen Elvira and Olga since our immigration to Jackson Heights; but Irma, the other member of the Colombian Parnassus, was a more recent acquaintance. They published *Colombian Queens,* a monthly magazine that my mother always saved for me. It was distributed free, financed through ads taken out by Colombian restaurants, travel agencies, and grocery stores in the Jackson Heights area. Carmen Elvira wrote the gossip column; Olga was in charge of the horoscope and the Colombian recipes, and Irma, who worked as a teller in a Wall Street bank, wrote the business column. The rest of the articles were reprints, exclusively about Colombia. The middle section of the magazine—which was the bulk of it—was packed with photographs of Colombian show biz personalities in the New York area (the women usually in bathing suits), and pictures of people recently deceased and girls in their *quinces,* etc.

On more than one occasion, Carmen Elvira had invited me to submit a section of my Columbus poem for consideration, but I had repeatedly turned down her request. Without consulting me, five poems of my book *Lirio del Alba* had been reprinted with many typographical mistakes. For a long time after that, I forbade Mother to mention Carmen Elvira's name in my presence.

I was about to ring the bell of Olga's home when the door opened and the hostess greeted me with kisses on both cheeks. The pleasant smell of burnt eucalyptus hit my nostrils. Walking down the wide-planked hall carpeted with cowhides, I experienced déjà vu: I felt as if I were in a house in Bogotá. Every detail was Colombian— the furniture, the pictures on the walls, even the plastic flowers.

I greeted Carmen Elvira and Irma, who were sitting on a couch drinking *tinto,* the espresso-like demitasse that Colombians swill nonstop. The air-conditioning was on and the curtains drawn, so that the room was in semidarkness, giving the scene a vaguely conspiratorial atmosphere. The three women, who ranged in age from their late forties to midfifties, differed sharply in appearance: Carmen Elvira, who was from the Cauca Valley, was tall and her complexion and features Mediterranean in color and shape; Irma, who was from Pasto, was on the short side, stocky, and her features were Incan. She wore her hair in a crew cut and was dressed in bermudas and sandals.

Olga, who was from Bogotá, was extremely petite and a natural blond. She was dressed in a sleeveless white cotton dress and wore high heels. It was spooky how, because of their close association, they seemed, at least in spirit, three weird sisters.

I was offered, and accepted, a *tinto.* Without asking for my preference, the hostess put two heaping spoonfuls of sugar in the inch-and-a-half cup. I decided to be gracious and drink it this way for fear of being labeled a gringo. The three women looked at me with curious but benign expressions.

"May I smoke a cigarette?" I asked in Spanish.

"*Sí, sí, por supuesto,*" Olga said in her tinny voice, pushing an ashtray on the coffee table in my direction. It was made of red clay and had the Colombian flag painted on it.

"We don't smoke anymore," Carmen Elvira said. "The group's New Year's resolution was to give up smoking."

"Thank God and the Holy Virgin," Irma said, and crossed herself.

Feeling like a criminal, I puffed on my Newport.

"How's Lucy?" Olga asked.

"She's fine, thank you," I said. Then, remembering I was among Colombians, I asked, "And how's your husband?"

For the next five minutes we inquired about each other's parents, husbands, brothers and sisters, children, and even pets. By then I had finished my cigarette and the sickeningly sweet *tinto*. It occurred to me that good manners required that I acknowledge the dubious honor of being elected a member of The Colombian Parnassus.

"Don't mention it," beamed Carmen Elvira as the unacknowledged spokesperson of the group. "We have to move with the times, and welcome the new generation."

"Personally, I'm not very fond of modern poetry. I prefer the old poets like Carranza. Ah, those sonnets. Do you love Carranza?" Irma asked me.

"Yes, I do." Like all Colombian children I had learned Carranza's poems in school, and did, indeed, favor his exuberant romanticism.

"The Sonnet to Teresa," Olga sighed, full of nostalgia for the poetry of the past.

Olga and Carmen Elvira looked at Irma beseechingly. Her expression becoming devout, Irma began reciting the sonnet:

> *Teresa, en cuya frente el cielo empieza,*
> *como el aroma en la sien de la flor.*
> *Teresa, la del suave desamor*
> *y el arroyuelo azul en la cabeza.*

Her eyes closed, her hands resting on her considerable breasts, Irma finished reciting the famous sonnet, which I will not endeavor to translate for you because its beautiful rhymes and music demand a greater translator than I could ever hope to be. When she finished, the women sighed and burst into applause. I joined them.

"That's poetry," Olga pronounced.

Carmen Elvira pontificated, "That's what I call great poetry."

"That's what I call love," elaborated Olga. "It's not enough to be a great poet. Oh, no. That's too easy. To write poetry like that, one must love very deeply and be a great lover. Like . . . like . . .

Petrarch. I hope some day you'll write a sonnet like that to your girlfriend, Sammy."

Unsure of how to respond, I said, "I hope so too."

"By the way," Irma interjected, "do you have a girlfriend?"

I assumed a blank expression and said nothing. It was one thing to join the Parnassus, but to have my life scrutinized by these ladies was out of the question.

"Yes, he does," Carmen Elvira said, to my astonishment. "Lucy told me all about it, Sammy."

"All about what?" I said.

Carmen Elvira flashed a maternal, approving smile. "About you and Claudia."

"Claudia!" I exclaimed, for the second time that day.

"Claudia Urrutia?" asked Irma in disbelief, giving me a long, searching look. "She's so . . ."

"So wealthy," said Carmen Elvira to settle the issue.

"Hey, look," I said, to no one in particular. "I—"

"I hope you don't mind my mentioning it," Carmen Elvira interrupted me, "but Lucy told me you're practically engaged, that you're proposing tonight at the Saigon Rose."

"Congratulations, honey!" exclaimed Olga, leaping from the couch. "This calls for a celebration. I have an *aguardiente* bottle I've been saving for a special occasion. Excuse me, I'll be right back."

"I'll help you with the glasses," Carmen Elvira offered, getting up too.

"We might as well have our lunch after the toast," Irma threw in. "I'll serve the *pasteles.* You do like *pasteles,* don't you?" And, without waiting for confirmation, she followed the rest of the Parnassus into the kitchen.

I could have killed my mother. I reached for the telephone, but in the middle of dialing her number, I changed my mind. "Maybe I'm dreaming," I blurted out. I shook my head in an effort to wake myself up. But dreams are odorless and I could smell the *pasteles.* The situation reminded me of something; I couldn't, though, tell quite what. *Rosemary's Baby, Macbeth,* and *The Trial* all came to mind. I wondered if Claudia had been let into this plot, or whether we were both just random bystanders snarled in the machinations of a bunch of crazed Queens matrons.

Toasting my induction to the Parnassus, we drank the *aguardiente* Colombian style—a small glass filled to the top, followed by a quarter of a lime soaked in salt, which I chewed until my teeth felt as if they would fall out. Tears choked my vision. Carmen Elvira proposed another toast to my imminent engagement. I figured it would be better to play along than to go into long explanations about my and Claudia's sexuality. We drank to love and happiness. I had never seen Colombian women drink *aguardiente:* it is essentially a man's drink, but then, I reasoned, I was among intellectuals, not conventional housewives.

My body temperature had shot up at least ten degrees. The ladies produced their fans and proceeded to cool themselves, their mouths open and blowing air as if to take off the sting of the *aguardiente* on their gums.

"How about another *aguardientico,* Sammy?" Olga said.

"No, no, thanks. Maybe later." I felt the insides of my stomach cooking.

Irma started giggling. Carmen Elvira and Olga joined in, and together they became hysterical.

"What?" I asked, feeling uncomfortable. "What is it?" They were certainly not being very polite.

"You should see the color of your face," Irma cackled. "It looks red like . . . guava paste."

"Like a brick out of the oven," Carmen Elvira chuckled, pouring herself another *aguardiente.*

I realized I had to put an end to the alcohol consumption before they became uncontrollable.

"I'm hungry," I said, pointing at the tray of aluminum foil-wrapped *pasteles* on the coffee table.

Irma unwrapped a *pastel* and served it to me on a plate, with a napkin and fork. It looked delicious; a steam cloud heavy with the aroma of vegetables and meats and corn traveled up my nostrils.

"Dig in, honey," Carmen Elvira said. "Don't wait for us; we made them just for you."

"I love corn *pasteles,*" I said, putting a piece of moist chicken in my mouth. "Ummm, it's wonderful." Closing my eyes, I chewed slowly. When I opened my eyes, the three women were leaning over the table, serving themselves.

"Ah," Olga exclaimed, setting her plate on the table and pressing her lips on the napkin. "I forgot the drinks. Now, Sammy, since you're the guest of honor, what would you like to drink with your lunch?"

"I don't know," I said, wondering what kind of exotic Colombian fruit juice or brew she had to offer. "What do you have?"

Opening her eyes wide and looking at the ceiling, she counted with her fingers. "Let's see: Diet Coke . . . ginger ale, Tab, Perrier, grapefruit juice, and beer."

I asked for a Classic Coke.

Carmen Elvira ordered a Heineken.

"For me too," said Irma. "Nothing goes better with a *pastel* than a Heineken."

While the hostess went to get the refreshments, I made small talk, asking, "Who made the *pasteles*?"

"I did," Irma said proudly.

"I never thought it would be possible to make a *pastel* taste like they do in Colombia. But they taste just as if you had cooked them in banana leaves," Carmen Elvira said.

"This is the best *pastel* I've had in a long time," I complimented the cook.

"Thank you, *su merced*. Have another."

"I will, when I finish this one. It's so big."

"Yes, Irma makes the most generous portions," Carmen Elvira said. "I follow your recipe, my dear, but they just don't taste the same."

"There must be something you're leaving out."

"Obviously. But I wonder what it is. I cook the pork with the chicken in the scallions and tomato sauce."

"Do you use fresh or dry coriander? That makes a big difference."

"Fresh. And I sprinkle the coriander on the meat just before I wrap the *pastel* in the aluminum foil."

"Maybe you don't use enough *guascas*."

"That's it. The *guascas*! Why didn't I think of it before? But it's impossible to get *guascas* in Jackson Heights."

"I bring it from Colombia. But you know they don't allow fruits or vegetables or spices into the country. I have to hide it in my panties. Once, I had to eat an *anón* at JFK because they were going to confiscate it. So, I said, 'Please, let me eat it.' And I did."

"I remember you told me. It was an *anón* from your mother's yard. I wish I had the guts to do something like that. Nerves of steel, that's what you have."

"In your panties?" I asked.

"Sure, sweetie. It was thrilling; I felt like a drug smuggler."

"Well, lucky you," Carmen Elvira complained. "The last time I went to Colombia, when I came back they made me take off my panties. I was furious."

"That's right. You wrote that marvelous column about it. It created an international uproar, Sammy. It was reprinted in two Colombian newspapers."

"That's the power of the press for you," Carmen Elvira said solemnly, looking at me.

"What's *guascas*?" I asked. It seemed to me that I was at least two steps behind in the conversation, but since I had never heard of this herb or spice or whatever it was, I had to ask.

Olga had returned from the kitchen, and was setting a tray with drinks on the table. "What's what, honey?" she asked, handing me my Coke.

"*Guascas*," said Carmen Elvira.

I realized that as the culinary expert of the group, it was up to Olga to explain the mystery. "*Guascas*," she repeated, as she distributed the drinks. With an air of authority, she sat down and smoothed her dress. "In pre-Columbian times, the Indians used it as an aphrodisiac. It's rare because it only grows in the *páramo*. I, for one, think that if we could cultivate and export it commercially, Western cuisine as we know it would be revolutionized overnight."

"I'll be damned," I said.

Carmen Elvira said, "Sammy, you're such a gentleman. Lucy is so lucky to have a son who appreciates our national dishes." Then, making a tragic face, she confessed, "My children only eat hamburgers and pizza."

"Mine too," Irma said. "I don't know what I did wrong."

Olga said, "I cook my *arepas, frijoles,* and *sobrebarriga,* and all the things I love to eat. If they don't like it, then they can go eat at MacDonald's. I cook to please myself; I'm not their servant."

"Right on," Irma cheered, making a fist.

"The last time I was in Colombia, everyone was eating hamburgers and pizza," I said. "Though Chinese takeout hadn't gotten there yet," I added.

"You were always so special," Carmen Elvira said to me. "From the time you were a boy you were so different from all the other children. That must be your poetic nature. You know, I used to say to my husband, 'If God had blessed me with a son, instead of five daughters, I wish he had been like Sammy.'"

I felt my face flush. "Thank you," I said.

"You have changed so much," Olga reminisced. "Irma," she said seriously, "you should have seen what huge ears he had when he was a boy."

"His ears look fine to me," Irma said in her curt, martinet manner.

"That's because you didn't know him back then. I have a picture of Sammy that now is of historic importance. Remind me to show it to you some day. His ears were not to be believed."

I had finished my *pastel* and was feeling terribly uncomfortable.

"Here, honey, have another one," Olga said.

"Thank you, very much. Not now." Seeing how disappointed she looked, I added, "Maybe later."

She said, "I promised Lucy I'd send her a couple of *pasteles* with you."

"She'll be so happy. She loves your *pasteles.* And I do too, but I had breakfast just a couple of hours ago. Maybe I'll take mine to Manhattan and have them later in the week."

"They taste better a few days later. Just freeze it, and when you want to eat it, warm it up in a *baño de María.*"

Carmen Elvira asked, "Do you cook all your meals?"

I noted that, as the gossip columnist, Carmen Elvira mainly asked questions. "Yes," I informed her, "though not much in the summer; it gets too hot in the kitchen."

Olga said, "He'll make such a perfect husband for Claudia."

The other women nodded in agreement; they had finished their *pasteles.*

Olga said to Irma, *"Mijita,* will you help me clear the table and bring dessert? Then we can discuss the details of Sammy's induction over coffee and a cordial."

I watched Olga and Irma clear the table and disappear in the direction of the kitchen. I'd just set down my napkin when I noticed Carmen Elvira reaching for her handbag and pulling out a small tape recorder. I lit another cigarette.

"Testing, testing. One, two, three," she spoke into the contraption. "Sammy," Carmen Elvira said, winking at me, crossing her legs and exposing her knees, "why don't you come over here and sit next to me?"

Thinking she was about to make a pass at me, I said, "What? You want to interview me?"

"Yes, honey. I'm going to ask you a few questions for *Colombian Queens,"* she explained, smiling.

"You know, Carmen Elvira, maybe this is not such a good time. I mean," I said, looking toward the kitchen door, "Irma and Olga will be coming back any minute."

"No, honey. They won't. They're doing the dishes and getting dessert ready while I interview you."

I realized I had been set up and that, as the guest of honor, it would be rude to decline the interview.

She interpreted my silence as acquiescence. "Here," she said pouring another *aguardiente* and handing me the little glass. "This will loosen you up."

I downed the *aguardiente.*

Patting the sofa, she said, "Come over here, Sammy. I'm not going to bite you. We'll just chat like two good old friends."

I sat next to her, feeling my forehead break into a sweat. "What kind of interview is this?"

She laughed. "You look as if you were facing a firing squad. Lighten up, honey. I'm just going to ask you a couple of questions, okay?"

"Okay." I put out my cigarette and lit another one.

"Ready?"

I nodded.

"We're here today with the award-winning poet Santiago Martínez Ardila, whose first book of poems *Lirio del Alba* (which, by the way, remains his only published title) will be remembered fondly by many poetry lovers, I'm sure. Today, however, we'll be talking to Santiago about other matters. Santiago, who has a Ph.D. in Medieval Studies from Queens College, and is a resident of Times Square, Manhattan, has announced today his plans to marry Claudia Urrutia."

"Wait a minute," I protested.

"Not now, honey," Carmen Elvira cut me off. "Claudia Urrutia, the import/export heiress of Barranquilla, Colombia; Jackson Heights, Queens; Miami, Florida; and Monte Carlo. Our Claudia, who trained in architecture at Yale, is also a great beauty and an accomplished . . ." Here Carmen Elvira looked lost. She motioned with her hand in front of my mouth, coaxing me to produce the word she wanted.

"Athlete," I ventured, remembering Claudia's fondness for motorcycles.

"Athlete. Yes. Athlete. Now, Santiago," she went on, pushing the machine against my nose, "tell us how you and Claudia met."

"This is preposterous. I'm not marrying Claudia Urrutia."

Carmen Elvira turned off the machine. She glared at me for a second and then broke into a big, fake smile. Her thin scarlet lips stretched taut over her big white teeth. "You're such a naughty boy, Sammy. It's a well-known fact in the Colombian community that you and Claudia are tying the knot very soon. Both your mother and Claudia's have confirmed the news. I understand how you want to protect your privacy, but honey, you're our foremost poet in the United States and this is news to our readers."

She must have thought that by flattering me I would simply

acquiesce as I had, after all, been doing all afternoon. Making an effort not to blow up (my mother would never have forgiven me if I offended her friends), I said, "Look, Carmen Elvira, I have no plans to get married at the moment. . . . But when I do, your readers will be the first to know. I promise. Cross my heart. Okay?"

Ignoring my speech, Carmen Elvira said, "Okay, Sammy. Don't you fret about it. I will fill out the details of the wedding. I know men don't like to talk about this sort of thing." Then she pushed the ON button and said, "Today, Santiago Martínez Ardila has been inducted as a member of The Colombian Parnassus, thus becoming the first male member of our society. Santiago, dear, we know that for the past ten years you've been working on a book of poems about Christopher Columbus."

"An epic poem, to be precise."

"We understand that this great . . . masterpiece, which will add glory to our national poetry, is almost finished. Is that so?"

"Not at all."

Totally unperturbed, she asked, "And is it in free verse or in rhyme?"

"Free verse, of course. I'm a modern poet."

"How innovative," Carmen Elvira said. "How avant-garde. May I ask what drew you to the subject of the Admiral of the Seven Seas?"

This was the first legitimate question she had asked. However, I had been writing the poem for such a long time that I could no longer remember why I had been drawn to Columbus originally.

"Could it have been his liaison with Queen Isabella?" Carmen Elvira (quick to dish everyone) came to my rescue.

"Certainly not."

She looked disappointed. "What is your opinion about the recent theory that Columbus was a woman?"

My jaw must have fallen open. In any case, Carmen Elvira did not wait for an answer. "We hope this long-awaited poem will be finished by 1992, the 500th anniversary of the discovery of America. We wish you great luck, both with it and with your forthcoming marriage." She turned off the machine and thanked me for the interview.

I was about to let her have a piece of my mind, when Olga and Irma burst into the room with dessert. Olga carried a tray with cheese, *obleas,* guava paste, stuffed figs and *arequipe,* and Irma the *tinto* service. While the sweets were being served on the saucers, I noticed Olga stealing glances at Carmen Elvira as if to find out how the interview had turned out. But the latter pretended to fuss with her glasses, ignoring Olga. We tasted the sweets in silence, making sounds of approval and sipping our *tintos.*

Olga said, "Tell us, Sammy, how does it feel to be a brand new member of The Parnassus? It's been so many years since I became a member. But I remember how honored I felt. I envy the way you feel right now."

"Yes," I said politely. "And what do I have to do now?"

"It's very simple," Carmen Elvira informed me. "We meet on the last Saturday of every month, except during August. It is suggested that all members attend the monthly meeting. Also, there are no dues or annual fees."

"Oh, good," I said, relieved.

"But to become a member there is a three hundred fifty dollar fee. Considering that it covers lifetime membership, it's a steal."

They offered me the perfect excuse, and I jumped at it. "I'm very honored to have been invited to join The Parnassus, but the truth is, I'm not solvent at the moment and three hundred fifty bucks is a lot of money for me. So maybe next year."

"Don't worry about it, sweetie," Olga reassured me. "Lucy was well aware of this and she has offered to take care of it."

"What? My mother is going to pay the fee?" I asked in disbelief, considering the many occasions she had denied me loans for small amounts.

"That's a mother's love for you, Sammy," Olga said.

"Treasure your mother while she's alive, and make her happy," Irma said. "I didn't know how lucky I was while my mom was alive, and I'll never get over it now."

"You just don't know how much you'll miss her when she's gone," Carmen Elvira prophesised.

"Let me explain a bit more in depth what is required to be a member," Olga said, taking a dainty bite of cheese and then licking her fingers. "A new member has to do some group service to join in."

"What kind of service?"

Carmen Elvira said, "Since you're a translator—"

"An interpreter," I corrected her.

"Well, it's the same thing, honey, isn't it?"

"Absolutely not," I said, setting down my saucer and glaring at her.

"It's almost the same thing," Olga said, "so why quibble?"

"Anyway," Carmen Elvira went on, "since you're an interpreter, we thought you'd be perfect for this. As you know, we are all poets. Not award-winning poets like you, but nonetheless serious poets."

"I've been writing poetry since I was seven," Olga said.

Carmen Elvira stared at me, waiting for me to certify their bona fides. "I didn't start quite that early," I said.

"In any case, I'm sure you've read our poems in *Colombian Queens*. We all publish quite regularly."

"Oh, yes," I lied. I had glanced at their gibberish on occasion to please my mother.

"I especially recommend this issue's selection," Olga said. "Carmen Elvira wrote the loveliest poem about the volcano disaster in Manizales, you remember? It's unbearably moving; Homeric in its ambition. If you encourage her, maybe Carmen Elvira will be gracious enough to recite it for you now."

Carmen Elvira was smiling and fluttering her hands and eyelids, so I hastened to say, "Thank you very much, but I promise you I'll read it tonight, in bed. That's how I read poetry. I never go to readings; I don't like people reading at me."

"How peculiar," Irma said.

"How un-Colombian," Olga added.

"What is it that you want me to translate?" I asked.

"Sammy, we've decided to go legit and to publish our poems in a collection," Olga said, clasping her hands. "And we've chosen you to translate them into English since you're such a talented poet, from our own country, and perfectly bilingual."

"What?" I croaked.

"And we'd love it if you could write an introduction. It doesn't have to be very long. We leave it entirely up to you, as long as it's written from the heart."

"But I've never translated any poetry into English. I think you've got the wrong guy for this project," I stammered.

"Your modesty is so appealing," Olga squealed flirtatiously, like a superannuated Lolita. "You'll do beautifully. We already have the title for you: *Muses of Queens*. Do you like it?"

"Can I have an *aguardiente*?" was my response.

"Of course, honey. You're right; this calls for a toast."

Once more we chugged down our drinks, toasting to poetry. It occurred to me that by joining the toast I was accepting their proposition just as I had already tacitly confirmed my engagement to Claudia. "Let me explain something," I said. "I have to think about this. I mean, as much as I'd like to do it, I don't know if I have the time right now."

"We understand, don't we, girls?" Carmen Elvira said.

"Take your time," added Olga.

"There's absolutely no hurry," Irma said. "What with your wedding and everything else, we don't want to put any extra pressure on you. When we meet again in September, we can discuss the details."

"What's more," Olga intervened, "we'd really love to pay you, but we have children going to college, so we live pretty close to what we make."

"We can't pay you in cash, that's true. But we have something much more valuable to offer you."

Shuddering, I asked, "Like what?"

"Power," she said. "That's right, honey, power! As a new member of The Parnassus you automatically become a contributing editor to *Colombian Queens*. You are aware of what that means, aren't you?"

"No. What does it mean?"

"It means you can reach one million compatriots in the greater

New York area. Our magazine reaches practically every member of this community. Think of the great audience you'll have for your poetry and your ideas."

"Did you know that the future of the next presidential election in Colombia is in our hands?" Olga giggled.

"No kidding!"

"We're a political force; we're a crucial element in the next presidential election. The candidates we endorse will receive about one hundred thousand votes, which is almost as many votes as there will be cast in all Colombia. You know our people are abstentionists, and only government employees go to the polls."

"Gee whiz," I said, genuinely impressed by their reasoning, though doubtful of their statistics.

Carmen Elvira said, "Your vote is of historical significance, Sammy."

"But I've never voted."

"Why not?" asked Olga, looking concerned.

"I don't know very much about Colombian politics."

She sighed with obvious relief. "That's all right. I thought it was something worse. Well, sweetie, this is your chance to learn. You couldn't ask for better teachers. We're all seasoned political campaigners."

"Do you always vote?" I asked stupidly.

"I can't vote," Carmen Elvira stated somberly.

This was interesting. "Why not?"

"She's an American citizen," Irma said.

"So are you," Carmen Elvira counterattacked angrily. "And you too, Olga."

"I don't deny it, *mijita*," a dejected Olga corroborated. "But I'm a Colombian at heart and will die Colombian."

"Me too," Carmen Elvira said, full of patriotic fervor. "I just did it so that my children could have a better chance in this country."

"I was practically forced to do it," Olga said. "In my ignorance, I thought I had to become a citizen in order to keep my federal job."

"Save your speeches; this is not the inquisition," Carmen Elvira said cattily. "We did it, and that's that. Period."

To cheer them up, I said, "My mother is an American citizen, too."

"Don't you ever become one," Carmen Elvira ordered me. "It would be disgraceful, a real tragedy of the first magnitude if our leading poet in the States became an American."

"I wonder if García Márquez is a Mexican," Olga pondered. "I think I read somewhere that he became a Mexican citizen a few years ago."

"I don't believe it for a second," snapped Carmen Elvira, slapping her knee. "Gabo would never do that. He'd never betray his country; he's one hundred fifty percent Colombian."

"But he's lived in Mexico for thirty years," Olga insisted.

"So what?"

"His children were born in Mexico," Olga expatiated.

"I don't care what the *National Enquirer* prints," Carmen Elvira scoffed, chugging down another *aguardiente*. Her speech was becoming slurred. "Gabo and Colombia will always be one, indivisible."

"Yes," Irma seconded her. "Like the Father, the Son, and the Holy Ghost."

The theological turn of the conversation warned me it was time to split. "I got to go," I said. "I have to go visit a friend."

Always the gossip, Carmen Elvira inquired, "Claudia?"

"No, my friend Bobby."

"Bobby Castro? Is it true he has AIDS?"

I stood up. "Yes, he's dying. Thank you for the delicious lunch. It was . . . nice to see you all," I said. Now that I was standing, I realized the *aguardiente* had gone to my head; my feet were wobbly, and the ladies and the room swam in front of my eyes. "And I'm really . . . pleased to be a member of The Parnassus."

"Wait," Olga said. "I promised Lucy a couple of *pasteles*."

Irma said, "Send her some figs. They're really fresh. My cousin brought them from Bogotá yesterday. These are Buga figs, Sammy. Be sure to tell that to your mother; she adores Buga figs. Actually, take all of them. I have plenty more at home," she finished magnanimously.

Minutes later, after another *aguardiente* for the road, and carrying a supermarket bag filled with Colombian delicacies, I staggered into the afternoon sun.

# 4

# Mothers and Sons

It was a ten-block walk from Olga's home to Bobby's apartment. The scene with The Parnassus women had unsettled me; memories that I had suppressed long ago were becoming exposed. Or maybe it was just the *aguardiente*, or the fact that I was ambling down the shady streets of Jackson Heights on a placid summer afternoon, going to see my oldest friend who was dying of a disease that seemed the product of a science fiction horror fantasy. At any rate, all kinds of freaky thoughts crept into my head.

Colombia is known as—among Colombians—The Country of Poets. Any Colombian worth his salt is at least a closet poet. It was our love of some poets—and our hatred of the Spanish Nobel Laureate Juan Ramón Jiménez (whose "Platero and I" we ridiculed cruelly)—that had brought Bobby and me together.

There are a couple of things I ought to clarify. I was born in the town of Barranquilla and, at age seven, after Father ditched us, we moved to Bogotá. However, four years later, in pursuit of a man she had the hots for, Mother moved back to Barranquilla. That's where Bobby and I met, at Colegio Americano, an American Baptist school that took all the rejects of the Catholic schools, in the hope that we'd all become militant Baptists. Bobby and I were chubby, unathletic, and loved movies and books. I was convinced that Bobby was a genius. While I barely managed to pass, Bobby made straight A's. He was a brilliant mathematician, and wanted to be a writer or a painter. He read books in both English and French.

On Saturdays, and during school vacations when I remained in the city, I'd go to spend the day at Bobby's house. I'd arrive early in the morning, and we'd usually play chess until lunchtime. Then we'd go to the patio, where we sat under the guava trees and read books aloud, especially *Hamlet,* which we never tired of rereading. It was at that time that Bobby encouraged me to enter a declamation contest, which I won. For the next few years, I entered, and won, many of these events. Bobby served as my coach. We favored the poetry of José Asunción Silva, a romantic, morbid suicide; and also the poetry of Porfirio Barba Jacob, Colombia's *poet maudit.*

Bobby and I came from different social backgrounds. His mother was an executive secretary for Cola Román, a soda pop company, and they lived in a modest house in a blue-collar neighborhood. I, on the contrary, was the son of a wealthy man. After Father left us, he had been generous with Mother, so we didn't have to worry about money. Also, Mother's lover was a high-ranking official in local government; he was director of the state brewery. We enjoyed luxuries such as a limousine and a uniformed driver. Most adolescences are unhappy, but mine was particularly miserable. I hated school, my classmates, and the town of Barranquilla. Books and movies were my only refuge; and Bobby, Claudia Urrutia, and my sister were the only young people I felt close to.

As I walked into a section of Jackson Heights that consisted mainly of small apartment buildings, I could feel the supermarket bag shaking in my hand. The closer I got to Bobby's home, the more upset I became. My last visit with Bobby had been at the hospital in May. Then, I thought he'd never leave the hospital alive. What was left of Bobby was in a respirator, so he couldn't talk. He looked like an extraterrestrial creature, with a big head and a shrunken body. His eyes, which had sunk a couple of inches into his face, were open, but unfocused. It was obvious to me that they were not looking at anything. I sat for what seemed like an eternity, staring at the bouquet of yellow roses I had brought him, aware of the noises of the different machines and of the nurses in white gowns and white gloves who entered and exited the room.

By the time I arrived in front of the brick apartment building where Bobby had moved over a year ago, I was feeling pretty frazzled. I lit a cigarette and stood at the entrance, wondering whether I should go in or postpone the visit. But I knew that Bobby wasn't going to be sticking around much longer. The possibility that he would again not recognize me at all upset me still further. I felt guilty that over the long period of his illness, I hadn't been by his side more often. I climbed the steps that led to the buzzer system. I was about to press the button for his apartment when a voice behind my back called, "Hey, Sammy."

Turning around, I saw my nephew on his bike.

"Gene, what are you doing here?" I demanded.

"I went by the crazy ladies' house and they told me you were coming here. Man, those women are a trip and a half."

"Anything wrong?" I asked, walking down to his bike.

"What's that smell? Are you loaded?"

"I had a couple of *aguardientes*. That's all."

"Yeah? Well, it smells like a couple hundred to me. You smell like . . . like . . . like . . ."

"It's the *pasteles*," I said, pointing to my bag.

"Oh, okay. Can I ask you a favor? I'm working until late tonight, and I rented a couple of movies. Could you take them home for me? I could lose them, going around on the bike." He reached into the basket on the bike's handles and handed me two plastic cassettes.

"Rocky Rambo Dumbo," I teased him.

"Man, I told you. I hate that shit." Suddenly, there was a loud metallic beep. "Got to beat it, man. That's my beeper."

"What kind of deliveries you make, anyway?" I asked, noticing a bunch of white envelopes in his basket.

"Can't talk now. I'm late. Thanks for taking the movies home for me." He lowered his sunglasses and put on his headphones. Grabbing the bike's handles, he shouted, "See you tonight at Saigon Rose. It's the big night, eh? Congratulations. Claudia's a cool chick.

Take care. Say hi to Bobby," he called out, and zoomed off, pedaling furiously.

The Claudia situation, I realized, was seriously out of control. However, there was nothing I could do about it now. Putting the movies in the shopping bag, I rang the buzzer.

I rode the elevator to the fourth floor. After years of visiting Bobby in swank lofts and apartments, coming here felt like going back ten years in time, to when Bobby still lived in Queens, working during the day and going to school at night.

A new nurse opened the door. I explained who I was. She informed me that there was nobody at home, except Bobby, who was asleep. "Mr. Martínez," she said as I headed toward Bobby's room, "Mr. Weisberg [Bobby's lover] called to say he won't be back until six o'clock, and I really have to go home. Would you mind taking over for me until he arrives?"

Being alone with a dying person made me nervous, but I said I would gladly stay. We went into the bedroom where Bobby was sleeping. The room was tidy and cool, and Bobby's body was covered with light blue sheets. On a wardrobe was a vase with red roses. The shades were open, and the afternoon light streamed into the room. And yet, there was something icy about it. Death had Bobby in its bony grasp already, as the French would say. On Bobby's night table was a large tray crammed with medicine bottles. However, I was relieved to see that he wasn't on a respirator. The nurse pointed to a card with phone numbers I should call in case of an emergency. Then, matter-of-factly, in the calm, blank manner of people who deal with death on a daily basis, she removed her plastic gloves, gathered her things, and left. I took a chair and sat next to the head of the bed. Three machines were hooked to him. One to his nose, one to an arm, and the last one (which leaked a greenish liquid that looked like mint liqueur) attached to a patch on his skeletal chest. The patch itself looked rotten, like putrid flesh. Bobby's hair was longish and had obviously gone unwashed for several days. I sat a foot or so away from his face and now I could study it in detail, something which on prior occasions, when he had been awake, I had been too self-conscious to do. He was beginning to look like a recently excavated mummy. The skin between the eyebrows and eyelashes had sunken even further than the last time I had seen him, so that even in repose his eyes bulged like golf balls. The skin that covered them seemed translucent and thin like a spider's web. The eyes remained open a third of an inch, so that only the whites of his eyes showed. His entire face, including his parched lips, was peeling off in white, crispy flakes. He had become a monster.

Bobby's faint, irregular breathing frightened me; I felt sad, depressed. It was hard for me to believe that this was the Bobby I had known since childhood. For a while I had hoped that a miracle would happen, but now it was clear that Bobby was going to die. What disturbed me most about it was how quiet, how undramatic it all seemed.

At his death, Bobby would be taking with him a big chunk of my life's memories. Even when we had been apart, we always kept up a correspondence. After I moved to America, I didn't see him for four years, until one morning when he showed up unexpectedly at our home in Jackson Heights. I hardly recognized him; he had grown tall, willowy, extroverted. He stayed with us for several weeks. Right away he informed me that he was gay—this was in the late seventies—and that he couldn't stand living in Colombia as a homosexual. He had come to the United States, he announced, to be "a free fag." I was still struggling to come out of the closet but when Bobby appeared again in my life I understood that I had to move out of my mother's house if I was ever going to accept my sexuality. His example was very important to me in this respect.

He got a job working in a factory that made plastic ashtrays, moved into an attic not far away from us, and enrolled at Hunter College, where he took evening and weekend classes. His main goal at that time was to move into Manhattan as soon as possible.

After I finished my B.A., I decided to return to Colombia, where I hoped to settle permanently. Bobby warned me that as a gay man I wouldn't be able to adjust. He was right: two years later, I returned to the States. By then, Bobby's fortunes had changed. He was now the manager of the plastic ashtray factory and a partner as well, had finished his B.A. with honors and enrolled in the N.Y.U. Graduate Business Program. He moved into a loft in SoHo. The building had gone co-op and he purchased the loft, which he converted into a beautiful place decorated with art and antiques, his new hobbies. He was also involved in a multitude of business enterprises, and was beginning to become extremely successful in his investments. He bragged his portfolio was worth almost a million dollars. Bobby became infatuated with the American dream. His goal was to be a millionaire by age twenty-five.

I resented his material success, his handsome and successful boyfriend, his possessions, his trips all over the world. Ironically, the freedom he had sought and enjoyed in America was the very thing that was killing him. Bobby was proud of my writing and encouraged me, but he disliked the fact that I was a poor poet.

In the early 1980s, he was on his way to becoming a Wall Street tycoon. He purchased a luxurious condo behind the World Trade Center, became thinner, more polished and elegant, took elocution lessons, and was the very image of the immigrant made good. Sitting next to him, it occurred to me that we were the first generation of immigrants who had skipped the ghettos altogether, who had been able to go directly to the suburbs and to college, who could return to our homelands for weekend trips. Our homelands were so near, by jet, that in spite of our adaptability and American ways, we did not feel the need to shed our Colombianness.

I decided to turn on the TV, hoping to catch an afternoon baseball game. Remembering the two movies Gene had asked me to take home for him, I took out the two plastic cases. They had no labels on them, which was peculiar. I turned on the TV set and opened one of the plastic containers. Inside I found a plastic bag full of a white substance. I unzipped the bag, stuck my finger inside, and tasted. It was pure, uncut cocaine. A bag of cocaine that was worth a fortune. "Shit," I uttered.

"What?" a voice said behind my back. I turned around.

"Sammy, are you all right?" Bobby said in English.

I was astonished to see him speaking. "Bobby, I thought . . ." The words choked in my throat. I hurried to his side and sat on the edge of the bed. I felt overjoyed: I thought I'd never see Bobby conscious again.

"Oh, how nice. You brought me a present," he said pulling his hands from under the blanket and touching the bag in my hands. His smile was like an open fan. "You brought me cocaine. But I could never snort all that coke even if I lived to be a hundred years old," he said, examining the bag. "Are you trying to become a yuppie overnight?"

I explained how I had come into possession of the cocaine. I pulled out the other plastic box. It contained only Marlon Brando's *Last Tango in Paris*.

"So he makes home deliveries," I said.

"This is Jackson Heights, you gringo. Not Times Square. I'm constantly getting flyers under my door. If I weren't about to croak, I'd love to take a hit. But go ahead; don't let my deathbed scene stop you from getting high."

"I gave up drugs, Bobby."

"Good for you. It only took me ten years of lecturing you before you finally caught on. I see you haven't given up alcohol. What's that smell—*aguardiente*?"

I gave him an abridged version of my induction into The Parnassus. Bobby looked amused, and struggled to pull himself up in bed, coughing like a lawnmower cranking without oil. His face became cherry red. I looked in the direction of the tray of medicines. "Is there anything I can get you?" I asked, when his breathing had settled a bit.

"Actually, yes. Here, help me to remove this thing," he said pulling out the plastic tube in his nose. He handed it to me and asked me to turn off the oxygen tank.

"Should you be doing this?" I was alarmed.

"Sammy, it's just oxygen. But I'm breathing okay without it, aren't I?"

I did as he told me. I was fidgeting and a tic began to twitch under my left eye. I wished that Bobby's lover would show up; I didn't want to be alone with Bobby in case his condition deteriorated suddenly. He asked me to help him sit up on the bed with some pillows behind his back. I was astonished at his weightlessness, and when I placed my hands under his armpits, his arms were thin and light, like breadsticks. Settling in his new position, Bobby said, "What does this remind you of?"

I was too muddled to think; I shrugged.

"Camille, you dummy. Remember how we used to play Camille during religion class?"

"We did?"

"*Ave María Purísima pues,*" he said, affecting a Medellín accent. "I don't know how you can be a writer with such a lousy memory. I sure hope you're not planning to write anything about me after I'm gone. Don't you remember we used to play Marguerite Gautier? We'd take turns coughing, and we'd imagine we were dying of consumption. Remember how Profesor Rincón—I swear he had a crush on me—for the most part ignored us. But one afternoon we must have pissed him off more than usual because he called on you. In that wonderful baritone voice of his he said, 'Mr. Martínez, since you seem to know so much about this subject that you don't even have to pay any attention to what I've been saying, would you be kind enough to explain to the slower students in class the meaning of Jesus Christ's immaculate conception?' I thought you were gonna shit in your pants; you looked whiter than chalk but you said, 'I hate to say it, sir. But in my opinion it means that St. Joseph was a cuckold, the Virgin a whore, and Jesus a son of a bitch.' Sammy, you used to be incredibly funny. I don't know what happened to your sense of humor." Bobby cackled, slapping his hands on the bed. I laughed too, until I remembered that my wisecrack had gotten me expelled from school for fifteen days.

"And who was our heroine?" He continued with his nostalgic vein.

"Vanessa Redgrave," I offered, remembering how we loved her in the life of Isadora Duncan.

"No, no, no, no, no, no," he chanted. "Close, but not quite right. Maybe this will help." He made a V with his arms; the pajama sleeves dropped to his elbows, revealing his emaciated extremities. "Now you remember?"

I shook my head.

"Diana Ross, you fool."

It might have been funny if he hadn't looked like a death camp survivor. It was a horrible sight. The only part left of the Bobby I had known was his humor.

"Okay, it's like this," he said. "I'm scared shitless of dying, but

48

I keep telling myself that it's important to die with a good attitude. You know what I mean? If there is an afterlife (and I sure as hell hope there isn't; one life is enough for me, thank you), I don't want to start it feeling sorry for myself."

In our adolescence, when we went through our existentialist period, we had become atheists. "Do you think there is an afterlife . . . now?" I asked.

"I haven't gotten any previews of it, if that's what you want to know. When I was in a coma, I saw myself walking down a dark, endless tunnel, and at the end of it, yes, there was the proverbial you-know-what beckoning me. But I resisted it. I dragged my feet. I refused to continue walking and sat down and just stared at it, without budging. I'm pretty sure it was death calling me. But I'll be damned if I go before I'm ready. I wanted to be conscious once more, so I could see Joel and even you, if you can believe that. Seriously now," he went on, "I had a good life. I sure got away from Barranquilla. I remember how I used to despair thinking I would never get away from that dreadful macho town. I knew I had to get away from there and become the gorgeous queen I was meant to be."

"You sure did," I said.

"And I had a good time with Joel these past five years so actually I don't give a flying fuck about all the other stuff. And you know, I'm glad that it's been such a long illness. This has been the first time since childhood that I've had time to think about spiritual matters. I became so wrapped up in making money that I thought only money and success could make me happy, but secretly I've always envied your freedom."

"Sure. Come on, Bobby. Get real. You wouldn't have liked Eighth Avenue all these years," I said referring to my place of residence.

"You'll be able to move now that you're marrying Claudia. Lucy told me all about it the last time she was here. Now you'll live in mansions for the rest of your life."

"Bobby, I can't believe you're talking such nonsense!"

"Hey, why not? Many of my fag friends are marrying women. And look at all the famous queens who've gone back into the closet.

Besides, it might save your life. Although, since you never have sex, you must be HIV negative. Tell the truth, have you had any in the last ten years since you came out?"

The uneventfulness of my sex life had always been a source of great amusement to Bobby. The truth is that other than the occasional vertical sex, I had practiced a single-handed celibacy for many years. Only recently had I realized that it wasn't so much AIDS I was afraid of, but of being sexually intimate with another person.

"Anyway," Bobby went on, "we were crazy about Claudia when we were kids; we had such great times. And she adores you. Plus she's rich. What more do you want? A true match made in heaven. A fag who's afraid of sex and a dyke who won't ask you for any! If she asked me to marry her—fat chance—I'd marry her in a second."

"Bullshit. You wouldn't. Just because you think you're dying I'm not going to let you take advantage of me. Is that your idea of having the last laugh?"

"No, it's not, *cariño*. I always said we were like Miriam Hopkins and Bette Davis in *Old Acquaintance*. You know me, a drama queen to the last. I really believe we were their modern-day incarnation. But the movie is over, Sammy. You've won the bet. This queen is dead."

It pleased me to see Bobby in such good spirits. Ironically, our most intimate times together since childhood had been during the past two years of his illness when we had been able to talk honestly and at leisure.

I said, "This is just like old times when I used to go by your house on Saturdays. Your grandmother cooked lunch for us. God, she was such a terrific cook. I loved her *plátano pícaro* and her *carne asada*. I can almost smell it now."

"The way you reminisce about food! You should have been a food critic instead of a poet. Maybe you should try to be a Colombian M.F.K. Fisher. This conversation is making me hungry. I'd give anything to eat something yummy."

"Are you still on your macrobiotic diet?"

"No, I went off it two weeks ago when the doctor told me I should get ready to die any minute. Since then I've been gobbling down pounds of ice cream, and chocolate, all the things I deprived myself of in my quest to be fashionably thin."

"I have a couple of *pasteles* in the bag. And Buga figs and *obleas*."

"My, my, you really go out well-prepared these days. Cocaine and *pasteles* and Buga figs. What else do you have in that bag?"

"The Parnassus women sent all that food to my mother."

Bobby perked up. "But Lucy will never forgive me if I eat her *pasteles*. Will she?"

"She might, eventually," I hypothesized.

"And what if she doesn't?" Bobby said mischievously. "I'll be dead anyway."

I touched the aluminum-wrapped *pasteles* inside the bag. "I think they're still warm, but I can heat them up if you want."

"This is perfect. It's now or never. I can't eat anything hot. Santiago, be a darling and go to the kitchen and get everything we need, and bring out a bottle of red wine. I've been dying to have a glass of wine."

I returned with the implements and cleared the medicine tray off the night table. Then I uncorked the bottle of wine and Bobby served the *pasteles*.

Bobby raised his glass to toast. "Here's a toast to . . . to all the good times I ever had; all the cocks I ever sucked. My only regret is that I never made it with an Albanian, but maybe it's not too late."

"Who was the best?" I asked with envy.

"Let's see . . . I know. The Belgian married count who sucked a bottled with baby formula while I whipped him."

I started to laugh; this was the Bobby I had known most of my life and loved like a twin.

Bobby began to chew the *pasteles* slowly and his face lit up with pleasure. "Superb. What a good idea this was!"

"It's the *guascas*," I informed him.

"But that's a sex drug. How interesting—a pornographic *pastel*."

"This is my second *pastel* of the day," I said.

Bobby smiled. I could see that although he was in great spirits he was also in pain. "Maybe tonight you'll pork Claudia."

"Cut it out, Bobby. Now, I wouldn't mind marrying one of her brothers. Those killers really turn me on."

"You know how Colombian men are, Sammy. If you marry the sister, you'll probably fuck all those hunky mafioso assassins."

Laughing, Bobby raised his glass, "This calls for another toast: To my last meal on earth."

"To our friendship," I said.

"I take back what I said earlier," Bobby said thoughtfully. "I'm not terrified of dying anymore. I mean, not hysterically so. As I told you, I've had a long time to think about spiritual matters during this illness. I know that you find the subject of religion fairly revolting, and I don't blame you. I haven't forgotten the pact we made at thirteen to be atheists forever. But I'm not an atheist anymore, Sammy. Sorry to disappoint you, old pal. Think what you want. Maybe my brain has gone soft because of this disease. I don't doubt it and I don't care. But the only way I can reconcile myself to dying is by believing in God. Otherwise, I would be terrrified of sinking into a bottomless void, for all eternity." He stopped to chew a chunk of *pastel*. Then he went on. "This way I know my spirit will find rest when my body goes. In these past two years, I've had a lot of time to study different religions and philosophies. Finally, only Christianity interested me because the Christian God sent his son to be one of us, and to suffer like all of us, and he knew how consuming and powerful love can be." He paused. There was a faraway look in his eyes, as if he saw something I couldn't see. "You know what my favorite passage in the Bible is? The Sermon on the Mount. Remember how it goes? 'Blessed are they that mourn: for they shall be comforted. Blessed are the meek: for they shall inherit the earth.' And it goes on and on. It's called the Beatitudes, and it's found only, I think, in the Gospel of St. Matthew." He took another bite of *pastel* and chewed slowly, munching and catching his breath at the same time. He handed me the plate. "This is delicious. Now I can die."

To distract him from his gloom, I said, "Would you like a Buga fig or an *oblea*?"

"An *oblea* would be lovely."

As I reached for the *obleas* wrapped in wax paper, a horrible burp erupted from Bobby's throat. The violent sound startled me.

I sat up very still, wondering what I should do next. I was struggling to dissemble my feelings. Bobby's face flushed crimson. With great desperation he sucked the air around him, as if he couldn't find it. His eyes opened wider, the light in them sparkled, and he stared at me with an enormous intensity and longing. Back in my childhood in Bogotá, when my mother went out at night, she would put belladonna in her eyes, and her pupils would enlarge and glisten so that they were both exciting and frightening to me—that was the look in Bobby's eyes, which were dilated, submerged in a face death had already claimed. And yet, his eyes were the only part of him that was still alive. It was as if his ravaged body had been dying bit by bit, but *life* had concentrated in that blazing, scorching stare. The light that sparked in his eyes was that of the supernatural, the other-worldly, a light that saw and bespoke of things to which the rest of us are not privy, and never glimpse until we approach the next world, if there is any such thing. By degrees, his face relaxed, becoming softer, fuller. Now that he was out of pain, a serene expression came over his features as if he had fallen into a deep, blissful sleep. He was dead. Just to make sure, I tried to take his pulse, holding his wrist until I realized I didn't know what I was looking for. Bobby's hand jerked spastically in my shaking hand. Spooked, I dropped his arm and put my palm on Bobby's chest, near the filthy patch. He was still as a board. Soon I started shaking all over. Oddly enough, I could accept the fact that Bobby was dead. But the fact that the IV and the other machine attached to his chest kept pumping liquids into his corpse really disturbed me. I turned off both machines. I wondered whether I should call the doctor or the hospital first. I dreaded the thought of a troop of paramedics bursting into the room and carrying away Bobby's corpse in a wailing ambulance. Yet I felt peaceful; now that Bobby was dead, there was nothing more that could happen to him. I called Joel at his office, and was informed he had already left for the day—it was, after all, Saturday afternoon. Next, I called the number I had for Bobby's mother (Doña Leticia was staying at a friend's house because she was afraid of catching AIDS) and told her she should come over as soon as possible—I didn't want to give her the news over the phone. The last call I made was to my mother; I told her not expect me back any time soon and the reason why. I sat on Bobby's bed and waited, staring at the ravaged corpse. I didn't cry or get hysterical or get down on my knees to pray for Bobby's soul. Afraid that the police might arrive and find the coke, I hid the shopping bag in the kitchen, under the sink. Then I cleared the dishes and put everything in the dishwasher. I was in the kitchen when the door opened and Joel came in. Speechless, I looked at him. He instantly knew because he froze on the spot, closed his eyes and clenched his fists. I walked up to him and we embraced and burst out sobbing aloud, clutching at one another, saying nothing.

Later, in the bedroom, I was recounting to Joel my last conversation with Bobby and how he had died, when the bell rang. I let Bobby's mother in. "How are you Doña Leticia?" I said. "I'm so glad you're here."

We had never liked one another. She was the stereotypical "stage mother." All her adult life she had worked extremely hard to give her son everything she had lacked—including great ambition. But this sacrifice had dehumanized her; she seemed more like Bobby's trainer than his mother. He loved her, but had been afraid of her and courted success desperately to make his mother proud.

She walked to the bedroom door and looked in. When she saw Joel sobbing quietly, she turned to me. "Santiago, what's the matter? Tell me!"

Lowering my eyes, I said, "He's dead."

Doña Leticia remained by the door, but she started banging her fists and her forehead against the door frame. She cried loudly, pulling her hair as if she were *Juana la loca*. Doña Leticia, who was a bilingual secretary in Colombia, spoke English well enough. Pointing a finger at Joel, she screamed shrilly, "You killed my son. *Murderer, murderer.* You killed my son. Goddamn you for turning Bobby into a homosexual. Bobby was no *maricón*. Not my son! I hate all homosexuals!" she screamed, turning to face me accusingly. "I hate them all! I hope they all die of this plague! I hate New York!"

After venting her hatred of homosexuals, she turned to Joel. "Where are the papers?" she demanded. "I want those papers! Don't think you're going to steal Bobby's money. I know my son left me a lot of money and I'm not going to let you steal it, you dirty Jew.

I'll hire the best lawyer in New York and you'll go to jail, you crook. That's where you belong, you degenerate corrupter. My son was a millionaire," she ranted. "I know that. Don't think I'm a stupid Colombian. I'll have my brothers come here and they'll kill you. Give me the papers!" Like an angry lioness protecting her prey, she paced back and forth in front of the door, growling. Joel ignored her. I took a chair in the living room, beginning to get really pissed. I felt that Bobby deserved much better, especially from his mother. Maybe this was the only way Doña Leticia could express her grief, but even now that her son was dead, she refused to enter his room. I thought about how heartbreaking it must have been for Bobby that his own mother would shun him when he was dying. All of a sudden, I could feel no compassion for her. I was angry. I was about to grab Doña Leticia by the shoulders and give her a good shaking when the bell rang. It was my mother.

"Lucy, Lucy!" Doña Leticia screamed, throwing herself into my mother's arms. They cried for a while. Mother kept saying, "Calm down, Leti. Calm down. The worst is over, Leti. Bobby is finally resting." When Doña Leticia quieted down, Mother went into the bedroom and, crossing herself, knelt at the foot of Bobby's bed and prayed silently, with her eyes closed and her hands clasped. When she finished, she kissed Bobby on the forehead and stroked Joel's head. Seeing this, perhaps wanting to do likewise but still afraid of disease, Doña Leticia resumed her histrionics. "You need a good cup of cammomile tea," Mother said with authority and, taking Doña Leticia's hand, dragged her in the direction of the kitchen.

I walked into the bedroom and closed the door. I sat on the chair and watched Joel, who seemed almost catatonic. Trying to collect my emotions, I breathed in and out deeply. A while later there was a knock at the door. Doña Leticia summoned Joel to the kitchen. She had calmed down now. For the next hour or so she worked Joel over about Bobby's will, insurance, holdings, etc. Mother watched all this with an expression of distaste. There was some ugly squabbling over Bobby's corpse. Doña Leticia claimed that it "belonged" to her, and that she wanted to take it back to Barranquilla and bury it there. Fortunately, in his will Bobby had been very specific about this matter; his last wish was to be cremated and have his ashes scattered in the Hudson. Joel must have seen all this coming, because he had all the papers ready and produced copies of all the documents. Bobby had left his mother his life insurance and real estate he owned in Colombia. The truth is that in the two years he had been stricken with AIDS, many of his businesses had fallen through and, except for the condo on Wall Street, which he had purchased with Joel, his art collection and antiques, plus some stock, he had lost most of his money. Again Doña Leticia accused Joel of being a crook and threatened to have her relatives in Colombia come over to fry him unless he gave her *everything*. Finally, she agreed to let Joel dispose of the corpse. Then she grabbed some papers, stood at the entrance to Bobby's room, announced that she was ready to go and once more began shrieking, cursing Joel, New York, and all homosexuals.

Mother offered to drop her off. I ordered a taxi, took my shopping bag from under the sink, and embraced Joel, telling him to call me if he needed anything. Joel stood by the door, waving good-bye, looking devastated, utterly lost, as we left him alone in the apartment with the corpse of his lover.

When the taxi arrived at Doña Leticia's address, Mother said, "If you'd like to have dinner before you go back to Colombia, I'd love to have you over."

Doña Leticia thanked Mother, and said that she would call her soon. As the taxi drove off, I said, "I hate that woman so much. I can't believe you're going to have dinner with her."

"It's more than just being polite," Mother said, staring at me. "I'm not crazy about her either. But Bobby was her only son, and I know how she must feel. Don't be too quick to judge harshly what you don't understand. If you ever have your own children, you may come to understand her a bit better."

Mother and I remained silent on the way home. Inside her kitchen, I removed the cartridges from the shopping bag. "The *obleas* and figs are for you. Irma wants you to know that the figs are from Buga." I paused. "They sent *pasteles,* but Bobby and I ate them."

Mother smiled. Eagerly, she asked, "Were they good? Were

they corn or rice *pasteles*? Did Bobby like them? He used to love my *pasteles*."

"He ate all of it," I said, which for Mother was the highest compliment one could pay to a dish.

"I remember how he used to come by on Saturday afternoon; I can almost see him now. He'd say, *'Tía'*—he always called me auntie—'what goodies do you have for me today?' He loved my *picadillo*, too."

"I'm going upstairs to take a nap," I said. "I feel beat."

I plodded upstairs. Spread out on my bed was a beautiful white Italian suit, a pink silk shirt, white Brazilian shoes, socks, and a gold designer tie. They were gorgeous. I hid the coke behind some books on the shelves and went back downstairs.

Mother was busy making pig's feet and chick-peas. Simón Bolívar greeted me, screeching, "Hello, stranger. Hello, stranger. Hello, hello."

Mother, who hadn't heard me coming downstairs, turned around to face me. There was an anxious look on her face, as if she had been worried I disliked her choice of clothes.

Regressing to my childish self, I said, "Thank you for the clothes, mommie. The suit is beautiful." I knew she wanted a hug, but I held back—it was very difficult for me to have any kind of physical contact with her.

"I'm so happy you like them. I know you don't have a nice summer suit. Anyway," she said, as she continued chopping scallions and tomatoes, "I want you to look nice tonight. You know Paulina and Claudia are such clothes horses."

"I really don't feel like going anywhere tonight, if you don't mind," I said, surprised that she still planned to go to the Saigon Rose.

"I don't feel so hot myself," she said. "But Paulina and Claudia will be disappointed if we don't show up. Paulina had a dress made just for the occasion. Anyway," she sighed, "I know Bobby would have wanted us to go out and enjoy ourselves. And I hope you do the same when I die, okay?"

The timing was wrong to confront her about the Claudia plot.

Chopping vegetables on the cutting board, all of a sudden she looked old, shrunken, defeated. The sorrow and weariness painted on her face deterred me from bringing it up. I thanked her again for the suit, and told her I wanted to nap for a couple of hours. As I climbed the stairs, I thought about how, for years, Mother had wished I had been a successful businessman like Bobby. His successes had made Mother proud of him. It was no wonder she took Bobby's death so badly. In my bedroom, I hung the suit, cleared the bed, set the alarm clock, and lay down, burying my face under the pillows. Immediately, I fell asleep. I began to dream about painful moments of my adolescence. I felt as if I were walking with a stick, using it to uncover the cobwebs that had accumulated on top of still-living and bleeding wounds. I dreamed I was in Colegio Americano, where Bobby and I had been classmates. I dreamed the principal called me into his office and for the millionth time asked me to bring my birth certificate to school. I promised to bring it soon, knowing deep down that it was impossible because my father had refused to acknowledge me legally and thus there was no legal record of my birth. The scene played and replayed in my mind, and with each new rehearsal the principal would get angrier until he threatened to expel me from school. In the dream, I experienced the acute feeling of inadequacy and rejection I felt at that time. At the first school I attended, the Jewish school, I saw the circumcised boys in the showers after gym class and I thought I was a freak. I saw myself during school recess, sitting at my desk, sobbing hysterically, while the other children were out in the yard playing. In the next sequence of dreams, I was eleven or twelve. I saw myself naked, holding my uncircumcised penis, trying to remove my foreskin with a razor. I made an incision and started bleeding. Afraid to call for help, I bled until I passed out in the bathroom where my mother found me. She wrapped a towel around my private parts and took me to her bed and applied Mercurochrome to my almost severed penis, then kissed me and hugged me, reassuring me that everything was all right, that I was not a freak, that a doctor would see me the next day and circumcise me if that's what I wanted. That night, I slept on mother's bed, embracing her, and when I woke up, I was kissing her, and we were both naked, panting and sweating and my penis was erect as if I had just stopped making love to her and I began to cry. I woke up, quaking. Was that what had really happened? Had I made love to my mother? Or was this just an incestuous dream of unfulfilled passion? Perhaps I would never find out and even if I did, what good would it do me to know the truth?

# 5

# Nostalgias

It was nearly midnight when mother and I arrived at the Saigon Rose. Red-carpeted steps led to a landing where we were greeted by a woman attired in a glittering scarlet gown and lots of costume jewelry. Upon giving our names, we were admitted, but not before two beetle-browed men, with gold canines, frisked us.

The interior of the nightclub looked like a set out of *Scarface*—the remake. Hot yellows and reds predominated; from the ceiling hung baroque chandeliers all ablaze. A conga was in progress. The long line snaked around the dance floor and the tables surrounding it. The shimmering gowns of the women, plus the substantial rocks they flashed, made the line look like a Chinese dragon. We stood by the bar, waiting for the conga to finish. Although the Saigon Rose is owned by Asians, Saturday night is Colombian night. It was a prosperous, plastic-looking clientele; the women, heavily made up and dressed in elaborate gowns; the men dressed mostly Caribbean style—in white and mauve suits.

When the conga was over and the exhausted but excited couples dispersed, a tuxedoed waiter escorted us to our table. I was impressed by Mother's numerous acquaintances. She glided around the tables, waving and calling names and blowing kisses, as if she were the queen of the ball. Much to the annoyance of the waiter, she stopped to introduce me to several "businessmen."

Near the back of the dance floor, Paulina and Claudia were sitting across from one another, at a round table for eight. Claudia stood up, stretching her arms. "Lucy, Sammy," she called out, laughing her deep, nervous, raucous laugh. She looked like a Latin Grace Jones: spiked orange hair, boa-constrictor pants and jacket, and diamonds, rubies, and emeralds cascading from various extremities and orifices. We exchanged kisses and embraces. As I sat down, I noticed two grim-looking men at the next table who must have been Claudia's and Paulina's bodyguards. Mother and Paulina engaged in a heated and giggly tête-à-tête. Claudia's French perfume made her smell like a voluptuous Barranquilla flower.

"Sammy, *viejo* man. It's good to see you. I'm so sad tonight," she said, putting her arm over my shoulder. Her long purple fingernails were pierced by thin gold chains with tiny diamond stars at their tips. If I had to use an adjective to describe her, I would have to say . . . unique. She seemed a bit sauced already, but her agate eyes shone like movie projectors in the dark. Claudia poured me a glass of Dom Perignon and we toasted Bobby. Since her arrival in America, Claudia and I had seen one another only intermittently. All I know is that her family arrived in Miami penniless immigrants, and a couple of years later they were millionaires. When Paulina purchased a house in Jackson Heights our mothers became fast friends. During her years at Yale, I saw Claudia infrequently. After graduation, she seemed to spend most of her time traveling to distant places and residing at her many homes on three continents. A few years ago, she had had a motorcycle accident, from which she escaped unharmed, but the friend riding with her, her lover, I assumed, had been killed. Since that time, Claudia developed her peculiar laughter which reminded me of Tallulah Bankhead's. In the late eighties, she had come to visit me on Eighth Avenue, and she had taken me to rock concerts and punk clubs on the Lower East Side. But she must have sensed that they were not my idea of fun because, much to my relief, she stopped asking me out.

"Sammy, *qué vaina. No joda*," she moaned, swilling her champagne. "I always thought of us as the three musketeers, and now is over and I feel old as hell."

I thought it was disarming that, in spite of her Ivy League education, Claudia retained the macho Spanish working-class argot of the Caribbean coast of Colombia. We began to reminisce about our adolescence, which seemed to be our favorite topic of conversation.

"I remember so clearly the first time I met you," she said. "I was playing with my toy soldiers in the backyard when I heard you over the wall. Even then your voice was so deep and spectral," she said, laughing and slapping my back. "Although Mother had told me she'd kill my ass if she caught me climbing the wall, I had to find out what was going on. I climbed the wall and I saw you with your eyes closed and your arms stretched to one side, reciting Silva's *Nocturno:*

> *Y era una sola sombra larga*
> and it was a long, lone shadow,
> and it was a long, lone shadow.

"Oh, man," she went on. "You sounded like Anna Magnani on valium."

"Yeah," I said. "I remember Bobby called you down and you climbed down the guava tree, and although you were nine or ten all you had on was a pair of shorts. And you had a Mohawk haircut even then; I thought you were a boy," I said, to get even.

"It was a mango tree, not a guava tree, man. How can you have forgotten such a crucial detail?"

"Are you sure? I always thought it was a guava tree. Sour guavas, if I remember correctly."

"Man, it must be all that LSD you did that fried your brains. I tell you, Sammy, it was a *mango de azúcar* tree. Don't you remember how during mango season we'd spend whole afternoons eating ripe mangoes? We'd only stop when Bobby's grandmother, Doña Guillermina, would come out in the backyard screaming, 'Boys, if you don't stop eating mangoes you're gonna grow hairs on your tongues.' " She was laughing hard, although the anecdote did not seem all that hilarious to me. I could see Claudia was lit.

We continued reminiscing about Bobby, gossiping about Joel (whom we both liked), and Doña Leticia (whom we both detested). The conversation was interrupted when the set of boleros was over and the dancing couples returned to their seats. The emcee came out and commanded the attention of the audience. *"Damas y caballeros,* ladies and gentlemen, the moment we've been anxiously waiting for: I give you the artist we all came to see, the heiress to Gardel's immortal throne, the supreme interpreter of the tango in our time, the incomparable international superstar, Lucinda de las Estrellas."

I looked at Mother, but she was already in another galaxy—all her concentration was directed at the stage. Five Japanese men in tuxedos appeared, bowed, and took their seats. They tuned their instruments, as all eyes riveted on the golden circle of light the spotlight made on the curtains. Lucinda de las Estrellas, a.k.a. Wilbrajan, flung the curtains aside and strutted onto the stage. All loud conversation ended, although I heard whispers and titters. My sister scanned the audience with an arrogant, defiant nod, as if she were displeased to find an audience in the nightclub. She smiled at our table, though. I hadn't seen Wilbrajan in several months, and I was struck how every time I saw her, she seemed to have grown more beautiful. She was wearing a simple, tight, white silk dress, cut several inches above the knees. She wore her hair in a tress, which she kept over her breasts. Wilbrajan walked toward the musicians with the grace of a mother swan. While she chatted inaudibly with them, she turned her back to the audience, showing the low cut of her dress, which exposed her back and carnal shoulder blades. In her fleshiness, she reminded me of Ingres's Odalisque. I realized that years after her metamorphosis, I still kept looking for the "grasshopper" of my childhood.

Wilbrajan had started her career singing boleros, *cuplés,* and *rancheras,* in disreputable dives all over the United States, wherever there was a Latin population that supported her act. Once a year, she traveled to Mexico and South America, where she claimed she was famous. She had cut an album in Colombia. In the early 80s, she became a *tanguera.* God knows her lifestyle suited her stage persona;

she had had many boyfriends and a few ex-husbands, whose only trait in common was their shadiness.

She approached the mike slowly, fussing with her tress. All in white, she seemed a moon goddess. She wore a gold chain around her neck and a single large pearl dangled from it. The hand that held the mike had a tattoo of a purple dagger.

"*Buenas noches,* ladies and gentlemen," she said in her husky voice. "I'm honored to have in the audience the person to whom I owe everything, my mother." The spotlight fell on us, and Mother, playing the moment for all it was worth, took a bow and then blew a kiss at Wilbrajan. I was miffed that the entrancing chanteuse had ignored me, while acknowledging our mother, with whom she didn't get along at all. The spotlight returned to Wilbrajan, who now was hugging the mike with both hands. "I'm happy to be back at the Saigon Rose, in front of this public I adore," she purred, stretching her exquisitely dramatic arms and opening her expressive hands. The audience applauded, responding to her fakery. "Tonight," she went on, "is a very sad night for me. A fellow compatriot, and dear friend of the soul, Bobby Castro, died this afternoon. To his memory, I shall sing '*Volver.*'" She signaled to her musicians, and the violins began rippling waves of melancholy notes throughout the nightclub. Closing her eyes, the way Gardel did it, she recited the first few lines of the famous tango:

> *Volver* . . . I can guess the city lights
> blinking in the distance,
> are marking my return.

Opening her eyes, she crooned:

> They are the same one that lit
> with their pale reflections,
> deep hours of pain;

She sang mournfully, as if delivering a dirge. But as the song progressed, her voice blossomed, taking dark, tragic tones:

And though I didn't want to return
one always returns to one's first love.
The old street that once echoed:
'Her life is yours, her love is yours,'
under the mocking glance of the stars
today indifferently watches my return.

Making a fist, Wilbrajan hit her breasts, as if she were stabbing herself. It was a most operatic effect. Then she ran her fingertips across her forehead:

To return
with a wilted brow
my hair silvered by the snows of time.
To feel
that life is just a sigh;
that twenty years are nothing,
that my feverish eyes
wandering in the dark
look for you and call your name.

Suddenly, the utter bleakness of the lyrics got to me, and watching my sister doing this striptease of her soul became unbearable. As I looked away, I caught Mother's profile and her beatific expression. Obviously, Wilbrajan had inherited her love of tango from our mother. To me, Mother was now just an old woman, but in her youth her story hadn't been much different from Wilbrajan's. The reason there was so much animosity between them was that they were like two different images of the same person: in Mother, Wilbrajan saw herself in old age. In my sister, Mother saw the woman she had been in her youth.

Vivir
con el alma aferrada
in sweet remembrance
that still makes me cry.

Wilbrajan paused, and, as if she were a latter-day but more glamorous and haunted Janis Joplin, she screamed at the top of her lungs:

I'm afraid of the appointed hour
when my past returns to confront my life
I'm afraid of the nights
alive with memories
that shackle my dreams.
But the wanderer who flees
sooner or later stops on his path
and though oblivion, smashing it all,
has killed my old dream,
I hide a flickering hope,
the only fortune left in my heart.

Wilbrajan's voice was barely adequate, but I had never heard anyone blast a tango in quite that way. She shook, and shivered, and shuddered, as she delivered her song in spasms of pain and despair, and I finally understood the old saying that tango was not sung but lived. When she finished, the entire audience leaped to its feet, and, banging tables, clinking glasses, it shouted: *"Viva el tango, Viva Gardel!"* Everyone clamored: *"Nostalgias, Nostalgias."* Smiling like a generous goddess, Wilbrajan obliged her fans. A few couples took to the dance floor.

"Come on, let's rip up the floor," Claudia said, standing and taking my hand.

"I can't dance the tango," I protested.

"Sure you can. Keep your crotch against mine, and push me around," she ordered me.

Ignoring the couples pirouetting around us in the lewdest manner, we danced, getting closer to Wilbrajan; the whiteness of her makeup made her look like a Kabuki performer. When we were about twenty feet away from her, we stopped and stood to the side, watching my sister's performance.

I hadn't lived until I heard Wilbrajan sing *"Nostalgias."* Standing with her feet apart, she raised her arms toward the ceiling, and with

her hands open, palms up, as if she were worshiping in front of a
pagan altar, begging to be sacrificed, she wailed:

*Bandoneón,* howl out your tango blues.
Perhaps you too have been wounded
by a sentimental love.
My clown's soul cries out
sad and lonely tonight
black night without stars.
If drinking brings consolation
then here I'm keeping vigil
to drown my sorrow once and for all.
I want my heart to get drunk
so that later I can toast to
the failures of love.

*"Nostalgias"* brought the house down, and Claudia and I returned to our table to listen to Wilbrajan interpret three more
tangos. After taking innumerable curtain calls, she joined us, while
the Japanese *tangueros* played their instruments to the total indifference of the audience who had come to drink, dance, and listen to
Lucinda.

Aware of being the center of attention, Wilbrajan embraced
and kissed Mother first, then she gave me a polite, cool peck; next
she embraced and kissed the Urrutias. Although it was true that over
the years my sister and I had grown distant, occasionally I missed the
closeness of our early years. Mother proposed a toast to her great
success. A bouquet of pink orchids, compliments of the management, arrived at our table. Wilbrajan pinned an orchid on Mother's
dress. Mother purred and purred, calling Wilbrajan *"Mi chinita
adorada.* My little angel." Several bottles of Dom Perignon, with
cards, arrived. When the waiter pointed to the sender, Wilbrajan
acknowledged him with a drop-dead stare.

*"Mijita linda,"* mother said to Wilbrajan. "I can't tell you how
proud you've made me. Now I can die; you've become a great singer.
I know that, in heaven, Gardel is watching over you and approves."

"Thank you, Mommie," Wilbrajan said, giving Mother a tiny smile.

"Next you'll have to sing in Radio Music Hall," Paulina elaborated. "I wonder if we could rent it for one night. I promise you, *cariño*, I'll fly all my family from Barranquilla for the occasion."

Mother kissed Paulina profusely on her cheeks to thank her for her generous, if far fetched, offer.

"You don't have to thank me," Paulina said, holding Mother's face. "More than friends, we're family. You know, I'll do anything for your children, *mi amiga adorada*."

"Right on," Claudia said, watching our mothers carrying on. "Lucinda, that's a heck of an act you've put together. Man, you're awesome singing that stuff."

Getting carried away, Mother said, "Maybe Carnegie Hall. Why not? I think you're better than Liza Minnelli, anyway."

Wilbrajan stared at me. I realized I was the only one who hadn't complimented her yet.

"That was good, Sister," I said. "I really enjoyed it."

She continued staring at me, fishing for more compliments.

"I especially liked 'Volver,' " I said sincerely.

"It was so sweet of you to dedicate it to Bobby's memory," Paulina said.

"I was practically in tears," Mother added.

"It was freaking great," Claudia opined.

"I shall always think of Bobby when I sing 'Volver,' " Wilbrajan said. "Tango is about pain." She gulped down a glass of champagne.

We continued praising her performance and swilling the bottles of Dom Perignon that Claudia kept uncorking. I noticed a tall, tanned, muscular blond in safari clothes. He approached our table, smiling. Jumping off my chair, I cried, "I'll be damned! Stick Luster!"

It was my friend Stick, with whom I used to play hide-and-seek in the morgue in Bogotá. We hadn't seen one another in over twenty years, but I recognized him instantly. We embraced, and then Stick hugged and kissed my female relatives and was introduced to Paulina and Claudia. It was a happy occasion and there were many toasts.

"Stick, *mijito*, how did you know we'd be here tonight?" Mother asked.

"Well, you do see, Mrs. Lucy. It was a most fortuitous coincidence," he said in something that was almost Spanish. His Spanish had deteriorated a great deal, but now he spoke it with a musicality that was Brazilian. He went on. "I go to visit my client in Queens today and they have a poster for tonight on the table, and there was a picture of Will and I thought, Aha, I think I know this singer. And you know, my friends, never once in all past years did I lose hope we'd meet again."

"Stick, are you a devotee of the *Virgen de la Macarena?*" my mother asked.

"No, Doña Lucy. I'm Protestant. If you must remember."

"The reason I ask, my dear," Mother explained, "is that la *Virgen de la Macarena,* if we pray to her with all our hearts, will reunite us with long lost friends."

"Most useful piece of information to know," Stick said thoughtfully. "I do remember *Virgen de la Macaroni, Virgen del Chilindrina, Señor Nuestro de Monsterate,"* he said, mangling the names of the most popular saints in Colombia.

Unable to restrain herself, Claudia burst into loud squeals.

"Claudia, *muchacha,* behave yourself," Paulina admonished her daughter.

Disregarding Claudia, Stick said, "And since when did you come to America, my friends? I see you're a very beautiful artist, Will, and a famous singer. I'm very happy about your success. But what about you, Señora Lucy, and you Sammy?"

"Sammy's famous, too," Mother said. "He won the most important poetry award in Colombia. And now he's writing a long book about Christopher Columbus."

"Ah, like me, a lover of high adventure. I always knew you'd be a famous writer, Sammy. You always had lots of imagination. Since you were a little boy. Remember how you read to me from *The Adventures of Dick Turpin?"* he said to my embarrassment. "And you, Señora Lucy?"

"I got married to the nicest man, Stick. I wish you could have met him a few years ago. But he has Alzheimer's now," she concluded with sadness in her voice.

"I'm so sorry to hear that."

"We choose neither our blessings nor our curses, my dear," she sighed. "And what about you? What have you been up to all these years?"

"Well, you see, Señora Lucy," Stick began, clearing his throat. "Afterward we leave Bogotá we go to Brazil. Ah, Brazil, land of the samba. What a beautiful country. But poor Papa had to go put telephone cables not in Rio or Sao Paulo or Bahia but in jungle. Ah, it was most exciting and wondrous experience for a child. Too many mosquitoes and bugs, snakes and tigers and alligators for Mother. But not for me. We live with tribes who do not talk anything we speak. I learned to hunt and fish with spears, and weave. I do love the life very, very much. But, since we move here and there, poor Papa catches deadly virus and after four years in jungle we go back to Sweden."

"Tarzan of the Amazon," Claudia cried, breaking into shrill peals of laughter.

"You must excuse my daughter," Paulina said. "Too much Dom Perignon."

Oblivious to Claudia's guffaws, Stick continued. "Back in Sweden, my soul was not Swedish but Amazon. But I could not go back, as I was only a boy. So after I finished college (I study archaeology), I return to Brazil. Ah, Brazil. I make my living traveling to remote tribes in deepest jungle—some of them I'm first blond they've seen—and I bring back pottery and weaving of most artistic tribes. I sell these in America and in Europe. And I will show you some whenever you want."

"We have an apartment in Trump Tower," Paulina said. "Do you think we could decorate it with jungle things, Mr. Stick?"

"Oh, yes, madam. Jungle motifs will look most beautiful there."

Wilbrajan, who had remained silent all this time, and looked bored out of her mind with the conversation, finally said, "Stick, come over here and talk to me."

Pretty much the same way she had hogged him all to herself when we were children, she drew him into an intimate conversation that excluded the rest of the party. I must admit that they looked stunningly sexy together. Mother and Paulina returned with renewed vigor to their interrupted tête-à-tête.

Seeing them all cozy and romantic, Claudia remarked, "Isn't it wonderful? They look great together, don't you agree, Sammy?" I nodded my approval even though I was quite pissed with Wilbrajan for taking Stick hostage. After all, as children, he had been my best friend, not hers. I was dying to have a long conversation with him, alone. Could it be possible, I wondered, that now that we had grown up, he preferred her company to mine?

"I predict they will fall in love," Claudia said. "Look at them, Sammy. *Qué cheveridad.*"

"God, I hope not," I said crankily. "Not the way she goes through men."

"You're pretty snippy tonight, aren't you? It must be Bobby's death that's affected you so much. You're not usually like this," she said, taking my hand. "Anyway, since it's getting late I might as well remind you that you're supposed to propose to me tonight."

I pulled away my hand. I had thought all along that the marriage plot had been concocted by our mothers unbeknownst to both of us.

"Sammy, I'm hurt," Claudia said, looking teary-eyed. "Here I'm proposing to you and you recoil from me as if I were a green mamba."

"You're joking, aren't you?" I asked, although something told me she was serious.

Claudia laughed hysterically, slapping my back. When she had collected herself she said, "No, Sammy. I think it's a marvelous idea. I think it'd be neat to marry you. I've been waiting for you to propose to me for years. It'd be so cool to have your child."

I chugged down a glass of champagne. I might as well take this with a grain of salt, I thought.

"Don't you love me at all?" Claudia asked pathetically.

I patted her shoulder as if she were a big dog. "You know I love you, but not like that. You're like my sister. I wish you were my sister and not Wilbrajan."

"So? You love me; I love you. It's perfect, man. Think of it. Have we ever had an argument? Have I ever been pissed at you? Never."

"But Claudia," I said gently. "You're a dyke; I'm a fag."

"Big fucking deal. Look at our mothers. Don't they look like a couple of sweet old dykes? I've never seen such devotion. I mean, this thing runs in our families?"

"Are you saying my mother is a dyke?" I said, outraged.

"Just forget it, will you? Anyway, don't you think dykes want to get married too? You're thinking about the dykes in the 60s. Now we want children just like all other women. Plus I'm going through changes. I'm sick of blowing heaps of money on mean bulldykes who just take advantage of me. And I've known you for so long. There aren't going to be any nasty surprises coming from you. I know you as I know the palm of my hand. Better. And the way you love that cat of yours. That tells me you have good parental instincts. When we get married you'll have your own child to love instead of a pet."

"You don't understand. I don't think I could love anyone more than I love Mr. O'Donnell. Nobody could ever need me that much." I could see this marriage thing wasn't going to work. If she couldn't understand something as obvious as my love for Mr. O'Donnell, what about my other dreams? For example, what about Christopher Columbus? "Mr. O'Donnell isn't just a cat," I said.

"Okay, he's not just a cat. He's a Bengal tiger, whatever you want. I'm not allergic to him. I'll be a nice mother. I'll buy him lots of nice, juicy mice to eat."

"That's so gross."

"Sammy, I will *not* let Mr. O'Donnell stand in the way of our happiness. In any case, as I was saying before, it's true you looked a bit weird when you were a boy, but not now." Claudia smiled her killer smile. "I really dig your looks, man. You've grown so tall and slender, just my type, if I were straight. And you have such beautiful cow eyes and your wonderful curly hair," she purred, running her fingers through my hair. "And even your ears, which were so peculiar back then, now make such a punk statement. And those nice, pink, fleshy lips of yours . . . I just want to bite them."

Before I understood what was happening, I saw her black, painted lips approaching mine and we kissed. It wasn't disgusting like I thought it would be: it was different. For the first time I had kissed a woman and not felt as if I were kissing my mother or sister.

In other words, it didn't feel incestuous. It must have been the *guascas* in the *pasteles,* and the champagne certainly must have helped. Suddenly I melted and found myself feeling chummy and mushy toward Claudia and her untold riches. I took both her hands in mine and she rested her orange hair on my shoulder.

"Listen to me, Sammy," she began after awhile. "This is very serious. Right now I'm footloose and fancy free. But not for much longer. My family is determined to marry me. They don't want an unmarried dyke in the family. And if you don't marry me, they'll make me marry some horrible mafioso. You know my brothers. Now, I know you wouldn't like that happening to me, would you? Besides, I promise to take good care of you."

"Oh, oh," I said, remembering her unpleasant brothers. "I wouldn't want to join 'the family,' you know what I mean? I disapprove of the drug trade. I think it's evil."

"I do too. I've nothing to do with that business. Mother and I just get the revenues, that's all. But they'll leave us alone. They know you're a poet. You know Colombians respect poetry so much."

"I'll have to think about it, okay?" I said, letting go of her hands. I noticed that Mother and Paulina were looking at us, smiling. If this were an early Dickens novel, I would conclude it now by saying that my sister and Stick and Claudia and I got married and lived happily in Jackson Heights ever after. But this is what happened next: the romantic, plaintive notes of the violin and the *bandoneón* in the background were drowned out by loud complaints and harsh, "Hey, you animal, watch where you're going, will you?"

Out of the corner of my eye, I saw my nephew rushing toward us. When he was a few tables away, I spotted two men with drawn pistols hot on his trail, pushing aside the seated customers, overturning chairs and tables, weaving through the crowd to catch up with Gene. People screamed and ducked as Claudia's bodyguards sprang forth and bullets were exchanged generously all over the nightclub. Gene's pursuers, with their faces, chests, and stomachs looking like bloody graters, fell dead on top of some freaked out customers. Several women fainted, and the ladies and gentlemen in the audience crawled and hid under tables, summoning their own bodyguards to protect them. Brandishing guns, Claudia's bodyguards fired at the chandeliers, and, for a moment, the room sparkled with a shower of glass. Yelling, "The Urrutias are leaving; nobody move," the bodyguards surrounded our party and herded us out of the Saigon Rose and into Claudia's limousine. And just like it's been done in a million Hollywood thrillers, the driver peeled rubber into the night.

Paulina was the first person to speak a coherent sentence. *"Qué taquicardia,"* she said, beating her breasts lightly with her closed fan. "Isn't it terrible how decent folk can't go anywhere these days?"

"It was worth the price of admission," Claudia said. "I haven't had so much fun since Carnival in Rio."

"How providential those nice gentlemen were there to help us out," Paulina said referring to her bodyguards. "Claudia, please remind me to have them over for coffee."

*"Qué horror! Qué horror!"* Mother exclaimed. Then, addressing Wilbrajan, "Cookie, I'll never come to hear you again as long as you sing in that place."

"Oh, Mother, get real," Wilbrajan said. "I'm used to it; it's like singing in Colombia all the time."

While the limo scudded down the dark Queens streets, Gene sat sullenly in a corner, staring out the window, his knees jerking up and down. To me, he looked guilty as hell; I would have to confront him later that night, I decided, but not in the car. I was sure the men had been after him, and I thought I knew why.

Checking her watch Mother said, "It's still early. Why don't we all go home and have supper? I made the most delicious pig's feet and *garbanzos.* There's plenty for all."

It was agreed we'd continue the party at Mother's house and we proceeded in that direction. As soon as we arrived, Mother and Paulina busied themselves in the kitchen, while the rest of us settled in the living room to get sloshed and chat with Colombian music in the background. Stick had just finished telling a gruesome tale about a young woman with her period who had been devoured by piranhas in a jungle river, when Gene excused himself. I took the opportunity to follow him upstairs. Wilbrajan and Claudia were so riveted by Stick's tales and hunky looks, that they couldn't have cared less if we had excused ourselves to go to Siberia.

Gene was lying on his bed, listening to the Grateful Dead, or the Dead Kennedys, or some such necrophiliac group. He looked scared as hell when he saw me come in. I asked him to turn down the damned music and sat down on his bed. "You got to return that coke," I said. "You almost got all of us killed. Do you realize that?"

He pretended not to know what I was talking about.

"The coke in the cartridge," I snorted. "You stole it."

"Oh that," he said, lying on his bed, closing his eyes. "I just want to buy a bike."

"There is enough coke in that package to buy a Honda dealership. Are you out of your mind?"

"Okay, so I did," he said, sitting up. "What do you want me to do now? They don't know who stole the coke, but I can't return it just like that," he said, snapping his fingers.

"Cut the crap. They know who did it. Those men were out to kill you."

"Where do you get your information? From the *Reader's Digest*? You're so wrong. Those men weren't after me; they were after Claudia's ass."

"Bullshit."

"Sammy, don't you know shit? There's a fucking drug war going on, and those men were out to fry Claudia and her mother to get back at the Urrutia brothers for some drug squealing or something. The Urrutias have been snitching to the DEA about Pablo Escobar."

"What episode of 'Miami Vice' was that? Do you think I'm an idiot?"

"I don't give a fuck what you think, Mr. Geraldo Rivera."

I sat there staring at him. If he weren't taller than me, I would have slapped his insolent mouth. To my utter astonishment, he started rapping:

"I'm just a boy
from Jackson Heights,
I ain't no criminal
All I want's a bike."

Then he burst out sobbing. "Oh, Sammy, I'm scared shitless."

This had the intended effect on me. "Okay," I said, patting his shoulder. "I don't mean to make it worse. We'll just have to think of something," I finished, feeling sorry for this pathetic boy who had no father (Wilbrajan wasn't sure who his father was), and a mother who carried on as the torch singer in *Blue Velvet.*

"You know, Uncle," he said. "Besides the Boners, you're the only friend I have in the world."

I knew he wanted something out of me—otherwise he'd never have called me Uncle. "What do you want me to do?"

He stopped crying. "You will help me? You're not shitting me?" he asked, smiling his killer smile.

"Of course I will. I said so, didn't I? You're my nephew and I care about you. I don't want to see you get fucked up."

"That's right. Because you know what they'll do to me? They'll chop me like *ropa vieja,"* he said, referring to Cuban brisket of beef dish. "So please, uncle Sammy, take the coke with you to Manhattan until I can think of something. Is that cool, dude?"

I vehemently refused. Gene cried some more, and like the sucker I am, I fell for it.

I went downstairs to join the party, which went on for hours. We munched on delicious Colombian *pasabocas,* until the pig's feet were served. After supper, Mother and Paulina, accompanied by Wilbrajan at the guitar and Gene on the drums, entertained us singing their favorite *rancheras.* We danced *cumbias, pasodobles,* and *merengues,* and consumed several bottles of *aguardiente* and *Ron Medellín.* It was the wee hours when I went upstairs quite tipsy. Although I was exhausted, I couldn't fall asleep. I tossed on my bed until my room spun like a roulette wheel and the bed tilted like a raft on the high seas. Feeling nauseous, I got up and sat on the sill of my open window. The branches of the cypress in front of the window were so thick they blocked the street. Looking up, through the leaves, I saw a handful of stars and maybe a planet. The sky was a milky black color that belonged neither to night nor day, but rather to a state of mind. I thought about the times I used to go to my grandfather's farm by the river: The motorboat would come to pick us up around 4:00 A.M., so we'd wake up after midnight and sit by a bonfire near the shore to wait for it. The mosquitoes were merciless at that hour, and my only consolation was the rococo sky and the hundreds of wishing stars that dropped from midnight until dawn. Grandpa would say that some of the stars were witches on their night errands, and he'd entertain us recounting the many times he had been bewitched, and how he had broken the spells and captured the witches. These stories terrified me, and even when I returned to the city after my vacations, they would haunt me at night. This line of thinking always weirded me out, and presently I thought I saw Bobby's ghost standing a few feet away from me. I don't believe in ghosts, so I immediately remembered I was sloshed. And yet, I could almost see it—this shape that was like Bobby's outline etched in mercury. I looked out the window and toward the sky and after awhile I looked back into the room, and it was still there. But there was no reason for me to be frightened of Bobby—not even his ghost. "What is it?" I asked, feeling quite batty for talking aloud to a would-be ghost. "What do you want?" As I spoke these words, the outline contracted until it became a little red dot that flickered before it went out. Now I was sure I had imagined all this. With the kind of day I had had, it was probably the d.t.'s.

A lovely, cool breeze caressed my face and I looked again at the night sky. I closed my eyes and in the camera obscura of my brain an old reel began to play. I saw myself and Stick and my sister when we were children. It was late in the afternoon and we were on our way to play hide-and-seek. We were ascending a long, steep street that led to the mountains above Bogotá; crossing *Carrera Séptima,* we entered the grounds of Javeriana University. Instead of walking across campus, we hiked up a mossy, unpaved trail that led to the shantytowns above the city. It was dusk. The sky above Bogotá was charcoal-colored, and the pallid sun had sunk in the horizon, buried behind the clouds. Beneath us, the city lights were beginning to go on, and, in the distance, the tall downtown buildings lit their skinny silhouettes against the ashen background of the mountains in the south. The mountain peaks were swathed in fog, and the ground was moist and cold. We walked until we reached a promontory, at the bottom of which rose the back of the building of the school of medicine; it looked deserted. Since the previous year, when the government had ordered a curfew, all evening classes had been canceled. We made sure that there were no guards around, and then raced down the pebbly hill. One of the windows on the ground floor was ajar. I went in first and Stick helped Wilbrajan. Inside it was dark, cold, damp, and reeking of the strong chemicals used for embalming. This was the morgue, a big, high-ceilinged room with four rows of slabs crossing it, whose walls were fitted with refrigerators stuffed with fresh corpses and loose organs in plastic bags.

"I hate this game," Wilbrajan whispered.

"Then why don't you go home," I said. "Nobody invited you."

We sat on the cold tiles with our backs against the wall.

"Okay, let's play now," Stick said. "Who will hide first?"

"I will," I said.

Wilbrajan offered to count.

"You count too fast. Let Stick count."

"He can't count in Spanish."

"You're the one who doesn't know the numbers," I said.

Wilbrajan and Stick turned to the wall, covering their eyes with their hands. Stick began to count to a hundred. I tiptoed down the aisles. Most of the corpses were covered with yellowing, stained sheets. Usually I'd climb onto an empty slab and cover myself with a sheet, or I'd lie next to a corpse and hide. There weren't too many hiding places. I heard the count of sixty-eight; I'd better hurry. I decided to try something new; I opened one of the huge refrigerators in the back of the room and stepped in. The door closed behind me. I realized it couldn't be opened from the inside. A small frosted lightbulb lit the interior of the icebox, revealing two corpses hanging from hooks, one male, the other female. In the dim light, their skins looked greenish. The man's body was old, skinny, its flesh corrugated; the woman's was young. Her face was smashed and caked with blood, and her red teeth appeared in a horrifying grin. Her eyelids were opened and she had no eyeballs. Her skin was taut, translucent, and her fingers stretched out, as if she were ready to jump on me. Seized with terror, I lunged against the door, and started banging on it and kicking it. I slipped on the icy floor and, as I fell backward, I grabbed the woman by a leg, knocking her off the hook. The corpse landed on me. Her breasts were on my face.

I put my hands on them to push her away from me—her breasts were hard, cold, sticky like ice cubes. I realized I was running out of air, that I was beginning to freeze. I screamed: white smoke came out of my mouth. The echo of my scream ricocheted off the walls of the refrigerator. "Oh, God, I promise to be good," I said. "I promise to make my mother baptize me and I'll have my first communion and I'll go to mass every Sunday. I promise to obey my mother." I felt dizzy, slipping into unconsciousness. I couldn't get the woman's breasts off my face. When I touched her, it felt as if I were being glued to her corpse. Now I saw that her throat had been slit, and the insides were brownish-red, like guava paste, and the edges blackish, rotting. Her face grinned inches away from mine. I tried to remember what I knew of the Lord's Prayer. It was useless; I didn't know it. Suddenly, I heard a tremendous pop; the door of the refrigerator opened, and I heard voices calling my name, and hands pulling me by my sneakers, and I knew the devil that my mother had threatened me with so often was finally here to drag me to hell.

# 6

## Just Say It

I woke up Sunday afternoon with a major hangover. I showered, shaved, dressed, and took a couple of Tylenols before going downstairs. I had decided to leave that afternoon. I was quite worried about Mr. O'Donnell.

*"Buenos días,"* Mother greeted me. Then correcting herself, "Good afternoon. I just woke up myself. What a rumba. Have a cup of coffee," she said pouring me a full cup of *tinto*.

"Good morning, good morning," Simón Bolívar screeched as I sat down.

"Mother, make him shut up, will you," I said, giving Simón Bolívar a nasty look.

"I can't," she said flatly, sitting at the table. "He loves to talk for breakfast."

I had never seen Mother so dishevelled. She had no makeup on her face, and her hair was completely out of shape.

"Have you seen Gene?" I asked.

"He left just right before you came down. He got tired of waiting for you. He seemed in a hurry. He said he was going by his job to quit. Why couldn't he wait till tomorrow, it beats me. I was happier with him working. I don't know what he's going to do if he's free all the time. That boy needs a father, Sammy." Mother frowned and finished her coffee. She left the kitchen, and while I was having my second cup of coffee and beginning to feel the effects of the Tylenol, I heard strange chanting in the other room. Mother entered the kitchen holding a burning stick of *palo santo,* singing in some ancestral African dialect. She seemed in a trance, as she walked to the counter where she opened the jar that contained my grandmother's ashes. Next she painted a cross on the floor. Since Mother had been into *santería* ever since I can remember, there was nothing odd about this, although I wished she had waited until after I had left for Manhattan. She lit a bunch of aromatic crystals in the incense burner and placed the burner at the center of the cross; with the smoking *palo santo,* she approached me and made the sign of the cross over my head. Mother grabbed my hand. "Walk over the incense," she ordered me, "and make the sign of the cross."

"What the hell is going on?" I snapped.

"It's a *despojo.* You need to cleanse your aura. Bad spirits are following you."

"What?" I yelled. "Are you exorcising me? I refuse to go along with this bullshit. Stop it right this minute, Mother."

Simón Bolívar mimicked me, "Mother, Mother, Mother."

When I refused to walk over the incense burner, Mother started zigzagging around the kitchen as if she were having an epileptic seizure, and began chanting, *"Yemayá, Yemayá, Quimba, quimba, quimbará."*

"He, he, he, he," Simón Bolívar giggled hysterically, flapping his wings. Too hungover to do anything, I sat down to wait until she finished.

This was the first time she had tried to exorcise me. I was too flabbergasted to comment on her performance. My feelings toward her were very antagonistic. I knew that some kind of breakthrough psychological unraveling had taken place this weekend and I wanted to run away and confront her about it, all at the same time. She was an old woman now and she was actually getting to the point where she would be needing my support to help her navigate through the passages of her old age. And yet, I was angry not at the old woman she was, but at the beautiful Gaugin goddess that had given birth to me; the first and only woman I had ever loved.

"I'm really pissed," I said, feeling the plug that held my feelings removed and a lot of steam beginning to blow out uncontrollably.

"What? What have I done wrong this time?"

"Mother, this whole Claudia thing is . . . insane. I'm not going to marry Claudia now or ever, is that clear?"

"But why, Sammy?"

"Because I'm homosexual and Claudia is a lesbian, that's why. Because I'll never love a woman that way." I couldn't believe I had actually said those words. I was shaking. For many years now I knew Mother knew, as she had known about Bobby since we had been kids; as she had always accepted our friendship, even when as boys we were probably in love with each other; when it had been adolescent romance. But the word homosexual had never been spoken, never been said in her presence, nor in connection with me. It was as if as long as it was unspoken there was still room for things to change some day, to declare that everything had been a passing fancy. As long as I didn't admit to it, there was hope that I would eventually marry like all good Colombian boys. Bobby used to say that the main difference between Colombian and American men was that all Colombians were gay until they married, whereas most Americans first married and then came out.

Mother looked crushed, deeply hurt. She seemed to be shrinking in front of my eyes. She began to cry, softly, delicately. "I just don't want you to die like Bobby. That's all, Sammy. I'm not stupid. I know about you and I don't care." The pain she felt must have been so severe that it left no room for histrionics. The moment was actually quite peaceful, serene. I wanted to put my arms around her shoulders; I wanted to say to her that I, too, loved her; and that I wanted to forget the past and to forgive. And yet, I couldn't. Perhaps in the future, I thought. Perhaps one day when all these feelings and revelations have been sorted out, I will be able to embrace you as a son, Mother, I thought.

An hour later, I found myself at the train station waiting for the number seven to take me back to Times Square. Clutching the shopping bags with clothes and food, and the valuable cache of cocaine I was smuggling into Manhattan, I thought about everything that had happened that weekend. As ridiculous as it sounded, I had come out to my mother in my mid-thirties. Perhaps because of this I felt freer, more liberated, than I had just a couple of days before. I was reeling with new knowledge that I trusted would lead me with clarity into the mature years of my life. Looking into the direction of the skyscrapers of Manhattan, I realized that for the first time they didn't look to me as the land of dreams, but the place where reality awaited me, at long last.

# PART TWO

THE CAT, THOUGH IT HAS
NEVER READ KANT, IS, PER-
HAPS, A METAPHYSICAL ANI-
MAL.

*Philosopher or Dog?*
Machado de Assis——

# 7

# The Cat Who Loved *La Traviata*

Nothing seemed to have changed in Times Square, and I found the familiar squalor somehow reassuring. As usual at this time of day, shoeless Muslims knelt on green towels, praying to Mecca in front of subway posters for Broadway shows. Squatting on the stairs leading to the street, begging aggressively for quarters, was the same woman I had seen for months, with the same shrinking baby, wrapped in a bunch of grimy rags. Nearby, bored cops chatted idly, petting their police dogs.

Forty-second Street was thick with a Sunday crowd of black and Latino teenagers looking for cheap thrills. Mormon-looking tourists with cameras strolled, sticking close together while taking in the scene. They were offered sex of all kinds, pot, Colombian coke, smack, hash, ecstasy, uppers and downers, designer drugs and, of course, crack.

It was one of those rare, mild late afternoons at the end of July when the air was like silk and Manhattan felt like an island. The multicolored neon marquees of the movie theaters advertised life-sized photographs of seminude porno stars in sexy poses. A naked man, looking stoned out of his mind, wandered out of a peep show. Halfway down the block, a young woman dressed in Salvation Army uniform and armed with a megaphone, was stationed under the awning of a sex palace, preaching to the depraved and indifferent denizens of Times Square. Two preppies stopped in front of her, swayed, twirled, wobbled on their feet and collapsed, overdosing on the sidewalk.

"You don't have to get high on drugs," the woman blared. "Jesus will get you high. You'll be so high on Jesus you'll never want to come down."

Waiting for the light to change at the corner of Forty-second and Eighth, I looked over my shoulder: the skyscrapers of midtown had bloomed. The Chrysler building caught the reflection of the setting sun; its silver top reminded me of a minaret crowned with a long, shimmering sword. Crossing Eighth, I saw the sky beyond the Hudson, which looked as if all the nuclear reactors from Hoboken to Key West had exploded, setting the air afire. Yet the color was not that of natural combustion, but synthetic, like the orange of a hot burner on an electric stove.

I live on the west side of Eighth Avenue, above O'Donnell's Bar, between Forty-third and Forty-fourth Streets, an address formerly nicknamed The Minnesota Strip. The good old days had ended when the famous Greek restaurant The Pantheon closed due to lease problems. Since that time the short block—which comprises a Citibank at the corner of Forty-third, O'Donnell's Bar, the Pantheon building, a porno joint (Paradise Alley), a Gyro coffee shop, the Cameo (a beautiful old theater now turned XXX movie house), and a four-story building at the corner of Forty-fourth, formerly a whorehouse and now a shooting gallery—had been taken over by crack addicts, who conducted their business on the premises of Paradise Alley. Now I looked back with nostalgia to the days when young hookers (for all tastes) decorated the block around the clock. . . . But wait a minute, not *that* young, I thought, standing on the east corner of Forty-third, as I spotted a tiny hooker standing in front of the door of my building. She looked about seven years old, maybe seven and a half. I had seen teenage hookers and hustlers, but this was a child. This was real depravity and decadence—no doubt a product of the crack epidemic. In spite of her spike heels, she barely reached the doorknob. She wore a vinyl miniskirt and red satin tank top. A pink plastic purse was strapped across her shoulder and her belly button was plugged with a blue stone. Her hair was streaked gold and punked-out. Long rhinestone earrings framed her cheeks and above the false eyelashes her eyelids were painted purple and sprinkled with gold glitter. Her tiny crimson lips were done in the shape of a heart. I stood in front of my door, open-mouthed, dangling the keys, waiting for her to move.

In her childish voice she said, "Want a date?"

I recoiled, aghast. Now she placed her baby hand on her hip and crossing one leg behind her knee she reclined lewdly against the wall. "Cheap blow job," she offered. I noticed now that her voice, though squeaky and reedy, had a sultry timbre. She was not a child—she was a midget hooker. I breathed a sigh of relief, "No, thank you," I said. "I live here."

She gave me a blank look, but made enough room for me to open the door. I ran up the stairs to my apartment on the fourth floor. I was worried about Mr. O'Donnell. The six months the vet had given him to live were over and even though Mr. O'Donnell seemed fine, I felt anxious when he was alone. Inside the apartment I set down my shopping bag and went to the closet to hang up my new suit. I was walking toward the living room calling Mr. O'Donnell's name when the phone rang.

"Santiago, is that you upstairs?" said Rebecca, my downstairs neighbor.

I picked up. "Hi, Rebecca. I just got here but I can't find Mr. O'Donnell."

"I'm so relieved it's you. I thought it might be a burglar. Mr. O'Donnell is down here with me."

"I'm coming down to get him. Is that okay?"

"Come on over. I'm so glad you're back."

Rebecca met me at her door. Her eyes were wide open, as if she had just had a major fright. Locking the door after I came in, she said, "Can I offer you a beer, iced tea, a glass of lemonade?"

"The lemonade sounds delish, but no thanks. Where's Mr. O'Donnell?" I looked around the room for him.

"I don't know whether we ought to disturb him right now. He's in my bedroom listening to side two of *La Traviata*."

Rebecca had discovered that Mr. O'Donnell would revive from

his periodic bouts of listlessness by listening to Monserrat Caballe's rendition of Violeta. He'd lie still, smiling, his ears pricked up until the opera was over.

"Is he in bad shape?"

"I didn't want to call you at Lucy's, but when I went upstairs Saturday morning to feed him, he was more dead than alive. He refused his Kal Kan, so naturally I was worried. I went to Barkin' Fish for some catfish since he likes it so much. I practically had to force feed him, but he ate one fillet, a teensy bitty bit at a time."

"Should I take him to the hospital right now?" I said.

"Goodness gracious, Santiago. You're making me more nervous, and I'm already a shitty mess. I called the hospital and was told there's nothing we can do except make sure he takes his medicine with his meals. Today he's much better. He's been listening to *La Traviata* all day. This morning he refused to eat fish, so I gave him a container of pineapple yogurt. Wait till this side of the record is over and you can take him upstairs. He's as good as new, thanks to my ingenuity."

"I shouldn't have left him alone, but thank you so much, Rebecca."

"Will you stop feeling guilty about everything. I swear, Santiago, I'm going to start calling you the Honorary Jew. I took real good care of the kitty; Florence Nightingale couldn't have nursed him better. So, how's Lucy? Did you have a nice weekend?"

I gave Rebecca a much abridged and sanitized version of what transpired in Jackson Heights.

"Honey, it sounds like a Flannery O'Connor novel set in Queens," she observed. "It's the planets," she added philosophically. "As long as Pluto is aligned with Scorpio it's going to be bad."

Willing to blame it all on the stars, I said, "Oh yeah, and exactly how long is that going to last?"

"Seven years."

"Rebecca, I couldn't take seven years of this!"

"That's why I'm going away. I might as well enjoy myself while there's a chance."

Thinking she meant her upcoming vacation, I said, "I'd love to get away from here, if I could."

"Santiago, darling, I'm beginning to doubt this area is ever going to get any better. All this time I bought your theory that it was just a matter of time before Donald Trump moved in to redevelop Times Square."

"I agree with you, Rebecca," I said, conceding defeat. "Donald Trump can't solve his own problems nowadays, much less ours. If only they closed Paradise Alley it would be okay. It wasn't all that bad when it was just hookers."

"The hookers were like girl scouts selling cookies compared to what's going on now," Rebecca said. "But I'm getting tired of calling the mayor's office and the midtown precinct and signing petitions. Somebody is getting paid a lot of money to keep that business open."

"Maybe we ought to go to the press with the story," I suggested. "A front page story in the *Post* would do it, I'm sure."

"Honey, I'm afraid nothing will get done until there's a massacre down there. By then I'll be a basket case. I tell you, if Francisco asks me to marry him, I'm saying *sí, sí*." She fanned herself with a letter.

"Is it a letter from Francisco?" I asked.

"Santiago," she said, "would you be a dear and do a little translating for me?"

"In that case I'll have some lemonade." I sat down and Rebecca went to the kitchen. Some months back, in a bookstore in Greenwich Village, Rebecca had met Francisco, a Venezuelan tourist and a hairdresser. Although she did not speak Spanish, nor Francisco English, they became lovers. After he returned to Caracas, I became the official translator of their correspondence. She entered the room and handed me a glass of cold lemonade.

"The weather's been so terrible, and the situation downstairs seems to be getting so much worse," she said in her melodramatic Alabamian twang, "that I declare I was ready to hang myself if something mighty good didn't happen to me soon. But there it was, in the mailbox, a letter from my beloved."

I took a sip of lemonade, cleared my throat and toasted to love. Striking a Cyrano de Bergerac pose, I pulled out the letter. It was written in Francisco's tiny gothic handwriting, which I had come to know so well. Rebecca sat very still and upright, holding in her lap her glass of lemonade. Her head thrust forward, her lips quivering, her aquamarine eyes wide open and gleaming; the intensity of her expression was almost frightening. I could have read the first paragraph blindfolded since it was always the same. "Dear Rebecca," I read. "I hope this finds you and your loved ones enjoying good health. God willing."

"Santiago, is that a South American convention of letter writing? He always says the same thing."

I ignored her and went on. "I was so happy to receive your last letter and to find out that you're doing well."

"Goodness gracious. He's so formal."

"Rebecca, my sweet, in case you haven't noticed, we South Americans are formal people. And now, shall I go on?" I asked, somewhat irked by her interruptions. She smiled for an answer. I continued with my translation. "I'm doing very well, thank God."

"Is that a South American thing, Santiago, to punctuate every sentence with God?"

I sipped my lemonade to control my temper. "Rebecca, don't be ridiculous."

"Well, better to have a Christian for a boyfriend than a druggie," she sighed.

Her reasoning escaped me, so I resumed my translation. "I've been incredibly busy lately, and I get to my apartment late at night, and I'm usually so tired that even though I want to sit down and write to you every night I fall asleep in spite of my good intentions." God is merciful, I thought. If he wrote to her like this every day, translating would become excruciating. May God keep him very, very busy.

"What is it? Bad news?"

"It's nothing," I said, and continued translating. "I have the most exciting piece of news. One of my clients has been elected Miss Caracas and she'll be representing our city in the Miss Venezuela competition. The girl is too divine for words, and very intelligent and has lots of personality, and I'm positively sure that she'll be elected Miss Venezuela and go on to represent our country in the

Miss Universe Pageant. Can you imagine what that will do for my business?"

"I smell a franchise," Rebecca exclaimed.

I looked up in disbelief. "I didn't know you were into beauty pageants."

"Beauty pageants are one of the interests Francisco and I share. Is that the end of the letter?"

I shook my head and continued. " 'In your last letter you mentioned wanting to visit me during your vacation. My humble abode is at your service, and I would be glad to receive you in my home.' "

"Glad? Is that what he says, Santiago? Are you sure?"

"Sorry. I would be *happy* to receive you in my home," I corrected myself.

"You know, Santiago, there is a difference. That's what's called a nuance of the English language."

"Even in the best translations something gets lost," I remarked, annoyed with her.

"Don't mind me, honey. Go on with the letter. You're doing beautifully. It always amazes me how well you do this sort of thing."

Predictably, the third paragraph referred to me. "All this part is about me, Rebecca. Do you want me to translate it also?"

"Would you, honey? I don't want to miss a single one of his words."

"Okay, here it goes: 'Please thank our dear friend Santiago for translating my letters. I hope everything is going well with him, and that he and Mr. O'Donnell are enjoying good health, God willing. I always include Mr. O'Donnell in my prayers and ask José Gregorio Hernández for a miracle.' "

"Who's that? Is it voodoo?"

"He may as well pray to Donald Duck," I said. "It might be more effective. José Gregorio isn't canonized, but he's Venezuela's national saint because he introduced the microscope to the country. And you want to know how smart he was? He was killed by the only automobile in Caracas at that time."

Rebecca frowned. "Well, it's real sweet and thoughtful of him, in any case."

"Yeah," I said. "It's real sweet of him. Now let me finish: 'I look forward to hearing from you soon, and I hope you're following my beauty tips and are taking good care of your hair and your lovely complexion. It's midnight now, and through my window I can see the moon illuminating the city below, and everything—the sensual breeze that comes from the Caribbean, the stars in the sky, the fires twinkling in the mountains—reminds me of you, my adored Rebecca. Love, Francisco.' "

"He's a poet," Rebecca said.

Folding the letter and handing it to her, I said, "He's a hairdresser."

"A hair stylist and a makeup artist," she corrected me, and started bragging about what a great lover Francisco was and how she had never met a man who cared so much about a woman's needs.

I studied her, marvelling at the change in her appearance since she had met this paragon. Before, she dressed like a receptionist in a funeral parlor. Tonight, she wore stone studded sandals and her toenails were painted a lurid purple. She had on khaki shorts and a Banana Republic shirt that depicted lush vegetation in an apocalyptic red. She wore too much glossy lipstick and mascara and green eyeshadow, but her gold-streaked, new wave haircut was becoming. I was alarmed, though, by all the gold and silver loops marching up her ears. I closed my eyes and saw Rebecca going all the way, like the Orinoco Indians in Venezuela, and piercing her lips, her nostrils, her . . .

"Santiago," she said, awakening me from my reverie, "is it very hot down there in August?"

"I don't know. I told you, I was there in November. It was pleasant during the day and cool at night. You might want to take a couple of sweaters."

"It sounds heavenly," she purred.

"So you've made up your mind to go?"

"I got to get away from these crack people downstairs before I crack up myself. Besides, I'm ready for adventure. Of course, I'm mighty apprehensive to be going there alone. I don't know what I'll do without you," she said, referring, I think, to my services as a translator.

I tried to reassure her. "Caracas is a cosmopolitan city. You'll have no problems communicating with the people."

"But, you know, Santiago. The truth is, when Francisco and I are together, we understand each other perfectly. Isn't that incredible?"

"I'll say. But you could learn Spanish too. It's an easy language to learn, unlike English."

"I purchased a dictionary, and I'm learning useful expressions: *Buenos días. Cómo está usted?*"

"Your accent is perfect," I lied.

"Thanks, honey. When I come back to New York (that is, if Francisco doesn't ask me to marry him), I'll take some lessons. Thank you so much for translating the letter. You're an angel, Santiago."

"Anything for love," I said.

"I hope it happens to you too. You'll be transformed, sugar." Rebecca sat with the letter on her breasts, blissed out. I could read love printed large over her face. Her happiness was becoming too painful to bear. I noticed side two of *La Traviata* was over and got up. "The opera is over," I said. "I'm exhausted and I have to get up early in the morning."

Rebecca followed me into her bedroom. Mr. O'Donnell was hiding under the blankets. "Uh-oh, Rebecca," I uttered in mock alarm, playing one of his favorite games. "Where's the kitty? I don't see him! He escaped again! Help!"

Mr. O'Donnell remained still. I sat on the bed and touched the bulge he made under the sheets, quickly pulling my hand away. In the winter this game was safe, because he was covered by heavy blankets; but in the summer his teeth and nails would poke through the sheets. I placed one hand on his head and the other on his thigh, immobilizing him. He struggled a bit to free himself but then started to purr loudly.

"It's a wonder to me how he can purr and be vicious at the same time," Rebecca said.

I uncovered him—Mr. O'Donnell was now on his back, smiling.

"Hello, kitty," I said, scratching him under his ears. "It's time to go home." As I picked him up, he felt lighter, bonier, as if he had lost weight over the weekend. On the spot where he had been lying remained thick chunks of his hair. In the summer Mr. O'Donnell shed copiously, but the way he was shedding lately he'd soon go bald. As I ran my fingers over his stomach, I noticed his coat of hair had lost all luster. Overnight, Mr. O'Donnell had become old.

I thanked Rebecca for everything and said good night. Upstairs, I stored the *pasteles* in the fridge. The cassette with the coke was harder to dispose of. Since I didn't own a TV, much less a VCR, its presence anywhere in the apartment was conspicuous. I threw the plastic case in the trash and then emptied the cocaine into a glass jar. I left it next to the salt, sugar, flour, oats, etc.

Setting the alarm for 6 A.M., I undressed, lay down, and turned off the overhead light. Although I was exhausted by the events of the past few days, I could not fall asleep. I was well aware of the strange turns and twists my otherwise dull existence was taking. I had in my possession what looked like a pound of cocaine. My brain went into overdrive. I needed to get some sleep, though. I turned on the air conditioner and tried to relax. I said to myself, "Your brain is out to kill you, Santiago. Stop thinking; remember your brain wants you dead." As the room cooled, I started to drift off. My eyelids felt heavy, as if they were glued. I thought of Caracas. Of huge, prehistoric leaves. And stars that had auras, like the moon. Of parks in which exquisite orchids nested in gigantic, emerald trees. And the smells: the tropical breeze scented with a million gardenias. And the Caribbean in the moonlight, silvery and smooth, and in the distance, riding shimmering seahorses, a chorus of mermaids serenading me with sensual, heartbreaking boleros.

I was hungry when I woke up around midnight. But I wanted something light, like yogurt or fruit, and there was nothing like that in the fridge. I splashed cold water on my face, combed my hair and went downstairs.

Both sides of Forty-third Street were lined with garbage bags, and the homeless huddled in front of the shops closed for the night. The after-theater crowd had dispersed and was replaced by the usual junkies, transvestites, and habitués of porno palaces.

I crossed Eighth Avenue and went into the *New York Times*

building to get today's newspaper. Then I walked to the Korean fruit stand at the corner of Forty-third and Eighth. I picked a piece of watermelon, oranges, carrots, and yogurt. I pulled out a twenty dollar bill. The woman rang the items as she placed them in a bag.

"Twelve-fifty," she said.

For some time I had suspected this woman of overcharging me. Tonight I decided to confront her.

"How's that possible?" I asked, grabbing the twenty from her hand.

"Pay, please. Next," she said, staring at me impassively.

Looking over my shoulder, I saw other customers in the store but no one behind me. I began pulling the items out of the bag. "Let's add them up one by one," I said.

"Four oranges, two dollars," she said, a flash of anger or annoyance sparkling in her eyes.

"Four oranges at fifty cents a piece, that's two dollars—if my math is correct."

"Watermelon," she paused, then looking directly into my eyes, "three dollars."

"It sounds like a lot for a small piece of watermelon, but it's too hot, okay, and I don't feel like arguing. So that's a total of five dollars."

With one sweep of her hand she grouped together the remaining items. "Carrots and yogurt, five dollars. Ten dollars total. Sorry for mistake. Pay, please."

"This is outrageous," I exploded, realizing my suspicions had been correct all along. "Yogurt is ninety cents at the supermarket, and a bag of carrots forty cents."

"Then go to supermarket."

I found it unnecessary to inform her that supermarkets in our neighborhood closed well before midnight.

"No want to pay price, no take," was her fortune cookie advice.

"Fine," I said. "I'll just take the oranges. And the yogurt."

She rang these items. I gave her the twenty dollar bill.

"Sorry, no change."

"You had change just a minute ago."

The woman said something in Korean, I guess. Wondering

which member of my family had been insulted, I prepared to call her a few names myself in Spanish when she turned and looked toward the back of the store. A man in a stained apron, looking like a cross between Gertrude Stein and a Sumo wrestler, emerged from behind a bamboo curtain holding a head of lettuce in one hand and a butcher knife in the other. They engaged in an animated conversation, and the man gave me a scorching look. Now Santiago, I said to myself, you don't want to engage in combat with that creature. I put my hand in my pocket and found a ten dollar bill. "Here," I said, looking at the man. "I'm sorry. It's this heat."

It was cooler now, but the humidity was unchanged and the sky looked cottony and gray. Feeling crappy, I dragged my feet on the sidewalk as I noticed several crack addicts milling excitedly in front of Paradise Alley, like hyenas around carrion. I unlocked the door and was about to go in, when a sharp object hit the middle of my spine.

"Don't move," a man's voice ordered me. "Just give me your money." His hand went into my right pocket, then into the left one where my money was. Thinking, This is where he busts my head and runs away, I closed my eyes.

"Give him back the dough," another voice screeched.

I turned around; the mugger's face was inches away from mine—these were eyes that hadn't seen straight in years. I grabbed the gun and snatched the bills. Out of the corner of my eye, I saw the midget hooker pressing a huge sparkling blade against the man's crotch.

"Now beat it, fuckface, before the cops get your stupid ass," she ordered him.

The man reeled backward until he reached the street curb. Pointing a finger at my rescuer he yelled, "You're dead, you fucking freak!"

I pointed the gun at the mugger. "You heard the lady! Piss off!"

The man ran across the street dodging the oncoming Eighth Avenue traffic. At the corner of Forty-third, he stopped and screamed a bunch of obscenities and threats. People were looking in our direction.

The gun shook violently in my hand; I felt dizzy. "I don't know how to thank you," I said.

"Don't mention it," she said, folding the blade and hooking it to a garter under her skirt.

"Here," I said, offering her the gun.

She shuddered as if I had offered her a cobra. "Are you crazy? I don't want that thing, man. It's yours. Who knows how many dudes he's killed with it."

Passersby were approaching. Like a gangster, I stuck the gun between my pants and my belly.

"See you around. I got to try to score tonight." She started to walk away.

"Hey, listen," I called after her, feeling that I hadn't thanked her enough. "What's your name?"

"Hot Sauce," she said. "And yours?"

I told her.

"Well, San-ti-a-go, it's been fun meeting you. Any time you want it, I'll give you a good deal, babe," she said, pouting and blowing me a kiss before she swaggered into the surrounding nocturnal sleaze. From behind, she looked like a child playing femme fatale.

The gun burning against my skin, I shut the door and dashed up the stairs. I locked the door and paced the length of the apartment looking for a niche to hide the gun in. Finally, I settled for the toilet water tank. Tomorrow I'll wipe off the fingerprints before I ditch it in the Hudson, I thought. I was still shaking and feeling slightly hysterical but it was too late to call anyone, even Rebecca. I lay in bed and tried to read the *Times,* but my eyes wouldn't focus. I ate an orange. Tonight, I wished I had a TV set. My mother was right—it was un-American not to own a television. Mr. O'Donnell jumped onto my bed. I set the paper aside. "You don't know how lucky you are to be a cat," I said. His face was on top of mine, and his breath stank, but I remained still. One half of his face was white and the other half gray, and he had the long pinkish nose of a tropical rat. I stared into his eyes. The black pupils were surrounded by a greenish circle that grew agate toward the edges. His whiskers were long and thick like plastic toothpicks stuck on his snout. I scratched him between his ears and he started to purr. "Yes, yes, I know," I said. Burying his nose under my chin, he went to sleep lying on my chest, his enlarged heart thumping against mine.

# 8

## Mrs. O'Donnell and Moby Dick

The alarm rang at six. I had to be at the Social Security office by eight. Consoling myself that I would be home before noon, I got up. Curled up on a corner of the bed, Mr. O'Donnell pricked up his ears.

After I showered, I put on some water for coffee and gulped my vitamins. While waiting for the coffee, I sat by the window that overlooks the alley behind my apartment building. On the far side of the alley is another building with an entrance on Forty-third Street between Eighth and Ninth avenues; the other half of the block is taken up by a parking garage several stories high. The alley is active day and night because it's used as blow-job alley by many office workers on their way to Port Authority. But in the early morning, looking out through the screen and my gate, all I saw was a family of alley cats playing below. These cats seldom came up the fire escape, but each day Mr. O'Donnell would spend many hours by the window watching their antics.

In April, he had broken an old window screen and escaped. He was lost for eleven days. I thought he had reverted to his old alley cat life and I searched for him in vain. My friend, the painter Harry Hagin, did a drawing of him and we posted hundreds of copies around the neighborhood. Since he was a sick cat and needed his medicine to survive, the story caught the attention of a *Daily News* reporter, and a picture of me, displaying Harry's drawing, appeared in the "Manhattan" section that Friday. My line was swamped by callers offering me other cats and animals; others claimed Mr. O'Donnell was their lost cat; I also received obscene letters and phone calls from heavy breathers, but no information as to the cat's whereabouts. I had given up hope he was still alive when, one morning, with one of his ears chewed up and his muzzle so badly scratched that I hardly recognized him, he came up the fire escape, looking guilty and tired. That same week I took him to the Humane Society to have him fixed.

The coffee was ready. I poured myself a big cup and looked out the kitchen window. The handsome flasher who lived in one of the studio apartments across the alley was sitting by the window in his underwear. I had gotten used to seeing him dancing and playing with himself. Mr. O'Donnell zigzagged into the room and, eyes still half-closed, started to beg. He did not meow, but instead made a weird noise that reminded me of the cry of a toucan. I fixed his breakfast, which he ate half asleep and then went back to bed.

As I went downstairs at seven, there was already a long line of applicants at Mike's, the employment agency on the second floor of my building. The men were Mike's usual crop of shabbily dressed Hindu and Arabic types, chattering in exotic languages. Sometimes they came to the agency with their cardboard suitcases, as if they had just arrived from Baghdad or Sri Lanka or wherever they came from. I always wondered what kinds of jobs Mike got for them.

Outside, Eighth Avenue reeked of uncollected garbage. Masses of stone-faced commuters wearing suits and carrying briefcases poured out of the Port Authority Terminal. The humidity was thick and oppressive but the A train was prompt, although crowded. Minutes later I resurfaced at Chambers Street.

To kill time I sat on a bench outside the Federal Plaza Building, under a rachitic maple. I lit a cigarette and watched the usually frantic Wall Streeters dawdle, struggling with the prevailing mugginess. For a few years I had been working as an interpreter in different boroughs of New York City, for the Department of Social Security, a trove of stories and characters. I found it hard to believe that in New York, the Mecca of the twentieth century, there were people whose squalid lives seemed as horrifying as anything one could find in the novels of Gorky. I was uptight about having to interpret for Judge Warpick, who was the most detestable person I had ever met. I felt reassured that my hatred was shared by the other department employees as well as all the claimants who came before her. On many occasions, I had felt like leaping from my seat and twisting her neck. To ward off these thoughts, I reminded myself that I was just the interpreter, a vessel of language, the invisible man, a passive and disinterested nonparticipant.

At five to eight I took the elevator to the twenty-ninth floor.

"Hi, Jeff, how's it going?" I greeted the security guard.

"Hey, Santiago. Good to see you, man. You up for a game?"

Jeff and I played chess while we waited between hearings. Although we had played hundreds of times, he still managed to beat me in the first dozen moves.

"I'd like to. But I have Judge Warpick, you know. And she's always on time."

"Good luck. She's in a foul mood. If you ask me, what she needs is a good fuck. But I'd rather go to the electric chair," he said smiling. "Here," he added, handing me the claimant's file. "She don't have an attorney. Maybe we can play when you get out."

"Okay."

The room was empty but for a couple of women sitting way in the back, near a tall fan which made a lot of noise all right, but blew no air.

I approached the women. Smiling, I said to the older woman, "Good morning. I'm your Spanish interpreter."

The women exchanged puzzled looks as if I had spoken in Chinese. The older woman said, "Thank you."

I sat next to her. Reading her name on the file, I asked, "Are you Guadalupe Rama?"

She nodded.

"Señora, why don't you have a lawyer?"

"Nobody told me nothing about getting a lawyer."

"Señora Rama, the letter you received with the date of your

hearing had a list of places where you can get free legal services. It's your right under the law."

"It would take someone with a very black soul to deny me help," she said.

That sounded to me like the perfect description of Judge Warpick. "The judge is not here to defend you, Señora Rama, but to interpret the law," I warned her, as I leafed through the thick file. "This folder contains all the documents that the judge is going to review to reach a decision about your case. There are twenty-eight documents here." I pointed to the list on the first page. "They go as far back as 1978, and the most recent entry pertains to your visit to Dr. Miller on June of this year. I also see that your claim has been denied four times."

"And if I lose this time, I will reappeal," she said, waving her crutches.

"If you had had an attorney, you might have succeeded the first time."

When I had explained the file, I informed Jeff that we were ready to go before the judge. We were led to Judge Warpick's chambers by her assistant. I indicated to the women where to sit, and sat down next to them. While the judge's assistant fiddled with the tape recorder and the mikes, I studied Señora Rama's daughter. A teenager of medium height, she was incredibly thin. Her complexion was caramel-colored and her hair shiny ebony. She seemed withdrawn and avoided my eyes. When our eyes finally met, I noticed that hers were dark and moist like a canna flower in the moonlight.

Judge Warpick entered the room, followed by the doctor. I rose, indicating to Señora Rama to follow me. She rose with great difficulty.

"Please be seated." The judge motioned with her hands without looking at any of us. The doctor sat next to me.

"Mr. Interpreter, have you explained to the claimant that under the law she has the right to obtain legal counsel?"

"Yes, your honor, I have."

"And she still wants to go on with the hearing?"

"Yes, your honor. She does."

"Very well, Señora Rama. I advise you to go ahead with the hearing; it will be to your benefit."

I started interpreting. Judge Warpick interrupted me, "You don't have to translate that," she growled. "This is not the United Nations. Please stand up, Mr. Interpreter, and raise your right hand. Do you"—she read my name on a piece of paper—"solemnly swear to interpret faithfully the questions posed from English into Spanish and Spanish into English to the best of your ability so help you God?"

I already wanted to strangle her. "I do."

Señora Rama was sworn, we were seated, and Judge Warpick began, "Guadalupe Rama, when did you come to the mainland United States for the first time."

"October 4th, 1964, your honor."

This was something I had noticed about all immigrants I had ever interpreted for: they remembered the exact date when they had first arrived in the United States.

"What was the highest grade of education you completed in Puerto Rico?"

"I never went to school."

"Never?"

"That's right."

"Do you speak any English?"

"I know a few words."

"Can you read or write in Spanish?"

"No, ma'am."

"Who do you live with?"

"My children."

"How many children do you have?"

"Four."

"Give their names and ages."

"Dorcas Antioco, twenty-five; Hennil Rangel, twenty; Sonya Altagracia, eighteen and Raisa Cococielo, here present, fifteen," she said, indicating her daughter.

The girl squirmed in her seat, and mumbled, "Sixteen."

"How many times have you been married?"

"Twice. My first husband died; my second husband divorced

me. The others, I didn't marry. I'm a useless woman. Men don't want me."

"Señora, just answer my questions. I don't want to hear long stories about your life. Is that understood?" She paused. Obviously she wasn't getting anywhere with this claimant. "Do you still live on Avenue A and First Street?"

"In the projects."

"On what floor?"

"Number four."

"Do you walk up the stairs or take the elevator?"

"I take the elevator when it's working, which is never. Otherwise, I walk the stairs one step at a time," she said, holding her crutches. Her hands shook violently now. There was a strange expression on her face, as if she were trying to smile. I noticed it was a grimace of pain; she was about to start crying.

"Señora Rama," the judge said, staring at her papers, "tell me about your present complaints."

Señora Rama's eyes were wet, but no tears came out of them. Eagerly, she extended her arms in front of her and opened her hands. It looked as if she were making an offering to the judge. "First, I had an operation on this hand," she said, looking at her right palm. "Then (shaking her left palm), I had an operation on this one."

I saw on each hand an S-shaped, wide, deep scar that ran from the joint of the middle finger to the wrist area. Now I noticed her gnarled fingers. "These hands are useless. I can't do anything with them."

"Who does the house chores?"

"Raisa," she said, nodding in the direction of the girl, who stared at her hands in her lap and sank lower in the chair.

"Don't you cook anything at all?"

Señora Rama shook her head; she squinted, as if trying to remember something. "I can boil two eggs and some potatoes. But I cannot peel them. That's all."

"Can you carry a five pound bag of potatoes?"

"I can't do nothing."

"Answer my question: Can you carry a five pound bag of potatoes?"

"If I hold it between my arms," she said, crossing her arms across her breasts.

"Do you have any other complaints?"

Señora Rama rose from her chair and, on her crutches, hopped to the side of the table.

"I have trouble with my feet. See? I have pins in my ankles." She pointed to scars the size of brown quarters on both ankles. "I had two operations," she explained.

The doctor rose and leaned over the table and took a look at the scars.

"You can sit down," the judge ordered her, looking very uncomfortable.

"And my knees, too," she said, refusing to sit down.

"What's the matter with your knees?"

"When I walk, the bones come out of joint, so I have to wear these braces all the time." She began to pull at her pants.

"That's enough. You can sit down." Visibly rattled, the judge waited until the claimant sat down and then went on. "And other than your hands and your knees, do you have any other physical complaints?"

Señora Rama lifted her blouse and showed three pink, corrugated scars that looked like scaly worms stretched across the width of her stomach.

"Please, señora," Judge Warpick screamed, hitting her desk with the palm of her hands. "You don't have to show us your scars. Please."

I took a good look at the judge. In her youth, she must have been a pretty woman. Now her still abundant hair was gray and cut short. Although her features were regular and firm, she was so skinny that she almost looked desiccated. But it was her expression of utter contempt and disgust—as if she hated her post, the world and its people, and maybe even herself—that I found so disturbing. Furiously, she scribbled on her pad.

Señora Rama went on. "I have to go back to the hospital for another operation."

In a voice filled with apprehension Judge Warpick asked, "In your stomach?"

"No, here," and she indicated behind her right ear.

"Can you bend?"

"No. I had an operation here." She turned sideways on the chair and pointed to her lower back. "The doctor gave me a shot in my spine."

"How many doctors do you see?"

I looked at Dr. McDowell, who all this time had been going over the woman's medical file. His beautiful green eyes darted back and forth between the claimant and myself.

Señora Rama asked her daughter for the handbag. She took out a stack of cards and handed them to me. I removed the rubber band. "Mr. Interpreter," the judge said, indicating that I should read the names on the cards.

"Dr. Bajit," I read.

"He's for my ankles," Señora Rama explained.

I handed the card to Dr. McDowell, who examined it on both sides. "Dr. Ramin Badrinthajanmon something," I read.

"He's for my stomach in Brooklyn."

"Dr. Dallon," I read.

"He's for my eyes."

"Do you have problems with your eyes?"

"If I didn't have problems with my eyes, I wouldn't see a doctor. I have great pain inside my eyes."

I read the names of at least twenty doctors. "Dr. Ramírez," I read the last card.

"Is he a psychiatrist?"

"Yes."

"And how long have you been seeing Dr. Ramírez?"

"Since 1969, when my son died." Suddenly, Señora Rama's eyes glistened and tears popped out.

"Do you want to take a break? Would you like to go to the ladies' room?"

She wiped her tears with the back of her trembling hand. "No, I want to finish this thing as soon as possible. I'm in a lot of pain."

"You can stand up if you'd like."

"It's worse when I stand up."

"So, Señora Rama," the judge said, breathing heavily. "Tell me, what do you do all day?"

"I sit by the window and look out. And I hear voices."

"What kind of voices?"

"Horrible voices; dirty voices. They tell me to jump off."

"And why don't you jump?" Warpick asked. "What prevents you from jumping?"

"I prevent her," Raisa said. "I have to watch her all the time."

"If you want to testify in your mother's behalf, I'll have to swear you in."

The claimant burst into loud sobs and stretched out her arms in her daughter's direction. In Spanish she said, *"No me dejes sola; no me dejes sola."*

"Silence," Judge Warpick yelled. "Silence. Mr. Interpreter, what's she saying?"

"Don't leave me alone; don't leave me alone."

"Señora Rama, listen to me," Judge Warpick said. "Forget about the voices. Nobody is going to do anything to you. We're all here to help you."

I noticed that my palms were sweating and my heart was pumping fast. I, too, was out of breath. I wanted to get up and run out of that room. I placed a hand on the claimant's arm—her flesh was very cold.

"So tell me, what else do you do?" the judge asked.

Señora Rama had stopped crying. "Well, on Monday mornings I go to see Dr. Bajit at Manhattan Eye and Ear. On Tuesday I go to see Dr. Ramírez in the afternoon. On Wednesdays I go to see two doctors. In the morning . . ."

"Okay, okay, okay," Judge Warpick interrupted. "I believe it." She paused, looked at the papers on her desk, and then asked, "Do you have any friends? Do any family members ever come to visit you?"

"I don't have any family here, just my children. There is a woman upstairs who used to come to visit me. She's so nice. But she's a sick woman . . . she's in a wheelchair. She had a stroke and . . ."

"I see," Warpick cut her off.

Señora Rama looked at me. I put a finger to my lips to indicate that she should shut up.

"Dr. McDowell," Judge Warpick said, looking exasperated. "I'm going to swear you in. Please stand up."

I could see the doctor didn't like having to stand up to be sworn in. He was tall like a basketball player and maybe a few years older than me. He wore a light brown summer jacket and a pale tie and a yellow shirt. When he was seated, the judge said, "Dr. McDowell, you have had an opportunity to hear Señora Rama's testimony. Have you gone over her medical file as well?"

"Yes, your honor," he said, turning to look at me.

"And could you tell me what you've found out?"

Dr. McDowell's handsome face turned red. He cleared his throat. "Based on my review of the documents, I've found no evidence, your honor, of severe physical impairment. According to Dr. Cummings, she can lift a twenty five pound bag of potatoes on an occasional basis. Furthermore, under article 11, 876, section B, rider H, paragraph 16," he read from a book, "Mrs. Rama doesn't meet the requirements for supplementary income. Moreover, it says here that . . ."

Señora Rama looked intently at the doctor, then at me, but I wasn't supposed to interpret his testimony. I observed Raisa, who did speak English and when I saw the expression of outrage on her face, I looked out the window, away from her anger. In the distance, I saw the Hudson and the Jersey shore, and tiny buildings billowing gray smoke. In the morning haze, this part of the world looked muted, ghostly, like an old painting whose colors are fading.

Señora Rama left in tears, but vowing to reappeal the decision in case it was unfavorable. I had the judge's assistant sign my form so I could get paid. Then I went to say good-bye to Jeff, who was disappointed I wasn't staying to play a game. Waiting for the elevator, I ran into the claimant and her daughter.

"Thank you, *guapo*," she said, opening her purse and pulling out a five dollar bill.

"No, no," I said, embarrassed but touched. "I get paid by the court," I explained. "You don't have to give me anything."

"Just for the cigarettes and coffee," she insisted.

"Thank you, but no," I said firmly. "Goodbye, Señora Rama; bye, Raisa," I said, heading for the restroom to escape them. When I returned, they were gone.

It was mornings like this that I wished I had kept my job as a reporter for *Modern Grocer*. Sure, it was dangerous and at least a couple of times I had come close to getting shot; but the lives and problems of *bodega* owners were glamorous Judith Krantz stuff compared to the plights of the social security claimants. And how could I change careers at thirty-three years of age? Wasn't that the age of Christ when he was crucified, anyway? I hadn't one skill necessary to do well in the Age of Libra, in which everything had its weight in gold. I hadn't learned to use a word processor—the most complicated machine I knew how to work was my answering machine. I cursed the fate that had made me be born in Colombia. If only I had been born somewhere in the California Valley, I thought, I would have been perfectly attuned to the needs of this age.

I was crossing the street, automatically heading for the subway entrance, when I heard someone call, "Yo, Santiago, are you ashamed of your old friends?" I turned sideways and saw my friend, the painter Harry Hagin, dressed in a white uniform and hat, standing on the curb next to an ice-cream cart.

"Don't you want to talk to me?" he called.

"Harry, I'll be damned. When did you start selling ice cream? Did you quit your job unloading fruit?"

"Yeah, man. I was becoming a hunchback. And it's not ice cream but ices, natural ices. Hey, you know, I figured there's no escape being a Rockefeller slave in America, so I decided to take it easy. I love being on my own; nobody gives me orders. I have delusions of being free: I go home in the evening, take a shower, drink a beer, eat something and paint for a few hours. So, how are you doing? How's old Mr. O'Donnell? Did you frame my drawing yet? Some day it's gonna be worth big bucks, you know."

Harry and I had met as students at Queens College, where he majored in arts and business, and I had majored in medieval Spanish studies. After graduation we had remained good friends.

"Mr. O'Donnell is living overtime. I took him to the vet a few weeks ago, and he says that he wished he had made a mistake diagnosing his condition, but Mr. O'Donnell is going to croak any day."

"That's rotten, you know. Such a nice cat. After all that trouble we went through trying to find him when he ran away. Sorry to hear that. That's a damned shame, you know."

"I know," I agreed, and shook my head, making an effort to push away the gloomy subject of death, which of late seemed to follow me everywhere. A customer approached to buy an ice. I stood thinking of how Harry, while still in college, had settled into a gutted building in the Lower East Side. It had taken him years to rebuild it, but now it was a hot piece of property. Besides, I knew he had invested successfully in the stock market and gotten out while it was still good.

"First sale of the day," he said, pocketing his change, when the customer wandered away.

"Harry, you're worth a lot of money. Why do you get these crazy jobs?"

"Look, Santiago," he said, becoming very excited, his big blue eyes dancing wildly. "It's heartbreaking, man. It took me ten years of heavy shit to fix my building and then, you know, I make a terrible mistake, all because I'm such a good-hearted asshole. Instead of renting the apartments to yuppies, I rented to Puerto Ricans. And you know, these Puerto Ricans, no offense, man (and you know I'm not racist!), will kill their mothers, fry their babies, jump out of windows to break every bone in their bodies, so they can sue the landlord. I'm involved in three litigations right now, you know. So I have to work to pay the lawyers to keep my building. And these fucking lawyers . . . man, the vermin capitalism produces! Santiago, let me tell you, never have anything to do with a lawyer."

If Harry had been a racist he wouldn't be my friend, but I was becoming alarmed. "Harry," I said, looking around nervously, "there could be a Puerto Rican going by."

He chortled. "Puerto Ricans on Wall Street? That's a hoot, man." He paused. "Hey, do you subscribe to *Business Monthly*?"

I shook my head.

"See, man, that's the problem with you. You're probably still subscribing to *The Tierra del Fuego Literary Review*, right? In any case,

I read this article that says that a guy who sells joints in Battery Park during lunch hour makes $125,000 a year, tax free. Weekends off, you know, plus ninety-day vacations in the can. And a hot dog seller makes twice as much. Of course, I wouldn't sell hot dogs. I'm sure they make them out of cancerous cats, no offense (you know I'm crazy about Mr. O'Donnell). So I says to myself, it's hot in the summer, you know. And what do people want when it's hot? Ices. Besides, if I want to play the market, if I get a hunch, I just push my cart to the stock exchange."

"It sounds good," I said.

"It sounds better than it is. Yet these capitalists warmongers love joints and crack and hot dogs. But ices, which are made of natural fruit—forget it! If I were selling diet drinks and other carcinogenic products, I'd be loaded. Even when it's 100 degrees they'll think twice before buying an ice. If it keeps going like this, I'm going to have to diversify. You know, Coca Cola or some degenerate capitalist product."

I didn't feel like getting involved in an argument about the final stages of the collapse of the capitalist state. So I said, "Harry, it just dawned on me. Why don't you bring your easel and paint when business is slow. You know, maybe a reporter from the *Wall Street Journal* will notice you and write an article, and you'll be taken by Castelli or somebody." I paused, remembering Harry's subject matter. "Are you still painting skeletons exclusively?"

"Santiago, that's a great idea. You know, just take a look at these people. Wouldn't you say they look like walking skeletons dressed in expensive suits? How about an ice? It's on the house. Maybe if they see you sucking on it they'll get the idea. Sheep!" he yelled at the passersby.

It was hot; an ice sounded like a wonderful idea. "What flavors do you have?"

"Tamarind. That's all I have this week. I make it myself."

"Tamarind? Are you crazy? No wonder you don't sell your ices! People buy watermelon, cherry, lemon ices. But tamarind is not a Wall Street fruit, Harry. It's not a Wasp fruit, or an oriental fruit, or a black fruit, either. It's for Colombians and Hindus—for brown people."

"The way you talk about colors you should have been a painter, you know. Anyway, I'm trying to give them something good. Tamarind is medicinal and it's also a laxative. I wanted to offer my customers an alternative, something unusual, you know. It's just that it hasn't caught on yet, you know." He filled a paper cup with two scoops of a shit-colored substance. I tasted it.

"Well?" Harry said, frowning and twitching his red Fu Manchu mustache.

"It's refreshing. Maybe a bit too acid."

"I don't want to use sugar, you know. Listen, Santiago, do you have any connections with the coffee crops in Colombia? You should invest in coffee commodities and make a pile of money that way. Isn't that where you grew up? A coffee plantation?"

"My father had a banana plantation."

"Hum, bananas. That's a thought. Banana ices, what do you think? Perhaps we can play the banana market. The market is very hot again, you know. And what I say is, let's make a killing before it collapses again. I don't see why Rockefeller has to be the only person who makes money in this country."

"I've got to go. I'm worried about Mr. O'Donnell."

"It's great to see you, man. I'll give you a call next week, you know. Maybe we can catch a flick, okay? Take care of yourself, and my regards to Mr. O'Donnell." He patted me on the shoulder and looking toward Broadway, he started yelling, "Natural tamarind ices. Treat yourselves to the fruit of Buddha and Montezuma."

It was noon by the time I arrived home. During the day, when the front door was open because of the employment agency, I'd go in and out quickly to avoid running into my landlady. But there were several items in the mailbox and I had to stop briefly to get them before the crack heads broke into the mailbox as they did almost on a daily basis.

One of the envelopes was from Unlimited Languages and it contained a check for $350. This was a lucky break. I had been hounding the agency to pay me for several jobs I had done for them back in June. For a second or two I stood there wondering whether I should run to the bank to deposit it and make a withdrawal. This interval of indecision was long enough for Mrs. O'Donnell to open the door leading to the bar. She grabbed me by the arm, as if I were a thief caught in flagrante delicto.

"Santiago, why haven't you answered my calls? Come in."

"Hi, Mrs. O'Donnell," I said, trying to fake a smile.

With her free hand, Mrs. O'Donnell indicated that I should go into the bar. Many alkies sat at the counter, and several of the booths were already taken up by the lunch crowd. We marched toward an empty booth in the back, near the kitchen. I said hi to Pete, Mrs. O'Donnell's oldest son, who was the head bartender; and to Sean, Pete's son. Both nodded, acknowledging me. I smiled to a couple of waitresses—they were Mrs. O'Donnell's relatives too. Need I add that the entire operation was run by Mrs. O'Donnell's many retainers? I wanted to become invisible. I knew they were all familiar with my situation, and although each and every one of them was always nice to me, I was under the impression they regarded me as the guy who ripped off the matriarch of the clan.

We sat at a booth. With her mass of auburn hair, and a map-lined face, Mrs. O'Donnell was the exact replica of Lillian Hellman. She also had the writer's whiskey-honed voice. "Well, Santiago, where's the rent?"

"I'm so sorry I haven't answered your phone calls, Mrs. O'Donnell," I said, trying to distract her from her one-track mind. "But I was planning to come to see you today."

"You're here now, so where's the rent?"

After eight years of being perpetually behind in my rent, I was hard up for excuses. "Mrs. O'Donnell, I was hoping I could give you one thousand dollars like you want, but I don't have that much in the bank. I haven't been working much lately. If it keeps going like this, I'm going to have to get a full-time job."

She had heard this argument so many times before that my words seemed to have no effect whatsoever on her. "I give you twenty-four hours to pack your things and move out. And don't make me evict you by force. That's final."

"Mrs. O'Donnell," I remonstrated, "you don't really mean that. You wouldn't do anything like that, would you?"

"What's to prevent me?"

So much anger flashed in her almond eyes that I became afraid of her. "Because . . . because you're a good woman," I said. "You know how fond I am of you."

"I'm a good person, that's true. But I'm not an idiot, Santiago. That's why you've been taking advantage of me all these years. My family thinks I'm crazy. My lawyer can't believe I've let this situation go on for years. I could rent that apartment for $1,500, even right now. You know I would've never let you move in if I had known you were Colombian. I thought you came from Venezuela, like Ben Burztyn," she said, referring to my friend Ben Ami who had lived in the downstairs apartment before Rebecca moved in.

Now that she had insulted my nationality, Mrs. O'Donnell softened. "I need some money today. Con Ed is turning off the electric if I don't pay the bill. You must have some money you can give me. Otherwise, I'll have to call Lucy. The poor thing; with all her problems with her husband, I hate to do this to her."

"Please, Mrs. O'Donnell, whatever you do, don't call my mother. I'll give you money right now. Here," I said, handing her the check from Unlimited Languages.

Instead of thanking me for the check, she became irate. "So you do have money! You must take me for the greatest jerk that ever lived."

"I swear to you that's all the money I have. But take it; it's all yours." I signed the check over to her.

She folded the check and pocketed it in her apron. "Here," she said, flinging some bills on the table. "I don't want you to go hungry."

I counted five twenties. "Thanks," I said.

"You now owe me $14,760 in back rent."

I couldn't repress a chuckle. "Mrs. O'Donnell, you do love to exaggerate; it must be your Irish temperament."

She cringed again. I should have never smiled; she was only forgiving when I acted remorseful. Maybe I should burst into tears, I thought. Or better yet, beg her for a job washing dishes.

"Santiago, you can't go on living like this. You're a young, bright guy. When are you going to get your act together?"

I wish I had a mother who owned a bar, I was going to say,

pointing at her children. But that was inappropriate, so I said, "When I finish my Columbus poem. Then I'll get a full-time job. I promise you."

Mrs. O'Donnell held her head between her hands. "Santiago, wake up. This is New York. People here don't care about poetry. If you must be a writer, for God's sake write a book that can be made into a miniseries. Why don't you write about," she stretched her arms toward the front of the bar, "Forty-second Street. Write about the crack people; how they're ruining my business, my family's way of life. That's what you should write about. That'll make money. Everybody already read about Columbus in high school."

I was sick and tired of people telling me what to write about, but I knew better than to argue with her.

"I fully agree with you," I said. "I hate those creeps. They're driving me insane, too."

"Whatever you do, don't do it."

"Mrs. O'Donnell, of course not."

"Santiago, I have an idea. This is also a good way for you to pay some back rent. We'll paint a sign, an anticrack sign, and you'll parade in front of the porno shop. A few hours every day. Maybe that'll get somebody's attention."

"No way," I said, getting up. "I'd rather become a homeless person, do you hear me?"

She got up too. "How about standing outside the Times building with the sign? Maybe we'll get them to write an exposé about it."

I was rendered inarticulate by her ridiculous proposition. I was infuriated too, and if it weren't that she was my landlady and I owed her some respect and a lot of money, I would have blown up. "I got to go," I said. "I'm worried . . ." about Mr. O'Donnell, I was going to add, but luckily caught myself in time. I lived in terror that she would find out I had named my cat after her late husband.

Reading my mind, she asked, "How's the cat?"

"He's fading quickly. I'm afraid this is the end."

"I know how it is. I had a cat like that; I had to crush his medicine and mix it with his food."

It seemed highly impossible that she had ever loved a cat; nevertheless, I said, "I'm sorry to hear that."

"Mind you, it was a long time ago. Before I married. I loved that cat so much I never had another one after him."

"Well, like I said, I have to go."

"How about a cheeseburger on the house? When was the last time you had a hot meal?"

I was hungry, but not hungry enough to stand the torture of having her whole family stare at me while I ate. "Gee, thanks a lot. But not today. I'm really in a hurry."

She pointed a finger at me. "I expect you to come with some more rent by Friday. Remember, you owe me $14,760."

"How could I ever forget it, Mrs. O'Donnell? Have a nice day. It's nice to see you."

As I slunk off down the aisle, she called out, "Santiago, pray for me that I can pay the Con Ed bill."

Mr. O'Donnell was in the kitchen in a carnivorous mood. He stood frozen by the refrigerator waiting for a mythic mouse to show up. He was so engrossed in his hunt that he glanced at me long enough to make eye contact, but that was all. "Suit yourself, ingrate, if you prefer dead mouse meat to my company," I said, somewhat hurt. I went to check my messages. No one had called. I sat down at my desk and went through the mail. It was all trash, except for an envelope that contained a newsletter with the ominous title the *Colombian Report*. It was eighty-eight pages long and written in English. I leafed through it; every item in it was about guerilla warfare in Colombia. Oh great, I thought, this is just what I need, to get on the mailing list of a terrorist group. What if the police raided my apartment and found subversive literature in my possession? I shook my head to expel these paranoid thoughts from my brain. This is New York, not Colombia, I reminded myself. My conscience was clear, I thought. And yet, regular guys did not keep pounds of cocaine stashed in their kitchens or illegal guns in their toilet tanks.

I started pacing the apartment. It was so hot and humid that I felt as if I were swimming against the current in a huge river of lukewarm pea soup. I thought about going to the park, to spend the afternoon cooling off under a tree. But Central Park in July is dustier than a ghost town in a western. At least Mr. O'Donnell seems okay,

I thought. Otherwise he would not be so intent upon catching that mouse. The phone rang.

"Santiago, pick up. I know you're there," said the sonorous voice of Ben Ami Burztyn.

"Hi, Ben," I said, picking up. "When did you get back in town?"

"Screening your calls, ha?" he said gruffly. "Hiding from Mrs. O'Donnell."

"Oh, man. I wish I could hide from that woman. I just saw her. So what's happening?"

"I'm calling to invite you to dine with me, on the off chance," he said sarcastically, "that you're free tonight."

"Sure," I said, delighted at the prospect since Ben Ami only ate at the very best restaurants.

"Meet me at Rupert's at seven-thirty." He gave me the address. "And look nice, will you? Wear a jacket and tie. Do you have a presentable tie?"

"Wait till you see me in the suit Mother gave me. I look like a million bucks."

"Humm," Ben said. "Anyway, please don't be late."

"Not a second late, I promise."

Benjamin chuckled at the other end. "See you tonight, *chico*."

"Ciao."

Ben's call had put me in a good mood. I knew it would be a great dinner. Besides, I hadn't seen Ben in a few months. Suddenly feeling energized, I changed into my shorts and a T-shirt. I decided to go to the pier on Forty-third Street to catch some rays, read, and maybe work on my Columbus poem. The river always made me feel as if I were in one of the caravels. I was just going out the door when the phone rang. It was Tim Colby, my literary agent.

"Santiago, I'm at the corner with coffee and doughnuts. Are you home?"

I told him where I was heading and invited him to come along.

"I'm game," Tim said.

Tim was waiting for me downstairs, perspiring, as if he had been doing a lot of walking. He was loaded with a briefcase, shopping bags, and large manila envelopes.

"You look like a Caribbean surfer," he said smiling.

"You can leave all that stuff upstairs if you want," I said, referring to the portable stationery store he was saddled with.

"That's okay. Just help me with the coffee and doughnuts."

Taking the paper bags from him, I said, "Let's get the hell out of here before the crack people see me going out of the building dressed like this."

Tim glanced in the direction of Paradise Alley. "They're taking over my neighborhood too. These people reproduce quicker than roaches."

At the corner of Forty-third, we turned west, heading for the Hudson.

"Are those books you're carrying in the envelopes?" I asked, watching him struggle with the bulky packages, although it occurred to me that dressed in sandals, khaki pants, and a red shirt depicting macaws and coconut trees, he did not look like he was coming from the staid world of publishing.

"No, I'm making deliveries for a friend of mine who works on Wall Street. But I'll deliver these tomorrow morning."

"Are you working as a messenger?"

"A couple of days a week to make some extra cash. I work for a friend I met at Princeton. Now he's a big shot on Wall Street and he helps me out this way. How are you doing?" he asked as we crossed Ninth Avenue. "Getting any writing done?"

"Not in a few weeks. I'm rethinking the whole concept."

Tim smiled broadly. "I've got good news for you."

"Oh, yeah?"

"I met an editor who's interested in you."

"In me? Are you kidding? Did he read *Lirio del Alba*?" I asked, although that sounded improbable.

"She doesn't read Spanish."

"How can she be interested in me if she doesn't read Spanish?"

"I told her I knew an up-and-coming Latin American writer. I told her I was giving her the chance to publish the next great Latin American sensation."

That hardly sounded like me, but I was flattered nonetheless.

"Gee, Tim, thanks. So she wants to publish Christopher Columbus?"

"I said you were writing an exciting book."

My high spirits sank a bit. "Did you tell her I was writing an epic poem?"

"No. But nobody calls Nabokov's *Pale Fire* a poem. It's called a novel. Anyway," Tim went on, "we were talking at a reception and she said that she had never read a South American thriller. She said she'd love to publish one."

"You mean, you want me to turn *Christopher Columbus on his Death Bed* into a thriller?" I sputtered. "It riles me up how everyone wants me to write what they don't have the guts to write themselves."

"Not me, Santiago. I want you to write *Christopher Columbus*. I really dig that poem. I told you I'll translate it into English when you finish it."

Tim's promise made me feel better since he was such a highly regarded translator. "What's the editor's name?" I asked in a conciliatory mood.

He told me her name and the name of the house, both of which meant nothing to me.

Becoming uptight again, I said, "I'm not even sure what a thriller is."

"You've seen thrillers at the movies."

"But she wants a book, not a movie. You mean, a thriller like Graham Greene's *The Third Man*?"

"Yeah."

I shook my head. "I just don't think I can turn the discovery of America into a thriller. I don't think Graham Greene could either."

"All I'm saying is that she's keen on publishing a young, unknown, Latin American author. Preferably somebody who's writing a thriller. You're kind of young and you're Latin, so that's two out of three. Just think about it. Don't get all worked up. Maybe the two of you could meet, and if you hit it off, who knows?"

We had reached the corner of Eleventh Avenue. A warm marine breeze engulfed us. I breathed in deeply, holding it in my lungs before exhaling. We crossed the avenue and entered the pier through the open gate.

Until quite recently there had been three wonderful old piers. Two were demolished and only Pier 43 remained, although an open-air summer concert hall had been built on it. Fortunately, half of the pier was still open to the public. It was extremely overcast yet there were a few men in tiny swimming trunks out sunning. The weather was only fit to be cursed but hardcore joggers trotted in slow motion. At the end of the pier a bunch of boys dove into the river and fished for eels; several Chinese men dressed in black, who lived at the Chinese mission on Eleventh Avenue, stood at the edge of the pier, exchanging looks I could not read, looking like conspirators about to blow up the Statue of Liberty or invade New Jersey.

We sat at the edge of the pier, our legs hanging in the air. It was windless and the Hudson seemed static, like a river of glue, but I was happy to be away from the stench of midtown Manhattan in midsummer. Here, at least, the city did not stink like a drunkard's breath. Tim opened the box of doughnuts and we sipped our warm coffees. Whenever Tim came to visit, he brought me doughnuts and pastries and we indulged in an orgy of sweets. I complimented the freshness of the doughnuts.

"Wall Street doughnuts. Only decent thing about the place," Tim said.

In the oppressive heat the tepid coffee was refreshing. Watching the excited boys diving into the river, climbing back up onto the platform and diving off repeatedly, made me think cool thoughts. We chewed and drank in silence. Tim seemed mesmerized by the eel fishers. Amidst much shrieking, the boys killed the eels with their shoes, bricks, or smashing them against the cement. Grossed out, I concentrated on the different crafts going up and down the Hudson. Yet the river's murky waters made me think of a channel of eel soup. I looked up and saw rain was imminent. I hoped for heavy rain to wash off the thick coat of dust and garbage that had settled upon the city like icing on a cake. The sky was a luminous milky opal, oppressively metallic and hazy. A filmy mist enveloped the world. An ocean liner floating by blew its horn, sounding like a gigantic, moaning cow. This melancholy mood made me want to jump aboard the ship and go off to an exotic island far, far away, a place where I could spend the rest of my life being a beach bum, sipping purple daiquiris at sunset.

"This is really nice," Tim said, lazily stretching his torso and arms. "You come here often?"

"In the summer I do. I read or write or just look at the boats. It's like going to the country."

"It must make you think of Christopher Columbus."

"Water always reminds me of him."

"You know what Melville says in *Moby Dick*?"

"It's a big book, Tim. He says a mouthful about everything."

"Melville says that the flood has not subsided; that two-thirds of the world is still under water. Did you know that?"

As it headed toward the sea, the ocean liner made the river heave with ripples that lapped the pillars of the pier, producing a gentle, caressing music.

"So Columbus knew how important it was to discover new land," I said.

"You make him sound like a land speculator. I'm sure there's more to it than that. Oh, wow," Tim exclaimed, "see the Statue of Liberty down there?"

In the distance, emerging from the shroud of gray that wrapped around the landscape, the statue was tiny, like a lit match.

"Did you know that when the French gave it to us it was the highest structure in New York? At that time, because there were no elevators yet, the tallest buildings in the city were only six floors high."

"So the statue was the first skyscraper."

"Yeah, that's right," Tim said, biting into a jelly doughnut. "Santiago, do you think Americans are naïve?" he asked me out of the blue.

I studied him. His tawny hair was longish and he needed to shampoo it and get a haircut. He was in his late thirties, but because of his intense, gleaming eyes and sunny disposition, he looked like a philosopher-child. I was going to say the polite thing. Such as, "Well, no more so than other people." But I said, "Yes, definitely."

"Why is that?"

"Who knows, Tim? You'd better ask Octavio Paz or one of those French deconstructionists who know everything. I haven't got a clue. But what I can't get over is how the pursuit of happiness is written in the Bill of Rights. I think that's why Americans are so miserable a lot of the time. They believe happiness is one of their inalienable rights. And, essentially, I agree with Freud that happiness was not written into the contract. You know, momentary happiness yes," I went on, totally unashamed of my clichés. "Like I'm happy right this minute with you. But if we ever tried to duplicate it . . . forget it. I think it's unrepeatable. But happiness as a way of life? How can one be happy in the face of death surrounding us?" I said, thinking about Bobby's death and the approaching demise of Mr. O'Donnell. "How can one pursue happiness as a main goal in life when there's so much pain and suffering everywhere? It makes for a nation of blind people. People who search for what doesn't exist."

"Shit," Tim exclaimed. "It's raining." There was no place to run for shelter on the pier. He bunched his envelopes and bags and sat on them. The boys swimming and fishing went berserk with joy. It was not rain, but the fireboat going by. It had started a practice drill in front of us, drenching the pier with a cool, abundant spray. The Chinese men ran away screaming as if they were demons being sprayed with holy water. The boat's many spouts shot sheets of very fine mist. It looked unspeakably beautiful, like a mythological benevolent beast that had risen from the depths of the Hudson to cool and delight us.

Always the man of letters, Tim said, "It looks like . . . like . . . like . . . Moby Dick. Like a white whale with a hundred spouts."

Indeed, the monumental, splashy ghost going down the swelling river looked as if it were heading out for the open ocean, ready to put out all the fires of the world.

# 9

# The Interpreter

I hailed a cab in front of the Port Authority building and directed the driver to Rupert's. Dressed in a snazzy suit, on my way to a fine restaurant, I suddenly felt grand, rich, glamorous. Being around Ben Ami Burztyn led me to fantasize like this. I had met Ben some nine years ago, standing in line to see Todd Browning's *Freaks*. A gigantic bearded man of ursine countenance wearing a red aviator's scarf and a green beret had wheeled around, almost knocking me off the line with his leviathan belly. Abruptly he demanded, "How many times have you seen *Freaks*?" I told him this was my first time and looked away, not eager to engage in conversations with a stranger. Tapping me on the shoulder, he informed me that he had seen *Freaks* twenty-eight times. I made up my mind to get away from this weirdo as soon as we entered the theater. I looked away. Ben Ami tapped my shoulder and said, "Is your schedule too busy to talk to me?" I decided to be polite. I said, "No, not really. . . ."

"I detect an accent. Where are you from?" he asked.

We discovered we had originated in neighboring countries. Ben's family had arrived in Venezuela from Russia after the revolution. We struck up a rapport and sat together during the film. Ben quoted entire sequences of dialogue as the actors spoke the lines. After the show, he invited me to his apartment for a glass of champagne. Although he looked freaky and acted like a nut, I accepted the invitation—I had few friends in Manhattan and fewer who loved the movies and were South American.

It turned out Ben lived on the third floor above O'Donnell's bar. At that time, he was the only tenant in the building. Ben opened the door into a pitch dark room and flicked his lighter. He lit a gas lamp on a table, and proceeded to light dozens of candles in an elaborate candelabra.

"What happened to the electricity?" I asked with some apprehension.

"I hate electricity," was Ben's curt reply.

The electricity was on in the apartment, but for illumination Ben preferred candles and gas lamps. He pulled a bottle of champagne out of the refrigerator. We sat on a huge bed by one of the windows overlooking Eighth Avenue and drank the champagne. Ben was going through his Edgar Allan Poe period at that time. He produced a couple of first editions of Poe's poetry and prose, a tattered manuscript of a letter and old, sepia-toned photographs of the author. Over champagne and caviar, Ben told me a bit about his background. His family was in oil and textiles. Among his childhood friends had been the children of the Kuwaiti royal family. Ben's parents had wanted him to pursue a business-related career, but he had dropped out of the London School of Economics and moved to New York to write the definitive biography of Poe. He had chosen to reside in Times Square because he felt that was the closest he could get to Poe's world. When I was about to leave, Ben told me he wanted me to meet his great-grandfather. From under one of the pillows, he removed a human bone. "This is my great-grandfather's femur," he said. "He was a general in the Russian army." I said hello to the bone. Ben kissed it and placed it under a pillow.

We became best friends. It was through Ben that I met Mrs. O'Donnell and moved into the apartment on the fourth floor. A year or so later one of Ben's maiden aunts died and he came into a large inheritance. He quit researching his Poe biography and moved to Paris, a city he preferred to New York. Over the next few years I saw him during his visits to Manhattan. The nineteenth-century French writer Gerard de Nerval had replaced Poe in his affection.

And now that he had lots of dough, he had become a great gourmand who traveled all over the world, eating at the best restaurants. He purchased a duplex at the Museum Tower, where he stayed during his overnight visits to the city. His most recent companion was a belly dancer named Scheherazade, who would break into dance whenever Ben was bored.

The taxi came to a stop; I had arrived at my destination. I gave the driver a three dollar tip. This was the danger of being around Ben—I, too, began to act as if I were rich. The restaurant was rather small and unpretentious in its decor. Inside the door the hostess greeted me. The woman sized me up from the tips of my shoes to the length of my sideburns and deciding, perhaps, that I was a wealthy South American or a coke kingpin (which is what I looked like in the clothes Mother had given me), she greeted me with a hale handshake and a cinemascope smile.

"I'm joining Mr. Benjamin Burztyn's party," I informed her.

Hastily, the woman withdrew her hand, as if I had just said, "I have the bubonic plague and want to kiss you on the mouth." Her fake smile transmogrified into a cold, unfriendly stare. "Follow me," she said.

The restaurant was sparsely attended and I assumed this was due to the fact that in late July its habitués were far, far away from New York or in the Hamptons. Ben was talking to a waiter.

"Hi, Ben," I said.

Ben looked up from the menu. "Hi, Santiago. Please sit down." Then he turned to the waiter. "I told you already," he said in the rotund tone of a pissed-off monarch, "bring me a bottle of what you personally think is the best champagne in the house."

The waiter's face reddened. "But sir . . ."

Ben crossed his hands, palms open, and pushed them toward the waiter's face. "I told you what I want. Now leave me alone." Flustered, the waiter headed for the bar, looking as if he couldn't make up his mind whether to curse aloud or kill Ben.

"Goodness gracious, Ben. What's going on?" I said.

"Santiago, my friend," Ben said smiling, as if he had just noticed me. He put his hand on my shoulder. "You certainly look dapper today. How are you?"

"Fine. But . . ." I was dying to find out why there was so much tension in the air, but now that I had a chance to see him in his full glory, my breath was taken away. He wore a magnificent white suit and a gold-leafed tie. Although he was a couple of years younger than I, recently his hair and his beard had grayed. Now he might have been mistaken for a sultan incognito, somebody who had been conceived in a womb of gold.

"Why is everyone acting so weird?" I asked.

Ben's eyes narrowed, his lips pursed and with hatred in his voice he growled as he looked toward the bar, "I'm about to sue this place for fifty thousand dollars."

"Why?"

Ben put a finger to his lips. The terrified waiter approached us with the champagne.

"Let me see what you have there," Ben said.

The waiter pulled out of the bucket a bottle of Dom Perignon.

"Dom Perignon!" Ben exclaimed. "Americans think that's the only champagne in the world."

"Sir, you told me I should choose the champagne," the deeply mortified waiter complained.

I was becoming embarrassed by the way Ben was bullying the waiter.

With the air of a grand lord who's grown up surrounded by servants at his beck and call, Ben said, "Well, what are you waiting for? The least you can do is open the bottle."

The waiter complied with Ben's wishes and we toasted to each other's health.

When we were left alone, Ben said, *"Chico,* I'm suing these people because the last time I was here they lost my umbrella, which was also my cane."

"I'm sorry to hear that," I said, full of sympathy, knowing that Ben had only the best of everything. "But there's no need to take it out on the poor waiter. Did he personally lose the umbrella?"

"But it was made in Paris," Ben said, with the total indifference of rich South Americans toward their inferiors. "It was especially designed for me. The knob was solid gold. It was unique. I haven't been able to replace it yet."

A few years ago, Ben had had a malignant tumor removed from one of his legs. The operation had been so severe that he ended up with a limp and thus needed a cane to get around.

"And you know how Americans are," he went on. "They don't take you seriously unless you threaten to sue them. As soon as my lawyer called the management they started listening to me. Anyway, they've promised to have the cane replaced. Exactly like the one I lost. They're having it made in Paris. But to mellow me, they invited me to a dinner, with three guests, everything on the house, including the drinks. I swear to you, Santiago, if anything goes wrong tonight, I'll put them out of business."

"I'm sure everything is going to be perfect," I said, feeling like I was going to break into a sweat, a knot forming in the pit of my stomach. I opened the menu and studied the appetizers and main courses and desserts. "Everything sounds delicious."

"I recommend the wild boar," Ben said. "The rabbit breast and the broiled snapper are good too."

The waiter approached us. We ordered the appetizers and main courses, and Ben asked the waiter to recommend the wine. Alone again, I said, "Where is Scheherazade?"

"She stayed in Chile. I just don't know about women anymore. I give them everything, take them everywhere, and there isn't one who understands what makes me happy. I went to a singles bar the other night just to try something different. So there is this beautiful woman sitting next to me—perfect-looking in that horrid Cher style—not exactly my type. Anyway, suddenly she turns to me and says, 'If you don't stop looking at me, I'll stub my cigarette in your eyeball.' "

"But Ben, you shouldn't go to those places. I'm sure there are plenty of women who'd give anything to make you happy."

Ben patted my hand. "That's the most romantic thing anybody has ever said to me. I wish there was a woman who talked to me the way you do."

"I had no idea you were in Chile," I said, to change this line of dialogue. "Why did you go there? I thought you hated Pinochet and had sworn never to return until Pinochet was shot."

Ben's rubicund face saddened. *"Chico,* one day I was walking

129

down the beach in Macuto with Scheherazade and suddenly, Santiago, something in the air, a smell, you know, like Proust's madeleine . . . it hit me so strong and took possession of me. And I remembered the great meat *empanadas* I used to eat in Santiago when I was a child and my father was ambassador. I don't know what came over me. Before I knew it, I was landing at the airport in Santiago." He fell silent, wolfed down a glass of champagne and looked devastated.

The suspense was so unbearable, I had forgotten to breathe. "So what happened?"

"Oh, Santiago. I have never been so disappointed in my life. The restaurant was still there, and they still made meat *empanadas,* but the old cook had died, and the new *empanadas* tasted plastic, like McDonald's food." Ben took out his pipe, filled it and lit it, creating a huge cloud of aromatic smoke. I sipped my champagne in silence. I didn't want to talk; I didn't want to spoil his moment of perfect dejection. Finally, he said, *"Chico,* I had traveled thousands of miles to recapture the *empanadas* of my childhood, and they had become plastic, like everything else." He finished, his voice quivering with grief. "They had become a fraud. I had a fit. The police were called and I was arrested and taken away. Fortunately, Scheherazade called the Venezuelan ambassador, who called the President and threatened to cut off all oil supplies to Chile unless I was released on the spot," Ben was saying as the artichokes arrived.

A gleaming white limousine was waiting for Ben when we got out of the restaurant. The air was so muggy and swamplike that I gladly accepted his offer to give me a lift home.

Although Ben Ami had found fault with the waiter's choice of wine, and had found the artichokes tough, the wild boar bitter, the rabbit overcooked, and the desserts mediocre, the dinner had been a success—the lawsuit had been averted, at least for tonight. I was pleased with my mediating role; for a moment I considered offering my services to Rupert's to placate their irate, displeased rich South American customers. I was feeling great—riding a limo on a night like this beats taking the grimy subway back home. And since I did not have Ben Ami's excruciatingly high gourmand's standard, the meal for me had been excellent, if not sublime.

We were seated comfortably, Ben puffing on his pipe, I smoking a Newport Light, when Ben said, "I'd rather be a *clochard* in Paris than a rich man in New York. You have to move out of this city, Santiago. You can stay at my place in Paris anytime."

"I'd love to," I said, wishing he would extend the open invitation to his empty place at the Museum Tower. I remembered Paris fondly yet vaguely. Ben had flown me there for a weekend expressly to show me Gerard de Nerval's grave. "But what would I do there? Here I can make a living, kind of. Besides, I'd feel more displaced there than here. By now, I feel kind of a New Yorker, you know."

"Marry my cousin Edna," he ordered me. "She's just as rich as I am. And she doesn't have parents or brothers or sisters. It's all her money. Plus she's a fag hag."

"Ben, you make it sound like I'm a fortune hunter." I had met Edna, a doctoral candidate for a degree in Divinity. I had found her nice, quiet, thoughtful, scholarly, and a lady to boot. She worshiped Ben, and I knew she would have married me just to please him.

"Anyway," I added, "if I haven't married a woman it's not for a lack of candidates. There's always Claudia. Come to think of it," I said, picturing close-ups of Claudia and Edna in my mind's eye, "I'd much rather marry Edna."

The limo had stopped at a red light on Forty-second Street and Eighth. "And to think I used to love Times Square," Ben said, denigrating his old neighborhood. "I don't know how you can stand living here with all that," he said, waving his hand in the direction of the porno palaces, the junkies and criminals outside the window. "*Chico,* that's the Reagan–Bush legacy. If you don't make $100,000 a year, and you haven't sold your soul to a multinational, you don't belong in Manhattan. You're supposed to live here in Times Square or move to the South Bronx and fuck yourself into extinction smoking crack."

"Gee, Ben," I said, "money has really made you wise. Do all rich people have your political savvy?"

"All rich people are assholes. I'm different because I'm an artist; I have the soul of a poet. With the right woman in Paris, I wouldn't mind being poor," he sighed.

I wondered if God, in his infinite inventiveness, had ever

conceived of such a creature. The limo stopped in front of O'Donnell's bar. "Ah, the abode of my bohemian youth," Ben waxed philosophic, his voice tinged with nostalgia. I knew that deep down Ben yearned to turn the high places where he lived into the gutter.

I gave him a hug. He smiled and nodded but sat very still. As I opened the door to let myself out, I saw, standing in front of my door, Hot Sauce's tiny figure. I waved at her, but she was so busy trying to lure customers that she didn't see me. Out of the blue, a brilliant idea came over me. This is indeed providential, I thought. "Ben, I think I have the answer to all your prayers." I turned toward the street. "Hot Sauce," I called out, "come here. There's somebody I want you to meet."

She recognized me. "Hi, Santiago," she said as she slithered toward the limo exuding carnality and lust. "How're you doing, you *latino* hunk?"

Sitting in the limo, with my feet on the pavement, my eyes met her eyes. "I want you to meet an old friend," I said.

Suspiciously, she checked the figure of Ben Ami nesting in the deep recesses of the limo. "He ain't a weirdo, is he?"

"Come on, Hot Sauce," I protested. "Would I introduce you to a freak?"

"Hot Sauce," Ben exclaimed, his eyes dancing with excitement. "Would you care to join me for dinner?"

"Delighted," she screeched.

I got out, helped her in and closed the door behind her. Ben and Hot Sauce took off into the mysteries of the scorching summer night.

Mr. O'Donnell was glued to his spot in front of the refrigerator. It was early for his midnight snack, but usually he'd start begging for it hours earlier. Tonight, however, he was oblivious to food, to me, and to the heat that usually knocked him out.

"You silly cat; you're gonna give yourself a heart attack waiting for that mouse to show up," I said. His tail wagged, as if to brush off my concern, but he did not even bother to cast a glance in my direction.

"Either that or you're gonna die a crazy cat," I went on as the phone rang. There was no message. Picking up the receiver I said, "Hello, hello." A click was the only response, and I was left there standing like a fool holding a dead telephone to my ear. Suddenly, I heard a deafening, abrupt noise as if a truck had crashed on the roof. The building did not crumble, though; the ceiling did not cave in. It occurred to me that maybe the refrigerator had fallen on top of Mr. O'Donnell. I burst into the kitchen screaming, "Kitty, are you okay?" Mr. O'Donnell repaid my concern by giving me a quizzical look as if to say, "What's the matter with you?" A flash of effulgence lit the kitchen, and looking up at the window that overlooks the alley, I saw lightning paint platinum slivers in the obsidian sky. Raging thunder made the glass of the windowpanes rattle. My eyes wandered down from the sky to the building across the alley. The flasher was standing by his window, dancing for me. I noticed he had shorts on and wasn't playing with himself. He was crisscrossing his arms to call my attention. I stood there, transfixed. He leaned out of the window holding a large piece of cardboard that read PHONE #. "No way, José," I replied, giving him the finger, and was about to turn away from the window when he started shaking the card-board frantically, and his desperation—he seemed about to fall out of the window—held me enthralled. Something was amiss, I thought. Or maybe he's just very horny, a voice said in my head; everyone is oversexed in the summer. But what if he was trying to tell me something else? And if he just wants sex, what would I do? Nothing ventured, nothing gained. With my fingers, I gave him the phone number. He signed it back to me and I nodded in confirma-tion and disappeared from the window. I ran to my telephone to turn off the machine. The phone rang and I picked up.

"Is that you?" a voice with an European accent said.

"Your neighbor across the alley," I said, choosing my words carefully, in case he was recording me.

"Listen, I want you to know," he said in an accent I couldn't quite pin down, "about a couple of hours ago, I caught two men trying to break into your apartment from the fire escape."

"What?"

"Yes, I saw them trying to break in. They had tools and were beginning to remove the screens on the window, so I started screaming, saying I was going to call the cops. One of them pointed a gun at me, but I ducked and continued screaming until they left."

"Did you recognize them? Are they crack people from downstairs?"

There was a pause. "Hum, let me think. No. Actually, they look more like you: slightly Oriental."

"I'm not Oriental," I remonstrated. "I'm Colombian."

"Oh, so I see. I knew you were a foreigner too because of the way you signed your phone number."

I didn't know whether to hang up, grab Mr. O'Donnell and run away from the apartment, or to call the police. In any case, it felt good to be talking to someone. I realized although I didn't even know his name, I felt almost close to this man; I knew more about his deepest sexual secrets than I knew about most of my friends.

"I'm German," he informed me. This did not surprise me at all. "What's your name?" he asked.

I told him, absentmindedly, aware that I was talking to him but was totally freaked out about the prospect of the Colombians breaking into my apartment.

"My name is Reinhardt," he said.

It occurred to me that the polite thing was to thank him for driving the burglars away. "Thank you so much, Reinhardt. I'm really grateful to you for what you've done. My cat could have escaped, and he's a sick cat. It would have been tragic."

"Now you know," he said. "It's better to be prepared."

"What do you mean?"

"You know: leave the radio and the lights on when you go out. Stuff like that."

"That's right. Thank you for reminding me."

"I wouldn't want anything to happen to you, handsome—or to your cat . . . maybe we can get together sometime."

A part of me wanted to say, "Sure. Why not." Instead, I mumbled, "Oh, oh, well, I . . ."

He interrupted me. "I don't mean sex," he said. "It's too dangerous nowadays. But we can go see a film."

"Sure," I said. "I go to the movies all the time."

"Well, then give me a call, Santiago. My phone number is

. . ." I took it down, thinking it might come in handy sometime. And, who knows, maybe some night . . . The truth was that I was extremely attracted to this tall slender blond Nibelung. And now that I knew he was Nordic I felt doubly turned on.

"Bye, Reinhardt," I said by way of conclusion. "Thanks a lot again."

"Don't mention it. Sweet dreams."

Sweet dreams? I shook my head. Rebecca was probably still awake, but what was the point of upsetting her? After all, the Colombians were out to get me, not her. It was my apartment they wanted to break into. Nevertheless, she should be aware of the danger. What if I got killed? Rebecca could help the police in tracking down my murderers. What did I care if justice was served when I was dead? Nothing was going to bring me back! At times like this, when I was afraid, restless, cracking up all over the place, I'd pick up Mr. O'Donnell and bury my face in his fur and smother him with kisses until the contact with a living thing calmed me down. Yet tonight something told me that if I distracted him from his ridiculous hunting, I was going to get badly scratched.

"I'll fight back; I'm not going down like a wimp," I said through clenched teeth. Feeling like Gary Cooper in *High Noon*, I removed the gun from the tank of the toilet and wrapped it in a towel to dry. I wondered if the bullets would still go off after having the gun soaked in water for two days. The Colombians did not know that, though. I was sure they would be scared shitless if I met them by the window aiming a gun at their balls. I decided to sleep on the couch by the window. If they returned, I would hear them coming up the creaky fire escape. Now that I was ready for a showdown with my persecutors, I stopped to reflect whom they might be. If they were indeed Gene's employers, should I call the police, the FBI, the CIA? Why couldn't they just be crack people trying to break in to steal anything valuable they could turn into quick cash? No. All they had to do was peek through the window to see that everything I owned was rubbish. Obviously, they were Colombian mafiosi who knew I had in my possession the coke Gene had stolen.

Even though it was only eleven o'clock, it was too late to call my mother's house. Tomorrow, I'll get in touch with Gene, I thought. You cannot afford to freak out, Santiago. Put away the bazooka; it's only a mosquito. You must muster all your wherewithal and clarity to control the situation. Tomorrow you can have an alarm system installed. I could borrow the money from Ben Ami. He'd always said he'd come to my rescue if I really needed him. Well, the time had finally come. Or should I take the money and move to Paris with Mr. O'Donnell until all this passed? I felt crazier than a shithouse rat. Perhaps the heat wave had done permanent damage to my brain.

I sat on the couch perspiring, the towel and gun in my lap; I looked down into the dark alley. Were they watching me? Were they at this moment aiming the gun and about to pull the trigger? I closed my eyes, took a deep breath and held it for a while and then, pumping my lungs as hard as I could, I puffed it all out. I heard a *clack, pop, clack*—the weapon had been fired, I thought. I'm a dead man. I felt as if I were falling off the face of the earth. Before it was too late, I opened my eyes to see Mr. O'Donnell for the last time. I seemed to be all right. I touched my head, and examined my chest, searching for the wound. They had missed me. I looked out into the alley again.

The rain had burst; a heavy wind blew fat drops through the window screens. I remained still, enjoying the refreshing wind. It was pouring with the violence of a typhoon. I hoped it would turn into a hurricane that would sweep away the killers down there in the alley, the crack heads outside the building, all the dirt and the grime of New York. There was nothing I loved better than a good summer shower. I flashed back to my adolescence in Barranquilla, when the rains were so heavy during the rainy season that the city became paralyzed and school was canceled.

My adolescence—roughly from my twelfth to my fifteenth birthday—had been the unhappiest period of my life. And yet, out of masochism, or the futile need to exorcise ghosts that would always haunt me—I kept regressing to those years over and over, with an insistence that was disturbing. We had moved from Bogotá back to Barranquilla, and I hated just about everything about my native city, except the rainy season when apocalyptic, violent downpours fed my fantasies of natural catastrophes of such severity that school would be shut down for weeks, months, years, and I would be left alone in my bedroom, forgotten, reading Dostoyevsky, Kierkegaard, Camus.

Bárranquilla is situated below sea level. *Barranca,* from which its name derives, means gorge, ravine. The city did not have then—and does not have now—a sewer system. When it pours—the way it does in Jean Harlow's *Red Dust*—the city floods, and the streets and avenues become raging *arroyos* that sweep away people, cars, houses, and buses full of passengers. Enterprising *Barranquilleros* make their living during this time of the year by installing over the street wooden planks a foot wide, so that the citizens can get across the streets without having to wade through the muddy, treacherous and filthy waters.

Whenever the rains would burst after lunch, I knew there'd be no school that afternoon. Wilbrajan and I would change into our bathing suits and go out on the patio to play in the rain. Our patio—which was planted with banana and plantain trees—overflowed, and our domestic ducks and turtles came out. We chased them, running among the trees, splashing in the water that came up to our knees. At night, the patio became a swamp full of thick clouds of mosquitoes, and scores of frogs that honked and croaked a cacophonous music. Then the huge orange moon of the tropics would appear, casting its reflection on the onyx waters, like a golden spotlight.

After our return from Bogotá, Mother had lived with Don Miguel, her lover, for five years. Don Miguel had a high post in local government and was a married man. He came every night for supper and slept with Mother until midnight, when he went home to his wife and family. This situation, though fairly common in Colombian society, was nonetheless painful for my sister and me. It was especially hard to explain to my school friends, though all the neighbors knew and understood. Don Miguel was kind and gentle with children, and was crazy about Mother, so Wilbrajan and I treated him as a favorite uncle. At night, when he and Mother closed the door of their bedroom, I would sneak out of my room and go through the kitchen to the patio and around the back of the house to watch them make love through the windows that opened onto the patio. Night after night I watched, discovering my own sexual appetites as I saw them go at it with a voraciousness and passion that to me was exciting, frightening, exhausting.

That must be why I'm still a voyeur, I said to myself, thinking of Reinhardt. I shook my head to stop this reverie. Yet I was drowsy, and I had to get up early the next morning to go interpret again for Judge Warpick. I decided to sleep on the couch by the window with the gun under my mattress. I changed into my pajamas and set the alarm clock in the kitchen. Soon, a heaviness descended upon me, and I felt sinking, parachuting down a pitch-dark, airless well. Before I surrendered wakefulness, the last image I saw was the golden eyes of Mr. O'Donnell, shining in the dark: feral, deracinated, like the eyes of Blake's tiger.

Mr. O'Donnell walking on my chest woke me up. His head hovered above mine. In the dark I was aware of something caressing my nose; I looked harder and I saw he had a squirming mouse in his mouth, hanging by the head. "Aggghhh!" I screamed in disgust, sitting up. With the mouse in his teeth, Mr. O'Donnell flew twenty feet and landed in the next room. My heart threatened to erupt in my mouth. I got up and turned on the lights. I was having an attack of *pavor nocturnus*. I knew I was cracking up and ran through the different rooms turning all the lights on. I poured myself half a glass of scotch, guzzled it and then sat by the windows overlooking the alley to cool off. It was 4:20 A.M. Mr. O'Donnell entered the room with his prey. With the broom I tried to coax him into surrendering it. Angered, Mr. O'Donnell dropped the unconscious mouse, and, like a rabid jungle beast, bared his teeth, growling, and then scratched my legs and bit me to defend his catch. I raced to my room and shut the door and threw myself on the bed. After a while, collecting half of myself and getting up, I turned on the light over my bed, and the air-conditioning. I didn't care whether anyone broke in or not; I would not get out of my room for a few hours, until the mouse was dead and devoured. Lighting a cigarette, I propped myself on the pillows and wondered whether I should try to go back to sleep or whether I should make an effort to stay awake. I began to daydream; I saw Christopher Columbus, on his fourth voyage, sick, crazed, broken, his caravel arriving at the coast of Paria. In the distance, he saw a pear-shaped mountain which he mistook for a huge breast, the huge breast of earth, reaching all the way to heaven.

# 10

## Ay Luna! Ay Luna!

"What's going down, dude?" Jeff greeted me as I walked into the Social Security office the next morning.

"Good morning, Jeff," I said, standing in front of his desk. He had his chess set out and a chair drawn to the side of his desk as a lure.

Jeff put the *New York Post* aside. "So how come you don't wanna play with me no more?"

"It's discouraging; you're too good for me," I said.

"Thanks. But you'll never improve unless you play good players. That's how I learned."

At that moment, Judge Warpick's assistant, who looked like a senior citizen version of Betty Boop, entered the room. "Are you ready, Mr. Martínez?" she asked me, batting her mile-long eyelashes.

I turned to Jeff. "Is the claimant here?"

"She was here before I arrived," Jeff informed me. "She's sitting way in the back of the room. Her name is," he winced, "Fridania Moquette. I wonder where these people get those names."

I called out the name. Today the room was packed with claimants, their relatives and friends, interpreters, lawyers and paralegals. In the back of the room a young woman got up with some difficulty. My heart sank a bit when she started walking toward us without a lawyer. The young woman pushed a baby carriage and moved with the help of a cane. As she lurched toward the front of the room, I saw that she used a golf club as a cane, and that she had braces on her legs.

Jeff tapped me on my thigh with the claimant's folder.

When the claimant reached the door, I accosted her with my usual introduction, "My name is Santiago. I'm your Spanish interpreter."

The girl stared blankly at me as if looking into a mirror. Slowly, we wended our way to the judge's chambers. The claimant stationed the baby carriage (which was covered by a cotton blanket) next to her chair and sat down, placing the golf club on the table.

I was feeling drowsy from lack of sleep. Presently, Judge Warpick entered the room swathed in her black robe, her gargoyle features truly frightening. She asked me to explain to the claimant her rights. We were sworn in and the hearing began. The first two questions—name and address—were asked and answered.

"Is it Miss or Mrs. Moquette?" Warpick asked.

"Miss," the girl said, blushing. I saw now that she was very young. She wore her black hair in two pigtails held with white and blue ribbons. Her eyes were decorated with gobs of purple eyeshadow and her nails were painted an aquamarine hue and dotted with silver stars.

"Where were you born?" Warpick asked with some disgust, as if she were sick to death of asking the same question over and over.

"In a hospital, I guess."

I couldn't repress a smile. Warpick looked at me as if she wanted to disintegrate me with her stare.

"The country, I mean."

"Puerto Rico."

"And when did you come to the United States?"

Fridania shrugged. "I don't remember; a long time ago."

"How come you haven't learned English if you came here so young?" the judge asked in disbelief.

A little voice chimed in, "Hi."

Smiling, Fridania tapped the blanket over the baby carriage.

Craning her flamingo neck, Warpick focused her eyes on the carriage.

"That's the baby," Fridania said, pulling off the blanket as if she were a magician about to produce a dove or a rabbit. A little boy's head was exposed. With his mop of black curls, he looked like a miniature Yanick Noah and was grabbing the side of the carriage with his hands. He smiled at us. There was something odd about him; although he seemed tiny, his face looked older.

"Hi," the boy greeted me, and reached over to touch me with his hand. I sat still. The judge's assistant sat up, snapping out of her usual torpor and put a finger on the tape recorder, ready to turn it off in case there was extraneous colloquy. The judge stretched an arm, opening her gnarled, knobby fingers to indicate to the assistant not to turn off the machine. "Miss Moquette, are you ready to continue?" Warpick asked.

I could see that by now she was on the warpath.

"Just a minute," Fridania said. She opened her bag, pulled out a milk bottle and gave it to the baby, who snatched it, squealing, before disappearing to the bottom of the carriage.

As if realizing for the first time the anomaly of the situation, Judge Warpick asked, "Miss Moquette, when were you born?"

"In 1974."

"So you are . . ."

Seventeen, I thought to myself, and took a real good look at the claimant. Then how old was she when she had the boy? That was Judge Warpick's next question.

"Thirteen and a half," Fridania said.

"So the boy is four and a half now?"

"He'll be five for Christmas."

"Isn't he a bit too old to be in a baby carriage?"

"No, ma'am. He can't walk."

"Why not?"

"Because he was born without legs."

"Why?"

"How should I know?" Fridania retorted angrily. "Ask God. He made him that way."

Warpick snarled back. "Miss Moquette, if you want to go on

with the hearing I advise you to control your temper. I will not put up with any tantrums from you or anybody else. Is that clear?"

Lowering my head, I interpreted all this in almost a whisper. I wanted to close my eyes and—

"Mr. Interpreter," Warpick shouted at me. "You have to speak up, otherwise the machine will not pick up your interpretation."

"I'm sorry, your honor," I said, giving her a look of hatred. Fortunately for me, she was staring at the claimant.

"Hi," the little boy said again. *"Ya terminé el tete, mami,"* he said. His head appeared again, and he handed his mother the empty bottle. For a moment, the judge, the assistant, and myself forgot about the hearing in process, and watched, galvanized, the interaction between mother and son. Fridania put the bottle in her bag and, taking the boy by his armpits, hoisted him out of the carriage. He was a perfectly developed boy from his head to his buttocks. The boy wore a red T-shirt with an image of Madonna grossly imitating Marilyn Monroe; his private parts were wrapped in diapers and covered with blue plastic. Fridania put the boy on her lap. Then she pulled a pad and crayons out of her bag, which she set on the table. The boy started to draw immediately.

"What's his name?" Warpick asked.

"Claus Pericles."

"Claus Pericles?"

"Claus after Santa Claus, because he was born around Christmas, and Pericles after my father."

"Where's Claus's father?"

"I don't know."

"What's his name?"

Impassively, the girl said, "I don't know that, either. I was raped by a gang of boys."

"Why didn't you have an abortion?" Warpick asked, to my utter astonishment. "I know why," she went on, "because you wanted to get on welfare as soon as possible."

"That's right," Claus answered in English for his mother, and resumed drawing fantastic beasts with red eyes.

"You have to tell the boy to keep quiet; otherwise he'll have to leave the room."

Claus set down his crayon and sat up straight, staring at Warpick.

"Tell me why you are asking for additional supplementary income."

"Because I don't have enough money to live on."

"But you get Medicare."

"Yes, ma'am."

"And food stamps."

"Sometimes," said Claus.

I sat on my hands as if this would somehow help me not to break into laughter.

Judge Warpick was becoming rattled; her features hardened as if set in cement. "What's wrong with Claus . . . I mean, besides the fact he was born without legs?"

Claus turned around to look at his mother, *"Dile, mami,"* he ordered.

Fridania ran her fingers through her son's black silky curls. "When Claus was born," she began, "he weighed four pounds; he had a bump on his back the size of a grapefruit and . . ." She paused; this part was obviously very painful to her. "He was born without a penis. So the doctors told me it would be easier to turn him into a girl than to make a penis for him. They said I should raise him as a girl."

"Why didn't you?" Warpick asked. "Why didn't you follow the doctors' advice?"

Fridania slapped the table; Claus imitated her. "Because if God had wanted Claus to be a girl, he would have made him a girl."

"I'm a boy," Claus shouted. "A boy, not a girl. Isn't that right, Mommy?"

*"Sí, Clauscito,"* his mother reassured him. Then she continued. "The worst part is that because he was born without a penis, his urine and excrement come from the same place. They've done two operations but haven't been able to fix the problem."

"No more operations," Claus said. He turned to me. *"Mijo,* no more operations."

"Why don't you live with your parents, Miss Moquette?"

"Because I have my own family now."

"You are a child, Miss Moquette. And an invalid. You seem to have a severe impediment with your legs; you should live at home with your parents. Maybe Claus would be more comfortable in a rehabilitation center. As he grows up, you won't be able to care for him. He seems like an intelligent child. He will have to go to school. Maybe he can learn a trade and be a useful citizen."

"I will not put Claus in an institution!" Fridania shrieked, the veins in her neck swelling, her features becoming distorted by rage.

"It's not up to you to decide that, Miss Moquette," snarled Warpick. "A higher court will have to deal with this matter. I certainly will recommend that the boy go to a rehab."

"Never!" Fridania shouted in English. "Over my dead body, you hear me?" she went on in accentless English.

"Never, never, never, never!" shrieked Claus, leaping onto the table and hopping all over it like a rabbit. The judge's assistant sprang off her chair and backed off against the wall.

"Miss Moquette, the hearing is over," the judge said. "Take the boy and leave."

Fridania stood up. Grabbing the golf club, she looked at me and raised it. I cowered, covering my head with my arms. But Fridania, inching her way toward the bench, started jabbing the club into the air, whipping it back and forth. Warpick stood up horrified, croaking hysterically.

Still hopping on the table, Claus started to sing, *"Bamba, bamba. Bamba, bamba."*

"Mr. Interpreter," Warpick called out imploringly. "Please stop her. You must stop her!"

I realized Fridania meant no harm to me and I had no wish to get in the way of her avenging club.

The judge's assistant, who was across the room from Fridania, ran out of the room wailing. Warpick began to pitch the objects on her desk at the approaching claimant, who batted them with her club.

"Mr. Interpreter," Warpick screamed again. "Stop her! I tell you to stop her. If you don't, you'll be fired. You'll never work again."

I got up and took a good look at Fridania, who moved as fast

as a convalescing snail, and decided that Judge Warpick could protect herself without my help. I turned around to exit the room.

"You'll never work again!" Warpick's voice trailed after me as
I traipsed down the hall. I walked into the office to say good-bye to
Jeff. I found the judge's assistant collapsed on Jeff's chair, blubbering
as she tried to explain what was going on in the judge's office.

"Hey, man, what the hell is going on?" Jeff asked.

"The judge needs you," I said.

"Oh, yeah. Well, I'm busy right now," Jeff said.

I offered to shake Jeff's hand, which he took with a questioning
look.

"I'm quitting," I informed him. "I'll miss you, though."

"Man, you can't do that. You're my chess partner." Realizing
I was serious, he said, "What are you going to do?"

"I don't know," I shrugged. "Write a thriller, I guess."

"No shit."

"Bye," I said, feeling a lump rise in my throat.

As I exited the Federal Plaza building, I knew that I would
never reenter it again as an interpreter. I knew Unlimited Languages
would never call me again and this was the only agency that sent me
out to interpret in Social Security and Welfare cases. I wished I felt
exhilarated and free, like heroes do in movies and novels when they
stand up for themselves—although in my case, Fridania had done
the standing up for me. What I experienced was terror. I told myself
it was unlikely that Judge Warpick would call all the agencies in town
to ruin my interpreting career.

Outside, the day was sunny. After last night's rain, the city
looked spic and span; the air was crisp, invigorating. We had just
entered the dreaded month of August, but today there was a touch
of autumn in the air. Usually, after leaving work I rushed back home.
Today I wanted to linger in the streets. The men who had tried to
break into my apartment were still present in my mind. Today I
longed to sit down with a friend, to chew the fat for hours. I'll pay
a visit to Harry Hagin, I thought. He always brightens my day. I put
on my sunglasses and started walking in the direction of the corner
where Harry had been selling ices the last time I had seen him. Harry

was not at his corner. I walked east for a few blocks, thinking maybe he had moved deeper into the financial district.

I found hot dogs, pretzels, books, sunglasses, and fruit ice vendors, but no trace of Harry. It's not like Harry to take Monday off, I thought. I began to feel depressed. I felt as if a huge hippopotamus were being lowered on my head, squashing me onto the pavement. It was time to go home. I couldn't walk through Wall Street feeling like that. My life was in crisis and I was reacting to it like an ostrich.

Think positive, Santiago, I said to myself. Do something; buy the *New York Times* and study the classified section under jobs. I started to perspire remembering how many times in the past years I had done this, and after reading the first column given up in despair, realizing how few marketable skills I had. The heck with the past, I mumbled—I have to change all that. I was talking aloud to myself and the Wall Streeters were eyeing me suspiciously. Obviously, whether I ended up writing a thriller or not, I had to support myself somehow. Moving back to Mother's house in Queens was no longer an alternative. To prove to myself my new-found seriousness, I purchased a copy of the *Wall Street Journal* and, tucking it under my arm, I bolted for the subway. The E train was empty at that hour, and I sat down to read the paper and to enjoy the air-conditioning. I opened the *Journal* to the classified—my heart sank; it looked forbidding, like the obituary page of the *Times* without the photographs. I shut the paper in haste as if I had just seen a picture of the devil inside. At home, drinking a cold beer, maybe I could stand reading it. But the train was taking so long to fill up at the Chambers Street station that to escape my screaming thoughts I opened the *Journal* again, hoping against hope to find an article that would vaguely interest me. I flipped through the pages and glanced at most of the headlines until the E train arrived at Times Square.

I felt excited, manic. As I approached the corner of Eighth Avenue and Forty-third Street I saw many people bunched at the corner. Besides the riffraff and the crack people milling around, there were policemen and firemen. Police officers were setting up safety nets and pumping to inflate a safety cushion on the street. Was it a fire at the hotel? Now I noticed priests, nuns, and, of course, photographers. I knew an event of major proportions was going on in Times Square. Soon the TV people would be arriving. Everyone was looking up. No smoke came out of the building, but a man on a high floor was sitting on a window ledge threatening to jump. Brandishing a crucifix, a priest started to climb up the fire engine's ladder. A couple of nuns were praying on their knees. The crack heads watched the scene as if they were in an action movie. The whole thing was a turn-on to them. Looking like angry, demented demons just expelled from hell, they began to chant: "Jump! Jump! Jump!"

I gotta get the hell out of here, I thought; I don't want to see this. I was about to start crossing the street when the crowd broke up in a shrill roar and the man on the window ledge dove headfirst to the pavement. I froze; I didn't know whether to shit or go blind. The suicide landed inches away from me with a dull thump. The top of his head opened and shot some blood like a fire hydrant. The man was naked, except for a T-shirt and his legs looked brilliant as if they were waxed. One of my arms was red, as if spattered with ketchup. Touching my face and my head, I discovered I was drenched with blood. I howled, shutting my eyes. The crack heads screamed and tittered and giggled demonically.

Momentarily insane, I darted across the street, barely escaping the oncoming traffic. Sprinting up the stairs of my building, I stumbled upon a figure sitting on the steps.

"Jesus fucking Christ, Sammy," my nephew Gene screamed. "What happened to you, man? Is that paint or what?"

"It's blood," I blubbered, breaking into loud sobs and collapsing on the steps.

"Sammy, did you just kill someone? Did you? Why? Why? Oh man, why?" Gene shouted hysterically.

A couple of clients of George's employment agency were coming down the stairs. I nudged against the wall, turning my face away from them, but making enough room so they could go by. When the men reached the door, I said, "A man just jumped out of a building and almost fell on top of me."

"Oh, man. What a trip! I gotta go see that!"

"No, you're not," I said. "Come on, let's go upstairs."

Inside the apartment, I asked Gene to lock the door after us as I ran into the bathroom. Turning on the lights, I was so shocked by my bloody reflection in the mirror I became dizzy and had to sit on the toilet. I managed to remove my shirt and undershirt and used the latter to towel off my hair, face, and hands. Feeling stronger, I took off my shoes and pants. I leaned my back against the cool water tank and closed my eyes.

"Sammy, are you okay?" Gene asked, coming into the bathroom.

I opened my eyes. He was carrying Mr. O'Donnell, the cat's face against his cheeks.

"Hi, kitty," I said. "Gene, will you do me a favor? Take all these bloody clothes and put them in a plastic bag and get rid of them."

Gene made a face and handed Mr. O'Donnell to me. I set the cat on my knees, feeling his back paws clawing into my thighs. Gene made all sorts of disgusting sounds as he carried the clothes away. I noticed Mr. O'Donnell looked better, almost rejuvenated. "It must be the protein in that mouse you ate," I said. At that moment, a black, shiny, metallic-sounding fly—the size of a bumblebee—hurtled into the bathroom. Mr. O'Donnell sprang off my lap, caught the insect in midair and alighted at the bottom of the bathtub where he proceeded to chew on his catch. He made scratchy, dry sounds and, sticking out his tongue, started to lick his chops, as if he had just finished a gourmet meal.

"Get out of my sight, you disgusting beast," I muttered, rising and chasing him out of the room with the towel. I sat down again; I was shaking badly when loud music began to blast in the kitchen. Gene was playing one of his incomprehensible tapes. Without knocking, Gene entered the bathroom almost running, awkward and impetuous, like a wild horse. He had two glasses with him and handed me one. "Here, I think you might need this," he said. I took a swig of the scotch and shuddered as the alcohol sizzled down my throat.

"Why don't you take a nice bath?" Gene suggested. "I can make it for you."

I was touched by his concern, whether real or fake. This was one of the few occasions ever he had offered to do anything for me.

He began to fill the bathtub with steaming water. He left the water running and came back with a bottle of extract of vanilla, which he poured into the tub. I was too upset to argue. Before he left the room, I said, "Gene, how about turning down the volume of the music?"

"It's the Beastie Boys," he said, looking hurt, as if I had asked him to shut off a sublime Brahms symphony. "I'm going up front to listen, is that cool?"

I nodded. Gene shut the door with a whack that made me jump. I took off my underwear and got into the scalding water. With the water up to my neck, I sat there taking deep breaths and wriggling my toes. The room looked foggy and mysterious in the rising steam. I bean to fantasize: This was not my bathroom but an ancient Inca bath. Instead of the pleasant, mild scent of vanilla, what I smelled was *palo santo* and burnt eucalyptus; instead of laying in tap water, I was floating in a pool of hot mineral springs emanating from a sacred volcano. I was beginning to unwind when, against my will, a babel of voices started having a conference in my head. What was Gene doing here? He seldom came to visit me, and never unannounced. He'd come to get the coke, of course! I could picture him now ransacking the apartment, turning everything upside down. That's why he had suggested my bath. It was not concern on his part but sly, devious thinking, and I had fallen for it, giving in to my avuncular sentiments that always made me act against my best interest. "Give the kid a break," protested the even-tempered voice of reason. "He's not bad, he's just scared." "Oh yeah," interjected the scoffing voice of paranoia, stepping up to the mike, "Keep thinking like a Miss Pollyanna suppository and soon you'll lie in the gutter with your head blown off by nice Colombian bullets." I was freaking out again.

I was about to leap out of the bathtub when the phone rang. I heard Gene's caveman footsteps galloping for the phone. I sat still. Maybe it was one of his friends calling to chat. Now the thumping steps approached the bathroom door. I reached for the towel as the door opened and Gene stuck his head in. "It's the United Nations, Sammy."

"The United Nations? Are you sure?"

"Yeah, something about the United Nations."

"Wait, I'll take it," I said, getting up, wrapping the towel around my waist, and rushing to the telephone.

"Hello," I said, slightly out of breath.

"San-tiaaaaaa-gooooo, San-tiaaaaaa-go," sang Virginia, from the Language Workshop, one of the interpreting agencies I worked for. "I've got a jooob for youuuuuu, at the Uniiii-ted Nations. It's a lunnnnn-cheon. Do youuuuuu want it?" she finished in her cracked quasisoprano voice. Virginia was a Viennese opera nut. She was in her seventies and still ran her own agency. I had run into her once at the Met when Rebecca had taken me for my birthday to see a performance of *La Traviata*. Since then, she was convinced that I went to the opera all the time.

"The United Nations, huh," I said very impressed. "Sure I'll take it."

"They asked me for my best interpreter, and of course I thought about you," she said, now in her normal speaking voice. Then she gave me all the information, which I took with great difficulty considering I was dripping wet and Gene stood next to me watching intently everything I said and did.

"Are you going to translate tomorrow at the U.N.?" Gene asked, visibly impressed, after I hung up.

"Yeah," I said, affecting a blasé tone as if I were used to interpreting at the U.N., when in fact I had never been there before.

"That's where you should get a full-time job, Sammy, instead of that welfare shit you do."

Gene's advice was undoubtedly not malicious, but I did not appreciate his tacit criticism of how I conducted my interpreting career. To punish him I said, "Will you make some coffee while I get dressed?"

"Can I use the Mr. Coffee I gave you last Christmas?"

"Sure. Do it any way you want."

He marched to the kitchen with the resolute, indelicate stride of a teenage Ollie Oop. In the bedroom, I toweled slowly, musing on the kind of day I was having. Just an hour ago, for all practical purposes, I had thought my interpreting career was over. And now, tomorrow I was going to work at the U.N. Who knows where that might lead? What if I screw up, though? I wondered. No, no, no, Santiago, I said, shutting off the negative tapes before they started running. I'm an excellent interpreter, I reminded myself. There are no coincidences; the U.N. is where I belong. I'll do beautifully tomorrow and they'll be so impressed I'll end up getting lots of assignments. My money situation will improve, and I won't have to interpret the squalid and horrifying lives of social security and welfare claimants anymore. Even my mother will be impressed, I thought, as I put on shorts, T-shirt, and sneakers. From now on, I would only interpret for statesmen and politicians. It occurred to me that the social security claimants were more admirable and honest than the corrupt politicians of the world—especially the ones from Latin America—for whom I no doubt would be interpreting. What's more, as grim as the lives of the claimants were, they were probably a more cheerful subject matter than Nazi criminals, famine, torture, genocide, and everything the U.N. had to deal with.

A plastic bag on my pillows distracted me from this line of thinking. I emptied its contents on the bedspread; Mother had sent the Colombian newspapers of the past few days with Gene. Wrongly, she assumed that I was interested in reading these newspapers; that I continued to be interested in whatever went on in Colombia. And yet, perhaps she understood something about myself that I denied; I always diligently perused the newspapers and found at least a couple of articles that interested me. I studied the front page of *El Espectador,* and read the headlines absentmindedly. I set the paper aside and let the back of my head sink into the pillows. Gene came into the room with two cups of steaming coffee. Mr. O'Donnell trotted after him and jumped on my bed while Gene set the cup of coffee on the night table and sat on my desk.

"How are you feeling?" he asked.

Mr. O'Donnell walked up the length of my legs and stretched out on my crotch. I sat up, brushing the cat aside. As he moved away, he stuck his back paws on my shorts. "Ouch," I uttered, covering my genitalia. I gave Mr. O'Donnell a hard look and tasted the sickeningly sweet coffee.

"How's the coffee?" Gene asked eagerly.

"It's very good. Thanks, Gene."

"You look awful, Sammy. I've never seen you look so shitty. It's like . . . it's like you need to relax or something."

I wasn't quite sure that whatever way I felt Gene wasn't at least partially responsible for it.

"Anyway, what are you doing in Manhattan?" I queried him, becoming suspicious of his motives for visiting me.

He shrugged. "Nothing." He ogled Mr. O'Donnell and sipped his coffee. "What a big cat," he said in admiration, as if he were praising Mr. O'Donnell for his genius or his poetic nature.

"Don't change the subject. You came to get the coke, didn't you?"

"No, man. I just wanted to get the hell out of Queens for a day. And I wanted to talk to you. You're like my only uncle. And you're my friend, aren't you?" he finished, looking hurt.

"I guess so," I mumbled, not being too thrilled at the prospect of being related to a future Al Capone. "I think your friends are after me," I said, giving him an accusing look. "We have to get rid of that coke. Last night there were two guys on my fire escape trying to break in."

"I just love the way you jump to conclusions," he said, exasperated. "How do you know they were Colombians? They were probably crack heads from the neighborhood. It's not like you live on Park Avenue, you know," Gene finished, with the cruelty of youth.

"Oh, yeah. I've lived here for many years and nobody ever tried to break into my apartment."

"Sammy, will you get off that horse? How would my . . . ex-boss know you have the coke? That's like so paranoid of you."

"If they didn't know before, they know now. I'm sure they followed you into the city."

"I can't believe this shit," Gene said, getting up and wringing his hands. "My own uncle trying to do me in. I'm gonna go and I'm never, ever no more coming back to see you."

"Not until you've learned to speak English properly," I snapped back. "Okay, okay, okay," I said. "I guess you're right. I'm overwrought by all the shit that's been raining on me lately. Please stay, okay?"

"Really, Sammy? You're not pissed off at me? How would you like to go to the park?" Gene proposed enthusiastically. Seeing me demur, he went on. "When was the last time you went to the park? You need the inspiration of nature."

"Sure, Mr. Wordsworth," I said, knowing full well that my allusion was completely wasted on him.

"We can have a picnic," Gene went on, "and spend the afternoon hanging out. I can chase the girls and you . . . can do whatever you want. How about that?"

"I just want to take it easy," I said.

"Remember how you used to take me to the park when I was little?" Gene said, waxing nostalgic as I wondered what had ever happened to the cute, lovable toddler I had known. "You used to say to me, 'Gene, want to go to the *patico* park?' That was so cute, the way you called the duck pond the *patico* park."

"Okay," I said, blushing. "That's enough. We'll go to the park for the afternoon."

"I'm raring to go," Gene said.

Now that I had agreed to do it, I got cold feet. "Wait, Gene. I can't go to the park just like that. Just cool it for a minute. Let me think about what we need to take with us, okay?"

Gene sat down again on the desk, although he looked like a race horse ready to take off. Mr. O'Donnell was now aware that we were leaving. He gave me the pitiful, longing, reproachful look he always used when he saw me getting ready to go out. Gene picked up on it.

"Let's take O'Donnell, too." He lifted the cat off the bed and started kissing his face.

"Put him down; he doesn't like to be mauled. It's not a good idea; forget it." As I said this, it occurred to me that the mafiosi might return, break in, and Mr. O'Donnell could escape. "Okay, we'll take him to the park," I said. "Let me get his box."

As soon as I said "box," Mr. O'Donnell torpedoed off Gene's arms and hid under the bed.

"What's come over him?" Gene asked, puzzled by the cat's bewildering reaction.

"He thinks I'm taking him to the ASPCA. He only sees the box when he has to go to the vet."

We tried to coax Mr. O'Donnell from under the bed—but to no avail.

"Wait," I said. "I know what will do it. Kal Kan," I cried out like a fool and started walking toward the kitchen. "Kal Kan, Kal Kan," I sang.

I opened the refrigerator and pretended to fetch the Kal Kan. As Mr. O'Donnell started rubbing against me, I grabbed him. Gene brought out the box and between the two of us we managed to put him inside it. Now I was afraid that the trauma of the skirmish might give him a heart attack. I was so exhausted by the ordeal that I didn't feel like going out anymore. But I knew Gene would be disappointed if I changed my mind.

In a duffle bag we packed blankets, cushions, paper dishes, insect repellent, suntan lotion, etc., and left the apartment as though we were going on a safari. In the street, Mr. O'Donnell started to bleat pathetically. We strolled up Eighth Avenue and stopped at a Korean grocery store to buy food for the picnic.

"It's been days since I ate anything that stuck to my ribs," Gene said. Living at my mother's house as he did, I wondered how that could be possible.

I reassured him. "Don't worry, we'll buy lots of food."

"I don't want to eat peaches and carrot sticks," Gene remonstrated. "You buy whatever you want to eat and I'll buy whatever I want."

That sounded fair enough. We marched up different aisles—I, carrying the cat box, he, the duffle bag. I bought a six-pack of beer, oranges, pears, rice cakes, and yogurt, and walked to the cash register to pay for my items. Gene had disappeared behind the aisles, so I waited, setting the box on the floor. Mr. O'Donnell was making blood-curdling sounds, as if he were possessed by the same demon that had gotten hold of Linda Blair in *The Exorcist*. The people in the store began to eye the box with alarm. I was getting uptight and restless when Gene appeared carrying three Hershey bars, a large Coke, a box of buttered popcorn, a bag of Chee-tohs, and two large containers of Pringle's Potato Chips. I was going to reprimand him on the junk he ate, but I decided it was wrong to begin arguing before the picnic started.

It was a cool, dry, golden afternoon crowned with an aquamarine sky. We dawdled all the way to Columbus Circle, where, in front of the statue at the edge of the park, a black trumpet player blasted to a large but hushed audience the melancholy notes of The Beatles' "Yesterday." The piercing notes of the melody felt like slivers stuck under my skin. I motioned Gene to move on. It was past noon and the park was alive with joggers and people having their lunches and smoking joints. We trekked away from the crowds until we reached a field where a baseball game was in progress. The teams wore uniforms and the players were young but serious. We chose a spot under a tree that was far enough from the action, but close enough that we could enjoy the game. We spread out our blanket and pulled out the cushions and emptied the shopping bags. Mr. O'Donnell had grown so strangely quiet that I wondered if he was all right. He was sitting up when I opened the box, and jumped out before I could reach in to pull him out. His eyes, like open yellow tulips, took in the scene, shining with the excitement of finding that he was someplace other than the Humane Society. He was ready to start exploring the surroundings.

"Oh, no," I said, "I'm afraid this is not going to work out. I forgot to bring some kind of leash. He could run away."

But, as if to purposefully contradict me, Mr. O'Donnell stretched out languidly and then collapsed on his side, facing the baseball field.

"Check that out," Gene exclaimed. "He likes baseball."

"No, no. He likes opera."

"He likes baseball, too. Don't you, O'Donnell?"

Mr. O'Donnell twitched his tail to indicate that he was both watching the game and listening to our conversation.

Gene opened one of the beers and took a long swig; with his teeth, he tore open one of the bags and stuffed his mouth, making loud, crunchy noises as he chewed. "Isn't this the ultimate?" he said with the fake sincerity of a budding thespian. "Nature," he expostulated, "summer, baseball, beer, everything. If I could choose one way to spend the rest of my life, I would choose this. Wouldn't you?" He finished as if he had just recited an immortal Shakespearean soliloquy. His face looked so enraptured that I wondered if he was already drunk from the beer. "Wouldn't you, too?" he insisted. Obviously I was not going to be allowed to brush off the silly question. I knew he was serious. I remembered how at fifteen I had been obsessed with the meaning of life, love, God, existence, the universe.

"I don't know," I said. "I don't think so," although I couldn't think of anything better. Perhaps the mountains, I thought; maybe the ocean. Life at a marina, sailing the pellucid sea. But I realized that "the ultimate"—Gene and I in harmony; Mr. O'Donnell happy, serene; the cool beer, the radiant afternoon; the guys hitting the ball—was very nice indeed, and despite my messy life, for the moment I could afford to be happy.

Gene and I became engrossed in the game. Mr. O'Donnell fell asleep, his snoring sounding like a pigeon cooing. After a while we got to know the names of the players, and when their teammates cheered them on, we'd join them. This was better than professional baseball, where I always rooted for the Mets. Here, I just wanted to see brilliant pitches, great hits, dazzling catches, no matter from whom. Whenever we'd scream too loud, Mr. O'Donnell would jerk awake, turn around and cast reproachful glances at us before going back to sleep.

We watched the game and drank and munched throughout the afternoon. At one point, Mr. O'Donnell woke up and begged for food. He ate an entire container of blueberry yogurt and a couple of Gene's Chee-tohs before he resumed his nap. By the time the game was over, maybe owing to the beers I'd had, maybe owing to the languid afternoon we were having, I felt relaxed and drowsy.

"Gene," I said, "I'm going to take a nap. Is that okay?"

"Go right ahead, man. Whatever makes you happy."

"I wonder if I should put Mr. O'Donnell in his box."

"Sammy, don't do that to the poor cat. He's so happy where he is."

"But I'm afraid he could run away."

"Not to worry. I'll watch over him. Just go to sleep, all right?"

"Thanks, Gene. I appreciate it. But don't let me sleep too long. Wake me up before dark, okay?"

"Okay."

I stretched out, my head on a cushion, and closed my eyes. In the darkness, I could hear the many sounds of the park; the twittering of different birds, traffic noises so far away that they almost sounded pleasant, bits and pieces of conversations of the people who walked near us. I began to dream of myself in Barranquilla when I was thirteen or fourteen years old.

In the afternoons, during vacation time or on weekends, I'd go for long walks in the best neighborhoods in town. I would pass all the great mansions, wishing I lived in one of them. I'd sit on a street curb, and then I'd proceed to create an entire fantasy about my life inside that particular house, complete with parents, pets, brothers and sisters I liked. Around the time I was Gene's age, I longed to escape my life. I wanted to go far away from everything that surrounded me, although the thought of leaving behind my dog, Spartacus, and my sister saddened me. Then my dream took on a different turn; it was nighttime. The moon was out and the sky was a rich, enamelled blue. I was on a farm with my mother, and we were strolling in a hilly, rolling landscape bereft of vegetation except for the grass we walked on. Spartacus appeared at the top of a hill, looking like a wolf. He stood erect, tough, vigilant, like a warrior. With his black and white markings, he looked as if he were dressed for a ball. I called him by his nickname, *Pita,* and he plunged down the hill to meet me. I patted his head and said to my mother, "Spartacus doesn't bark anymore," to which she replied, "It's because he's so fat, like you." Then a lovely and pure tenor's voice sang, *"Ay, luna que brillas; Ay, luna."*

When I woke up the afternoon was quite advanced; it was six-thirty but still very light. Another baseball game with different teams was in progress. I opened Mr. O'Donnell's box, thinking Gene had put him inside before going off by himself. The box was empty; my heart stopped. I refused to believe that the worst had happened, that Mr. O'Donnell had run away and now Gene was desperately roaming the park trying to find him. I was about to get up to start looking for them, when I saw Gene approaching. He carried a shopping bag but no cat.

"Where's Mr. O'Donnell?" I screamed.

"He's in the bag. I took him for a ride; we had a great time. He's so kickass bad. You should have seen him in the woods trying to get those birds and the squirrels and . . . ."

"Asshole," I interrupted him. "You could have given me a fucking heart attack."

"Didn't you see my note?"

"What note?" I grumbled.

"Next to your pillow. See it?"

Indeed, next to my pillow there was a piece of paper bag with something scribbled on it. "Sorry, Gene," I apologized, feeling ashamed of myself. "I guess I woke up in a state."

Gene dumped Mr. O'Donnell out of the bag. As if to cheer me up, O'Donnell sat on my lap and began to purr. Gene sat next to me.

"Where you having a nightmare?"

"Not really. I was dreaming about when I was your age," I said, scratching the cat under his chin. "Lately I've been dreaming a lot about my childhood. I wonder what it means. All I know is that I had an unhappy childhood and adolescence."

"Sammy, you didn't have a bad childhood, just a long one," Gene said.

"In the past couple of weeks, though, I've felt as if my life were going from monochrome into color."

"Sure. Your best friend died, you got engaged . . ."

"I'm not getting married to Claudia, is that clear?"

"Why not?"

"Because I'm gay. And because . . . it's none of your business." I lit a cigarette and took several quick, furious drags like Bette Davis in *Dark Victory*. I looked up; the sun had traveled three-quarters of its way from sunrise, and now it hovered above the gothic, malignant structure of the Dakota, where God knew what Satanic ritual was taking place. The sun's rays fell obliquely; they felt warm and gentle. The treetops swayed in the tranquil breeze, and a flock of noisy geese flew northward. The sky was still immaculately blue, but the light was golden, like twilight in a luminist painting. The nippy air promised a crisp evening.

"You wanna go home now or you wanna stay a bit longer?" Gene asked.

"What do you want to do? Want to stay? I don't mind catching some of this game," I said, nodding in the direction of the players. "Those guys look really good."

"That's cool with me," Gene said.

I construed this to mean we were staying. I looked toward the baseball field and began to space out again. This time of day made me think of my grandparents' town. The air became charged with the acrid smell of cow manure. It was my favorite time of day. If I didn't go by the quay to watch the sunset, I'd sit on a rocking chair outside the house and watch the young girls carrying baskets loaded with fresh fish, returning to their homes before nightfall. Then, as the sun sank, vapors rose from the muddy river bed, where litters of squealing pigs rolled and vultures searched for carrion. Later, as dusk set in, the smell of ripe *ciruelas,* mangoes, *nísperos,* and cashew fruit turned the evening into an aphrodisiac. My grandfathers and uncles approached the house, riding their horses after an afternoon at the farm. They rode up the mossy street, which was decorated with huge white boulders set in the middle of the road like fossilized dinosaur eggs. Barefoot, almost naked, children led their family burros back into their corrals. The African-looking *palenqueras,* advertising their coconut sweets, sashayed their way up the street singing in their soprano voices, *"Alegría, alegría con coco y maní."* As night fell, the mosquitoes arrived, myriads of bats took over the sky, fireflies glowed on the patios, and the sweet smell of honeysuckle spread all over town, like an elixir, mixing with the dinners being prepared in the open-air kitchens.

"Want a hit of this?" Gene asked, waking me up from my reverie; he was smoking a fat joint.

"No, it makes me paranoid." I took the opportunity to scold him. "You should quit drugs; they're not good for you," I said sternly, aware that I sounded like the detestable Nancy Reagan.

"I'm gonna quit soon. I promise you."

"The trick is to quit while you're alive."

"I know you want to have a hit of this. This is the best pot in Queens, man."

I took a long drag and felt the marijuana resin singe the insides of my lungs; I also felt pleasantly stoned.

"What did you do in Colombia all those years after college—besides being a garbage head?" Gene asked.

"I can't remember a lot of it."

"It sounds to me like you were fucking vegged out on drugs," Gene said.

"It was like being in a spiritual coma, if you know what I mean. I'm only beginning to wake up from it now," I said.

"I think you should still get hammered once in a while, before you're too old."

"Gene, when I was your age, cigarettes were the strongest stuff I did."

"Mr. O'Donnell looks so happy on your lap," Gene said, changing the subject. "What do you think he's dreaming about? Look, he's smiling."

"Whatever cats dream about: a fat mouse, perhaps. A saucer heaped with Kal Kan, pigeons, juicy flies. Maybe he's dreaming of Monserrat Caballe singing Violeta."

"He really likes opera? That's like so fucking bizarre, man."

"He likes Monserrat Caballe singing *La Traviata*. I don't know that he likes anything else."

"You shoudda seen him in the woods; he was awesome. He was one happy cat. Sammy, do you think cats have like a last wish? You know, like prisoners before they die?"

I thought about it. "It's different, I think. Prisoners know they're going to die; I don't think cats know."

"How do you now? You're not a cat." Gene paused. "I think I know what his last wish is."

"What?"

"To be free."

"What do you mean?"

"To be free in the park. To be loose. To go wild killing pigeons and squirrels and birds. I'd bet you anything that's what he wants. Before you got him, wasn't he an alley cat, anyway?"

"Just because all you think about is guns and killing doesn't mean my cat wants to decimate the endangered fauna of Central Park."

"I'd bet you anything he'd rather have his last heart attack while munching on a pigeon or something."

This vision made me shudder. I lifted up Mr. O'Donnell in my arms and kissed his cold nose.

"When is he supposed to croak, anyway?"

"Any minute," I said, "but I'd rather not talk about it, if you don't mind."

"Sammy, if you really loved him, you'd rather let him go. You'd let him die a free cat."

"Hell, no," I boomed, nettled by his insistence. "When you have your own cat you can do that, if you want. I could never forgive myself if I did anything that stupid."

"You should have been in the woods with me. You shouldda seen how his eyes shone when he spotted the wild animals, especially the squirrels. He'd die a happy cat, that's all I'm saying to you."

Maybe there was something to what he was saying, although it sounded suspiciously like pseudo-hippy new age talk. "Mr. O'Donnell," I said, poking him gently to wake him up. "Is that what you'd prefer? Do you want to be set loose in the park?"

"Sure, man," Gene answered for the cat. "If you were dying wouldn't you rather die in nature than in Times Square or in a hospital?"

"Let him speak for himself," I said, setting Mr. O'Donnell on the blanket. I got up. "Let's go," I said. "Help me pack." I began to pick up the garbage without looking at Mr. O'Donnell. When we finished packing, Mr. O'Donnell's box remained open. He sat next to it, looking up into the trees.

"Okay, Mr. O'Donnell," I said. "This is good-bye, old man. You are a free cat; you can go."

Mr. O'Donnell turned around to look at me. He stared me in the eyes, sprang to his feet and jumped into his box, without any coaxing on my part.

I slapped Gene on his back. "You see? He prefers me to squirrels and rabbits. He loves me as I love him."

Gene's jaw fell open. There was a look of total perplexity on his face. "Man, what a cat! That's so fucking unbelievable."

I scratched Mr. O'Donnell between his ears and closed his box. It was the perfect way to end the day. It almost made up for the horrible morning I had had. Shadows were taking over the park. A couple of stars and a planet gleamed in the cobalt sky.

# 11

## This Island, This Kingdom

The alarm woke me at eight. I had to be at the U.N. at noon but I
wanted to have plenty of time to get ready. Gene was sleeping on
the couch in the living room. In his underwear, he looked gigantic,
fleshy and amorphous like a pale sea lion. The sheets were on the
floor, and he had fallen asleep reading *Rolling Stone*. Mr. O'Donnell,
who was sleeping on a pillow, leaped out of bed when he saw me
enter the kitchen. I fed him, put on the water for coffee, and went
into the bathroom to wash my face and brush my teeth.

Around ten o'clock I got dressed. Since Gene was still asleep
and I had to tiptoe around the apartment, I decided to leave early.
For some months now, I had been thinking about taking my typewriter to be cleaned. I put the machine in its case and left. I walked
to a repair shop on Fortieth Street, between Seventh and Eighth
avenues. The store was empty, except for the clerk behind the
counter.

"What can I do for you?" the man greeted me.

I told him several of the typewriter's keys were stuck and I
wanted to give the machine a complete overhaul. The man asked me
to open the case. I hadn't finished removing the top when he
diagnosed, "We can't help you."

"Why?"

"Because we don't carry parts for that kind of machine anymore."

Ha, I thought. He's trying to sell me a machine; I know this trick.

"Well, do you know of another place where they might repair it, since I can't afford to buy a new machine?"

"There's a store up the block, on the other side of the street. You can try them, but I doubt it. The manufacturer doesn't make parts for that model anymore."

"What do you mean?" I asked in disbelief. "It's almost a new machine."

"It's about ten years old, right?"

I nodded.

"You can see for yourself," he said, making a sweep with his arm around the store, "we don't carry typewriters that old."

I glanced at the different models on display, and I observed that all the machines for sale had a high-tech look unrelated to my primitive-looking electric typewriter. I thanked the man and headed for the other store. It was a replay of the same story. What's more, the salesman told me I should throw the machine in the garbage. Something told me these men were right. At the corner of Broadway and Fortieth, as I lowered my machine slowly into a trash receptacle, I also felt as if I were unburdening myself of a different kind of weight—my Rip van Winkling of the past decade. Where had I been all these years? How had I gotten so out of touch with everything? Was it possible that the typewriter was a symbol of everything I had to get rid of? By what process had I become an anachronism at age thirty-three? Was it in any way related to all the memories that I had been having in the past few weeks about my childhood and adolescence? I shook my head. I knew this was not the most cheerful line of thinking to be engaged in before starting my interpreting career at the U.N. I would concentrate on the sunny morning. We were having a spell of gorgeous days, which for New York City, in August, amounted to a miracle. As I walked in the direction of the East River, it dawned on me that I had lived half of my life in New York and I had never passed, much less gone inside, the U.N. building. Instead of getting depressed over this fact, I told myself I should look at the positive side of it; today was a new beginning. Feeling much better, I strode to Forty-third and Lexington, where the Language Workshop was located and I had to get my admission pass to the U.N.

I had seen the U.N. building in the movies, so that in a way it was déjà vu. I flashed the blue pass on my lapel to the guards at the main entrance. I was an hour early, so I decided to take a stroll in the expansive, well-kept grounds. Hundreds of colorful flags made snapping sounds high in the wind. Variegated groups of tourists headed excitedly in all directions. I walked east down a series of steps that cut through rows of what looked like cherry trees, leading to a promenade above the East River. The industrial, ugly carcasses of buildings on the other side of the river contrasted unfavorably with the gleaming structures of the U.N. The only sign of beauty across the river was provided by the pink, white, and blue neon Pepsi Cola sign, which was lit even though it was nearly noon. The chartreuse waters of the East River teemed with sailing vessels, small motor boats, yachts, and even a monumental tugboat. To the north loomed the imposing structure of the Queensboro Bridge. All this was very scenic, but I was nervous; the palms of my hands were clammy and I felt an uncomfortable tightness in the pit of my stomach.

I could have stayed on the promenade another twenty minutes, but I decided the sooner I stepped inside the building and reached my destination the less there was to fear. I took several deep breaths, taking in the seemingly fresh but undoubtedly polluted air. After wending my way through a maze and further scrutiny and frisking, I walked into the cathedral-sized lobby. This is what being inside the Tower of Babel must have felt like, I thought, as I overheard the well-dressed herds of tourists speaking in exotic languages, darting excitedly from display to display, led by the tour guides. At the Language Workshop I had been given the details of where I had to report to; I was going to interpret for the annual luncheon of the meeting of Parliamentarians for Global Disarmament. As I moved deeper into the inner chambers of the U.N., the security outposts became more thorough, the crowds thinned, and only diplomats and U.N. employees were visible. I felt more and more like a character in a Hitchcock thriller—*The Man Who Knew Too Much* or something

167

like that. I took an elevator to the second floor. It dropped me off inside a small reception room. A security guard in a blue blazer promptly demanded to know my business. He gave me brief and precise instructions where to go. I stepped into a spacious dining room. It was barely noon, but there were people having lunch already. All the tables had arrangements of orange and yellow flowers and through the twelve-foot glass windows streamed the silvery noon light. Heavenly smells hit my nostrils and I felt envious of the elegantly dressed people sipping aromatic wines and conversing in hushed tones. I turned left down a corridor that led into a small dining room. The tables were arranged in a U shape, the bottom of the U against the south wall. The people catering the affair gave me inquiring glances. I informed them I was the interpreter, which was acknowledged by blank stares. Since none of the world parliamentarians or the U.N. officials had arrived, I stood by the huge windows watching the multifarious crafts going up and down the East River.

The waiters were putting the finishing touches on the luncheon; more flowers were brought in, French rolls were distributed around the table, a shrimp and lobster salad on a bed of wonderfully fresh Romaine lettuce was served, wines were uncorked. I had forgotten to eat anything for breakfast and the smells perfuming the room made me feel faint with hunger. I decided to concentrate on matters other than food; I had to get a new typewriter. Because of the expense, a word processor was out of the question. I needed a machine if I was going to finish my Columbus poem, or start my thriller. This purchase would severely deplete my nest egg. Perhaps my mother would give me a loan—although I was aware how hard it was to squeeze a penny out of her CDs.

Suddenly, a rising murmur of voices approached and the delegates entered the room. I had been instructed to introduce myself to Mr. McClanahan, who had contracted my services from the Language Workshop. I approached a thin man in his early thirties, quintessentially the executive type: clean-cut, efficient-looking and impeccably and conservatively dressed. McClanahan gave me the tiniest smile possible and absentmindedly shook my hand and told me to hang around until all the delegates had taken their places.

When everyone had sat down in a hurry—they all looked as hungry as I was—I saw there was no seat left for me. McClanahan motioned to a waiter to produce a chair, and a place was made for me near the window, at the tip of the upside-down U. Quickly, plates, bread, salad, and wine appeared. A pink-looking man in his midfifties sat to my right. He nodded, smiling, and asked me where I was from. I told him. Then he introduced himself as the delegate from Botswana. I wasn't sure where Botswana was, so I was speechless.

Mistaking me for a delegate, the man said, "I didn't see you this morning at the sessions. Did you just get here? Have you met the other members of the Latin delegation?"

I told him I was the interpreter.

"Oh," the man said frowning, and immediately turned to talk to the woman on his right.

Racist creep, I thought to myself, bunching together Botswanians and South Africans. I imitated the people buttering their rolls and sipping their wines and was about to take my first bite when a very Ivy Leaguey, lean man, stood up and introduced himself as the vice prime minister of New Zealand or something like that.

"Good afternoon, ladies and gentlemen," he said, beginning the session. "Welcome to the annual luncheon of the Third International Congress of the Security Commission of the Parliamentarians for Global Disarmament," and he extended his open palm in my direction to indicate I should start interpreting his introductory remarks. Much to my dismay I had to put down my roll and begin to interpret. "The U.N. has provided us with the services of an excellent interpreter for the members of the Latin delegation who do not speak English," he said. Everyone stared at me; I tried to smile the best I could.

The vice prime minister launched on a long and convoluted explanation of what the Parliamentarians for Global Disarmament stood for. I realized I wasn't being paid to have lunch; nonetheless the man's explanation struck me as an utter waste of time designed to prevent me from enjoying my lunch. The vice prime minister then went on to talk about the recent origins of the organization, the main resolutions of the past congresses, and the goals of the current summit. While the man pontificated, and I interpreted, the delegates gobbled their salads, bread, and wine. The vice prime minister was still talking about the importance of the organization, how necessary it was in order to keep the world from self-destructing with nuclear weapons, when the salad plates were removed and replaced by large, juicy salmon steaks and done-to-perfection steamed vegetables. The aromas of the fish, broiled in a light butter and lime sauce, and the vegetables made me dizzy. The vice prime minister concluded his peroration hyperbolically, though in a dispassionate tone: "World Parliamentarians for Global Disarmament, remember that the future of mankind is in your hands."

The delegates stopped chewing in order to clap. I reached for a glass of wine and took a long sip. I was perspiring; I had been interpreting nonstop for twenty minutes and my throat was dry. I was about to cut into my salmon steak when the vice prime minister stood up again and said, "If there are any questions, I would be delighted to answer them." I put the chunk of salmon in my mouth, praying that there'd be no questions and I could have my lunch in peace. I washed it down with a little more wine. To my enormous displeasure, the Malaysian delegate raised his hand.

"Mr. Frost," he addressed the New Zealander, "the Malaysian delegation was wondering who funds the Security Commission of the Parliamentarians for Global Disarmament."

Disgusted, I put my fork down and averted my gaze from the scrumptious lunch. Something told me that to justify their having been flown to New York for the session, some of the members felt compelled to ask all sorts of inane questions.

Looking poleaxed, Frost fidgeted before answering. "Our main backers are the Rockefeller family and the MacArthur Foundation."

*"Los Rockefellers,"* exclaimed a delegate in Spanish.

"The Rockefellers," I echoed in English, forgetting my lunch and becoming interested in the proceedings. It was the Peruvian delegate who had extrapolated thus. Who's this nut? I wondered. A member of the Shining Path?

"Had we known the imperialist Rockefeller family funded this congress, Peru would have abstained from attending," I interpreted for him, both amused and embarrassed at what I was saying. I noticed the Colombian delegate next to him. He was dressed in an

English three-piece gray suit and a red tie and he looked like an Andean cousin of Peter Lorre. The man reminded me of one of my mother's Colombian "businessmen" friends in Jackson Heights.

"The Rockefeller family," I caught Mr. Frost saying, "is very interested in nuclear disarmament, yes, sir."

The Latin delegates turned to me for an interpretation. I interpreted the last words I had heard. Then, in Spanish, I said to the delegates, "I'm sorry, but I couldn't hear what he was saying; he was talking too softly."

A Central American delegate raised her hand. Oh, my God, I thought, she's going to complain about me.

"Sir," she said, "will you please speak up so that the interpreter can hear you?"

I wanted to die right then and there. My incipient career as a U.N. interpreter was certainly over.

"Mr. Interpreter," Frost said.

"What?" I cried, jumping from my seat.

"Please, sit down, sir," Frost ordered me in his even, computer manner. "If you have trouble hearing me, please let me know."

I sat down as the marvelous salmon was being removed from my field of vision.

"What the Latin delegates want to know," said the Peruvian representative, "is what the Parliamentarians for Global Disarmament plan to do about the difficult situation in Central America."

Luscious strawberries and aromatic coffee made their appearance at the table.

"The Parliamentarians for Global Disarmament deals exclusively with the subject of nuclear disarmament. There are many other committees at the U.N. where you can bring up the concerns of Central America for discussion."

"But Mr. Chairman," the testy delegate went on, "none of the nations here present have nuclear weapons. In Latin America the threat of nuclear war is not perceived as one of our more pressing problems."

Good question, I thought, realizing that none of the nations present had the economic might to create or purchase nuclear weapons. So what were they doing here?

"Perhaps I should stress to all delegates the fact that the Parliamentarians for Global Disarmament is a nonpartisan organization. Our only concern is how to contain the spread of nuclear weapons and the threat it represents to all of mankind, not just the industrial nations. This afternoon," he said by way of concluding, "there will be many interesting sessions that all of you will find enlightening. On behalf of the United Nations, once more I extend my welcome to the third congress and I wish you all a pleasant and fruitful stay in the Big Apple."

He smiled, sat down, and attacked his dessert. Frost was obviously as hungry as I was. Although he did not live on my starvation budget, I was sure he, too, mourned the sumptuous lunch.

I ate my dessert slowly and relished the marvelously brewed Colombian coffee, second only to my mother's coffee in Queens. An hour later, after many cordials of which I did not partake, the delegates rose to leave the room. I got up to follow them and was about to exit when Frost approached me, smiling.

"Mr. Interpreter," he said in the oily, insincere manner of all politicians, "thank you very much for doing a difficult job so well."

I must have blushed, I'm sure. "Oh, thank you, sir," I said politely, thinking I should be nice to this cold fish, who in a few years would undoubtedly be ruling over a big chunk of the world.

"I will certainly recommend you to your superiors," he finished and shook my hand. Then he turned to greet a bunch of delegates from faraway countries.

As I walked back home thoughts tossed in my head like wet clothes in a tumble dryer: Had I done well? Would I be hired by the United Nations? Did I want to spend the rest of my life interpreting for those people? Interpreting at all? Being an interpreter for the rest of my life, in every aspect of my life?

In this unserene frame of mind, I arrived at the east corner of Forty-third Street and Eighth Avenue. As I looked up I shuddered, remembering the man who had killed himself yesterday. On the spot where he had landed there was still a moist black stain. As I waited for the light to change, all I could see on the other side of the street were scores of crack heads panhandling outside Paradise Alley. I felt incredible anger rise up in my throat; I was thankful at that moment

I did not own a machine gun, because otherwise I would have sprayed thousands of bullets on these vermin. Maybe I should burn the porno place one night, I thought as I crossed the street. Late at night, I would douse the premises with gasoline and light it up. Thinking these incendiary thoughts I reached my front door. I was about to go in when something pulled at the sleeve of my jacket. I swung around ready to strike whoever it was.

"Santiago, what's the matter? Are you okay?" Hot Sauce said.

"Hot Sauce," I exclaimed, breaking out of my mood and smiling. "You don't know how glad I'm to see you. If you only knew the kind of days I've been having lately."

"Man, you tell me. I'm gonna have to move my business; this block has gone to hell. Anyway," she chortled, "thanks for introducing me to Ben Ami."

"Did you hit it off? I haven't talked to him since that night."

"He's in Paris. He wanted me to go with him. He'll be back tonight, I think. Yeah, he's nice. Thanks, Santiago."

"Don't mention it. Anyway, I'd love to chat more with you but I'm anxious to get upstairs. Maybe we can get together soon, all of us."

"Wait. I don't know if I should mention this to you. But a couple of minutes ago I saw some real sleazeballs go in."

All kinds of alarms went off. To reassure myself I said, "Maybe they were George's customers."

"They didn't look Pakistani to me, if you know what I mean."

"Were they crack heads?"

"No. They looked like . . . like . . . like . . ."

"Colombians," I offered.

"Yeah, man. No offense."

"Jesus, I gotta go! This could be serious."

"If you need help, just yell."

"Thanks." I raced up the stairs; the partition door at the second floor was ajar. I went in and left it open in case I had to leave my apartment in a hurry. I sprinted up the remaining sets of steps. As I put the key in, the door caved in. "Gene, Mr. O'Donnell," I screamed, bursting into the living room.

A not-too-distant relative of the apes stood a few feet away, pointing a nasty-looking gun at me.

*"Entra, pues,"* he said in what I recognized as a Medellín accent. "Close the door," he ordered me. Extending my arm behind my back, I slammed the door.

Jerking the gun, the man motioned me to go into the next room where I found Gene sitting at the table, still in his underwear, puffing frantically at a Marlboro, and looking scared shitless. Next to him, also armed with another revolver, sat another *paisa,* as people from Medellín are called.

I looked anxiously around the room trying to spot Mr. O'Donnell but I couldn't find him.

*"Qué pasa?"* was all I could say.

The seated killer, who was small, razor-thin, dark, with swarthy hands and puffy eyebags, barked, *"Este vergajo* stole a pound of cocaine. Just hand it back and nobody will be hurt. Otherwise . . ." He put the gun against Gene's temple and something told me he wasn't kidding.

"Sammy, tell them . . . I don't have it," Gene said, whining like a child about to burst into tears.

"Okay, okay," I said, knowing I had to act quickly before the electric saw appeared and our limbs started painting red spots all over the place. Yet I knew that if I gave these men the cocaine, we would be killed afterward. "Señores," I said diplomatically, trying to disguise my fear and distaste, "we'll give you back the coke. Just relax, *por favor?"*

Gene's eyes seemed about to pop out. He shook his head ever so imperceptibly as if to say no.

"The coke is in the bathroom," I said.

*"Dónde?"* hissed the seated simian.

"Just follow me and I'll show you."

"Get up." The killer slapped Gene's cheek with the gun's muzzle.

I went in first; the Colombian who had greeted me at the door poked the end of his gun against my tailbone. The four of us crammed into the tiny bathroom.

"It's in the water tank of the toilet." I informed them. I

removed the top of the water tank and was about to put my hand in, when the mafioso who had Gene at gunpoint hissed, *"Cuídado, it could be a trap. Dario, you get it."*

"Not me, *ave María purísima,*" Dario hissed back. "There could be a snake in there."

"Okay, you get it out," the nameless man said to me.

As I put my hand in, I heard Mr. O'Donnell galloping in the other room, making quite a racket.

"What's that?" the man yelled, turning to look in the direction of the living room. Quickly, I grabbed the gun at the bottom of the tank, and, in one motion, hooked the man's neck with my left arm and stuck the dripping gun's muzzle into his mouth. "If you try anything, I'll blow your fucking brains out," I barked in my best Jimmy Cagney manner.

The other mafioso placed the gun on Gene's temple. "Drop the gun before I count to three or I'll kill the boy. One . . . two . . ."

I had no choice but to aim at the man's head and pull the trigger. The gun went *clack;* I pulled again and nothing happened.

The man I had been grabbing struggled free. *"Mátalo,"* he said, spitting on my face.

"If you kill him," Gene interjected, "I'll never tell you where the coke is, no matter what you do to me."

"What's a pound of coke?" the man said with hatred. "Kill the son of a bitch."

Well, this is it, folks, I thought, when a shrill scream pierced my ears and I heard Hot Sauce say, "Cool your bones, motherfuckers, or you're dead fish." And two shots were fired in succession at the men's feet. Gene and I jumped on top of the astonished killers and disarmed them. We herded them out of the bathroom.

"Put them hands up against the wall," Hot Sauce said, jerking the gun from man to man.

I began to frisk one man when I heard a loud stampede of heavy shoes come up the stairs. "Oh God," I said, "their friends are coming."

"Nothing doing," Hot Sauce reassured me. "It's the cops. I sent word before I came up."

"You sent for the cops?"

"Santiago, I'm an undercover agent," she explained and pulled a walkie-talkie out from under her skirt. "Hot Sauce speaking. Reinforcements have arrived at 687. Thanks. Over." She smiled at me.

Gene and I exchanged flabbergasted looks. "You should get dressed," I said to Gene as three gun-happy cops arrived on the scene. I recognized Lieutenant McGavin, with whom I had had many conversations concerning the crack heads downstairs.

"Hi, Santiago," he said, giving Gene an inquisitive stare.

"Lieutenant, this is my nephew Gene. He's staying with me for a couple of days," I said.

McGavin and the other cops were panting from the exertion of making it up to the fourth floor in a hurry. He addressed the Colombians, "Hi, fellows. You'd better have your green cards in order."

My fellow countrymen betrayed no emotions; they looked at each other as though in a daze, as if this new development was the last thing they had expected. The men were handcuffed, their rights were explained to them in English and translated by me into Spanish. Seldom had I enjoyed my role as interpreter as much as I did on this occasion.

Gene excused himself to go into the bathroom to get dressed. While the cops checked the killers' IDs and reported their findings back to headquarters, I sat anxiously, wondering what would happen next. Would I, too, be charged with illegal possession of a firearm? No, I thought; Hot Sauce saw how I got that gun. And what if the mafiosi talked? What if they snitched on Gene? Should I turn in the coke before the killers implicated me?

The report from headquarters threw the cops into a loud celebration. These men were on all sorts of most wanted lists, and had been identified as important links in one of the most powerful cocaine rings in Queens.

"Lieutenant," Hot Sauce said, "take them away and lock 'em in the can. I'll stay here with Santiago and Gene to write the report of the break-in."

As they were about to depart, Lieutenant McGavin stopped to

ponder and said, "The one question I have is why did they break in here? What were they hoping to get here?"

Confess, a voice screamed in my head. "Well, Lieutenant, I hope you . . ."

"Oh, no, no," McGavin interrupted me. "We're very aware of your efforts to try to clean up this block; you've helped us to smash one of the most vicious drug rings in America. We've been trying to catch these guys for a long time, but it's impossible if they remain in Queens. You and your nephew will have to come to the midtown precinct tomorrow or the next day and we'll have a press conference. I'm going to recommend that the mayor's office awards you the medal of civic service. You and your nephew are heroes. I wish there were more concerned citizens like you. Now, amigos," he said to the downcast drug fiends, *"vamos."*

We shook hands, expressed our thanks and said good-bye. Gene, Hot Sauce, and I were left alone in the apartment.

Hot Sauce and I lounged on the couch and Gene sat around the table. Gene, who had just now met Hot Sauce, could not get his eyes off her. Mr. O'Donnell walked into the room cautiously to make sure the commotion was over. Then he jumped on the couch, sniffed Hot Sauce, and crouched on my lap. I looked around me and saw a teenage mafioso, a Times Square hooker, and a dying alley cat, and wondered at the principals in my life.

"You have to write a report now?" I asked, still amazed she was an undercover agent.

"Oh, no. I can do that later. I just said that so I could stay here to chat with you."

"That's nice," I said. "Oh, God, I'm about to croak from hunger."

"Me too," Gene said.

"How about going out for lunch?" Hot Sauce said. "I'll treat you guys."

"Thanks a lot, but I'm too tired; I don't think I could make it down the stairs."

"We could order Chinese takeout; how's that?"

"I hate Chinese food," Gene said.

I sighed. "Well, as I said before, I'm starving."

"I know what," Gene said getting up. "I'll make lunch while you two guys talk."

I shuddered at the prospect but had no choice but to accept the offer. "I don't think there's much in the fridge."

"That's cool," Gene said. "Just leave it to me, man. I'll improvise. Lunch will be ready in five minutes. In the meantime, how about a cup of coffee? I had just made some coffee before my . . . before the *paisas* broke in."

"A cup of coffee would be lovely," Hot Sauce said. "Black, no sugar, please."

"The same for me. Thanks, Gene."

Gene served the coffee and disappeared in the kitchen. Mr. O'Donnell, who was always a persistent beggar when there was any activity in the kitchen, followed him.

"I can't get over that you're a cop, not a hooker," I said.

"Yeah, undercover agent. That's my job. We're conducting an investigation. You know, gathering enough evidence so we can shut down the crack den downstairs. But it ain't easy, Santiago. First, the place belongs to the mob so there are big bucks involved. Second, since it is a porno place, we're dealing with freedom of speech. And that's the law."

"But your real name is not Hot Sauce, is it?"

"No," she blushed. "My real name is Rosita. Rosita Levine."

"Are you Latin?"

"Do I look Latin to you? I'm a Jewish girl from Brooklyn. When I was born, my mother's best friend was from Cuba. Her name was Rosita Matamoros; so my mother named me after her best friend. Rosita means Little Rose, as you know, being an interpreter and all that. So I came up with Hot Sauce, which is a compound name, you get it now?"

"Oh, oh," I uttered, feeling more and more discombobulated all the time. In the kitchen, Gene had turned on the radio very, very loud, but through the heavy pounding of the rock music I heard the blender going on, and what sounded like a machine gun firing hundreds of bullets. The toxic fumes of hot dogs invaded the room.

"I wanted to talk to you about something else."

"Shoot," I said.

"It's about Ben. You know the way he is so . . . like romantic, you know. I'm worried that when he finds out I'm a cop instead of a hooker he won't like me no more. Watcha think?"

"Well, yeah, I don't know," I said. "I'm sure the hooker part probably seemed very . . . interesting to him. On the other hand," I said, recalling Ben's fondness for the leading lady in *Freaks*, "I also think he likes the fact that you are . . ." I didn't quite know how to put it.

"A little person."

"That's right. A little person."

"You mean there's hope? You really don't think it's over?"

"Do you like him that much?"

"I'm crazy about the guy, Santiago. He's the nicest person I've ever met. A girl like me doesn't meet too many guys like that."

Gene stuck his head out of the kitchen. "Lunch is ready. Please sit down at the table."

"Gene, hon, can I help you?" Hot Sauce offered, for the first time showing her motherly instincts.

"That's cool; it's under control."

We sat at the table while Gene brought out the place mats, dishes, silverware, napkins, and glasses. First, he produced a tray heaped with steaming hot dogs plastered with mayonnaise. Next, he brought out a pitcher of chocolate milk shake. "And the chef's masterpiece," he announced, producing a huge bowl of popcorn swimming in melted butter.

"Well?" he said, beaming, standing in front of us, fishing for compliments.

"You'll make a good husband," Hot Sauce said.

This compliment didn't go over very well with Gene. "It looks just . . . great," I lied, digging into the popcorn.

After lunch, when Hot Sauce announced she had to go, Gene informed me he was going to walk Hot Sauce back to the precinct and then was going back to Queens. I was tired and feeling so muddled that it didn't occur to me to stop him.

When I was alone in the apartment, I remembered the cocaine was still in the kitchen, so I decided to wash it down the toilet. The glass container on the shelf was empty; it had been rinsed not too long ago because the inside glass was still wet.

I had been experiencing so many contradictory emotions for the past week or so that, instead of getting frantic, I merely shrugged it off. Later, when Gene had had enough time to get back to Jackson Heights, I would call him to straighten out the situation. I felt drained; I felt as if I were dragging a dead horse behind me. I decided to lie down for a while. I picked up Mr. O'Donnell and closed the door of my bedroom and turned on the air conditioner. Mr. O'Donnell went into the closet to investigate God knows what and remained there.

This was perhaps the first moment of quiet and solitude I had had in days. I thought of Bobby, and I thought of how he was dead and it was almost as if he had never existed and that somehow did not seem right. It occurred to me that I had known Bobby for most of my life, and I had no tangible memento of him, not even a photograph, just memories, which time would eventually distort and flatten out. I made a mental note to call Joel and ask him for a picture of Bobby. Then I felt Bobby's presence next to my bed. I was sober today, not like the last time I thought I had seen him. It was invisible, whatever it was, but it felt like a warm spot in the air, throbbing to express itself. I closed my eyes. "I surrender," I said. "You can talk to me, Bobby, if that's what you want." Then I fell asleep.

In my dream, I saw Paradise Alley in flames, and hundreds of wailing crack heads trapped inside. Standing on the street curb, I watched. There were no other witnesses: no cops, no firemen, no gawking New Yorkers, nothing, nobody except myself watching them as if they were on a window display of a chamber of hell. As I watched, I started to shrink, growing smaller and smaller until I was a boy of seven or so. The scene in front of me changed: the chamber of hell turned into our house in Barranquilla, after my parents separated, but before we moved to Bogotá. I was wearing short pants, sneakers, and a cotton shirt. It was nighttime. Mother and a stranger, a foreigner, were in the living room, sitting very close. Mother wore a tight, white dress, and her hair was done and she had makeup on. She radiated sensuality. She had sent for me to introduce me to this man, who was obviously drunk. The stranger was tall, blond, heavyset, and he was sweating. His pink face revolted me. The man spoke in English and gave me some sticks of bubble gum. I accepted the gum out of politeness, but then changing my mind flung the sticks at Mother's lap and stormed out of the living room. I hid in the garden, behind some leafy *yucca* plants, where I crouched, crying. The dark night frightened me, but I was too upset to go back inside the house, and no one, not even my nanny, came out to look for me. Bolero music played and Mother's laughter rippled in rich, high-pitched notes through the tropical night, reaching me. I hated my mother for bringing this man to the house; I hated my father for abandoning us. I longed to run away to another city to become a gamin. I wished a kindly couple without children would adopt me and take me far, far away to another country.

I crouched there for what seemed an eternity, alternately feeling hungry and cold. Finally, the music and the laughing died out and lights were turned off inside. I entered the house unobserved. On the way to my bedroom I had to pass by the door of my mother's alcove. Loud moans and writhing sounds reached me and I peeked in and saw my mother and the stranger making love. Shaking with anger, I went into the next room, where Eduardito, my little brother, slept. He was nearly a year old, and had been born with a defective heart and was not expected to make it to adulthood. In a corner of the room, there was a shrine to St. Jude Thadeus, with several votive candles lit. Irrationally, I flung myself at the shrine, smashing the saint's statue on the floor and with my arms I swept the votive candles aside. Before I realized what had happened, the curtains caught on fire. Terrified at what I had done I ran out of the room and into the next bedroom, where Wilbrajan slept, and I woke her up and told her there was a fire and we left the house, Wilbrajan still half asleep. Wilbrajan started crying when she saw smoke coming out of the house and she knew that Mother and Eduardito were still inside. The maids ran out of the house coughing and crying; the neighbors woke up; and curious people stood on the street watching the house go up in flames and there were many screams and Wilbrajan cried, "Mommy, mommy, mommy," and then it struck me that my little brother was probably dead and I, too, started screaming and

. . . I woke up, Mr. O'Donnell's nose nuzzling me as if to wake me from my nightmare. I squeezed him tight against my chest. "Kitty, I'm so happy you're here," I said. "I don't know what I'd do without you." Realizing he was uncomfortable I let go of him. Mr. O'Donnell jumped onto the night table and then leaped into the air, doing a flip-flop before he plopped to the floor. He was having a horrible seizure.

The moment I had been dreading for so long had finally arrived. Mr. O'Donnell's eyes looked as if they were about to pop out of their sockets; he was foaming at the mouth, baring his teeth like a feline with rabies; his chest swelled and collapsed, gasping for air; his tail curled, and his hind legs kicked the air as if it were an invisible yet solid wall.

"Kitty," I screamed, unsure of what step to take next. I was afraid he'd bite me if I touched him. Mr. O'Donnell did not seem pathetic, broken, but phenomenally angry, as if he were locked in a fierce confrontation with death and he was unwilling to go like a wimp. I ran to the telephone and dialed Rebecca's number and got her machine. She was out; nevertheless, I left a message. "Rebecca, Mr. O'Donnell is dying. Please, come upstairs if you get home soon." I hung up and returned to my bedroom. Mr. O'Donnell's eyes had turned emerald, but the violence of the convulsions had diminished. "Mr. O'Donnell, kitty, please don't die," I said to encourage him. It occurred to me that perhaps he might be saved if I took him to the hospital; he might survive for a few days or weeks or who knows. I pulled his box out of the closet but I still didn't dare pick him up. I looked for a beach towel and covered him with it and placed him inside the box. I wrote down the hospital's address, made sure I had enough cash to pay for the taxi, and slowly made my way down the stairs, making sure the box did not rock too much. Pandora's box couldn't have made more horrifying noises.

The taxi ride to the hospital seemed interminable, as I remembered other taxi rides when I had taken him to the Humane Society to be neutered, for his shots and checkups. He'd always cry pathetically and I'd have to talk to him, sticking my fingers through the holes of the box to reassure him that I was with him and there was nothing to fear. On this taxi ride, once or twice he made shrill, piercing noises, and his paws scratched the insides of the box violently.

Arriving at the hospital, the size of the building surprised me—it seemed like a real hospital, not a toy one like the Humane Society. The woman at the reception desk took down my name, address, a brief medical history of the pet, and then gave me directions to the elevators. I went to the fifth floor where I stepped into the waiting room. A man with manic eyes approached me and told me his cat had jumped from the living room into the street seven floors below and broken two legs. Two hospital vets in white uniforms came rushing from behind glass walls and asked me to turn Mr. O'Donnell over to them so they could place him inside an oxygen tent. The man opened the box and pulled him out. My hands reached out, as if to wrestle Mr. O'Donnell away from the doctor. Mr. O'Donnell's eyes and mine met, and he gave me a look I had never seen before. He was saying at the same time, "I love you; I'm scared; don't leave me alone; good-bye." His eyes were very yellow, like lighted lanterns, and they expressed horror. I thought of Bobby, of the last look he had given me, and at that moment I understood one of the differences between man and cat: man knows he's going to die, so he can get ready and be willing, even eager, to go. A cat knows the end is near, but that's all. He can't accept death: he can't trust in it; cats are perhaps too metaphysical an entity to need to believe in the idea of a beyond; a cat is his own god and man his creation.

I sat there, numb, staring at my hands, listening to the crazy man tell me stories about his cat, the many times he had jumped before. I was grateful when the nurse came out and told me that Mr. O'Donnell was on a respirator and to call the hospital tomorrow to inquire about his condition. She was sympathetic, I thought, but it sounded like a mere formality. Downstairs, before I left the hospital, I had to finish filling out the forms. Outside I lit a cigarette and walked to the nearest subway station. It was 10:00 P.M. and the station was almost deserted. I waited, leaning against the wall of the station. As the train rumbled in, I moved forward and stared at the tracks which, as the train neared me, became conduits for rushing gold rills that were almost an invitation to jump in front of the oncoming car. I had known all along that Mr. O'Donnell's days were numbered, but now that the moment had come the notion of joining him in death was appealing.

I got off the train at Times Square, and was about to turn west on Forty-third when loud music coming from the island on Broadway between Forty-sixth and Forty-seventh streets reached my ears. I really didn't want to go home to be alone with my feelings. Welcoming any distraction, I headed for the little island where a big crowd had gathered. As I approached it, the music got louder and brassier along this stretch of Broadway. It was hard to find an inch of cement to stand on on the island. The band had stationed itself in the middle of it, between the statues of George M. Cohan and Father Duffy. Six players blew on huge instruments. It was crazy, happy honky-tonk music that could have resurrected the dead. As the players puffed their shiny cheeks and stomped their feet, swaying with their tubas and trombones, the crowd rocked sideways. Most of the spectators looked like summer tourists and suburban theatergoers, but there were also many regulars of Times Square, including myself. Black kids climbed on the large cement pots where scraggly trees grew. Everybody was smiling, and many people were clapping, surrendering to the rambunctious sounds.

Behind the band rose the red Coca Cola sign displaying geometric combinations of lines and colors; and the blazing lights of Broadway, the legendary White Way that was anything but white, had never seemed so beautiful, so glittering, so inviting, so dazzling. It was one of those rare moments when a mass of people surrender to the city, embracing everything that gets pressured out of us as we grow up and become responsible citizens and assume obligations and conform. I turned to look behind me and, to the east, a full ivory moon was poised on top of the red tip of the antenna of the Empire State Building. I stood with my back to the crowd, feeling the music surge through my veins, and rush to my head, and I thought about this island, this city, where the homeless and the rich, the powerful and the powerless, the radiant and the sick, the lovely and the hideous, the arrogant and the humble, and the crazed and the hopeful, where Blacks, Asiatics, Hispanics, WASPs, Europeans, their descendants, refugees, exiles, where people from all over the

world came to, as if this were their Mecca, a Byzantium throbbing
with thieves, and hookers and hustlers and murderers and suicides,
and cops and tourists and stockbrokers, and the rootless and great
stars and beggars, all commingling, coming together for a slice of the
elusive dream these neon signs promised, for moments like this one,
when the night was like red wine and it was summertime and for a
moment we could forget all our wounds, all our pains.

I looked up and saw the Times Square zipper going round and
round, flashing news about the weather, bankruptcies, murders, and
catastrophes from all over the globe, and then, at the tail end of it,
just for me, to show me that I, too, belonged here, in gold letters,
against a black velvety background, through the tears that clouded
my vision, I read: MR. O'DONNELL, THE MOST WONDERFUL CAT OF
FORTY-SECOND STREET, DIED TONIGHT, AUGUST 2, 1990.

# 12

## Everyone Happy in Manhattan and Mr. O'Donnell Enters Heaven

I didn't set the alarm clock for the next morning because I didn't have to work that day. I thought I would sleep at least until noon, but I awoke by ten o'clock. I realized things were different as soon as I opened my eyes; for the past two years I had gotten used to seeing Mr. O'Donnell upon waking up.

I went to the kitchen to make coffee, and the saucers on the floor, the steel comb hanging on a nail, the bag of dry food, and the cans of Kal Kan in the cupboard reminded me of him. Although I knew Mr. O'Donnell was dead, I called the hospital to make it official. The woman who gave me the news was nice and gentle; she informed me that Mr. O'Donnell had passed away last night, shortly after I had brought him in. I thanked her and hung up. I was about to return to the kitchen when the phone rang. It was Rebecca; I gave her the news.

"Actually," I said calmly, but feeling a big hole open up inside my chest, "would you like to come upstairs for a cup of coffee?"

"I'd love to."

I opened the door and waited for Rebecca to come up the stairs. She was dressed to go to work. We embraced, patting each other's backs. As the person who had found Mr. O'Donnell in the alley, she had taken the role of adoptive mother and she too had grown to love him.

We sat on the couch sipping our coffees. She was giving me such a look of commiseration that just to break up the silence, I said, "Aren't you late for work?"

"I start at noon today, but I'm going to call in sick."

"I'm okay. Really," I said, assuming she was doing this for my sake.

"I'm just sick and tired of that place. Thank God I'm going to Caracas next week." She paused. "Santiago, I have an idea. I think we should have a memorial service for Mr. O'Donnell tonight."

"Rebecca, you've got to be kidding!"

"Not at all. We owe it to him. We ought to celebrate the fact that he's gone to kitty heaven. Because I have no doubts whatsoever that that's where he is. Any old how, his friends should all get together to reminisce."

"You mean, we should have a wake?" I asked, totally astonished and wondering if Rebecca's elevator was ever going to make it to the top floor. "Anyway, what friends are you talking about?"

"Mr. O'Donnell had legions of adoring fans. He was absolutely beloved by everyone who ever came into contact with him. He was the most perfect bundle of joy that ever drew breath."

"We could invite Harry Hagin," I said, remembering the drawing he had made of Mr. O'Donnell when he had run away in the spring.

"And Francisco would come too if he were in New York," Rebecca said, not missing the opportunity to bring in her paramour. "He always said hello to the kitty in his letters, didn't he? But there are lots of other people," she prattled on. "It'll be a lovely gathering. A wake for Mr. O'Donnell as well as my bon voyage soirée. After all, I may not see you all for a long, long, long time."

"For goodness sake, Rebecca, you make it sound like you're going to Jupiter. But anyway, maybe a party is not a bad idea. It's very Colombian to celebrate someone's passing."

"Leave the details to me. I once organized the loveliest *fête champêtre* for Aunt Annabel back in Jackson. Is seven o'clock okay with you?"

I shrugged.

"You *poor* darling, you've been through so much lately. You don't have to lift a finger; I'll take care of everything. All you have to do is straighten up the place a little bit."

"I'll be here all day, if you need anything," I offered just in case.

She finished her coffee. "Thank you, doll face. Now I've got to run. There are a million pressing details that need to be attended to."

We embraced again. As soon as she left the room, I felt the full weight of my aloneness. When Mr. O'Donnell was alive, I'd always felt as if I shared the apartment with a roommate. I became aware of an uncanny silence creeping all over the house. Feeling spooked, I decided to get busy tidying up the place. I got the broom and duster out of the kitchen, but realizing how much I would have to work before the place looked decent, I was overwhelmed by the task ahead of me. I headed back for the security of the bedroom and threw myself on the bed where I tossed around despondently. I found myself staring at the spot where Mr. O'Donnell had collapsed the night before. To my horror, the image of him contorting and gasping for breath replayed in my mind's eye. I closed my eyes and when I opened them, I noticed one of his whiskers on the floor. I picked it up. It wasn't a particularly long or beautiful whisker, but I decided to put it in the box where I kept all the whiskers I had saved in the past couple of years. I ran the end of it up and down my cheeks and then I pressed it between my lips. I took all the whiskers out and spread them on my open palm, fingering them. I realized that unless I found another whisker lying around somewhere, this was the end of the collection; these were all the mortal reminders I had of my cat. I closed my fist, clutching the white, prickly things, and I broke down crying.

I spent the rest of the day tidying up the apartment, which was no small chore. I was mopping the floors when Mr. O'Donnell's loss hit me again; he loved to see the mop in action, and always attacked it as if it were a wild animal to be conquered.

Around six o'clock I was so exhausted all I wanted to do was take a nap, but Rebecca asked me to come downstairs. I could barely walk around her living room; she had bought many large arrangements of assorted flowers, a baked ham, two cases of white wine, half gallons of vodka, scotch, gin, rum, hundreds of candles, huge breads, three or four kinds of olives, what looked like an entire farmers' market of vegetables and fruits, dips, club soda, Coca Cola, diet drinks, juices, Perrier. . . .

"Have you gone crazy?" I said. "You must have spent a fortune."

"I may never get another chance to give a party in New York, so I'm gonna go hog-wild."

"I'd say. You could feed all the homeless people of New York with that spread. I thought you were just going to invite Harry Hagin."

"Wherever did you get that notion, sweetie? It's going to be a bacchanal, an authentic, honest-to-goodness hoedown. Everybody accepted, of course. And I asked everyone to bring something. I'm so excited I can barely breathe."

I was too astonished to say anything.

"Honey, are you okay? You must start taking everything upstairs," she said. "We have not a minute to waste. I have to attend to my toilette. I want to look lovelier than a catalpa tree in May."

"Who's coming besides Harry?" I managed to ask with great apprehension.

"Lucy is coming, and she's bringing some friends. And I invited Tim, and Ben, and he's bringing his new girlfriend and lots of other people are coming. The list of guests is too long to mention them all."

"My mother is coming! She hated Mr. O'Donnell, Rebecca."

"No one hated Mr. O'Donnell, Santiago. Your mother is just partial to Simón Bolívar. Besides, this is the time to let bygones be bygones."

"And what friends is she talking about?" I asked, horrified, thinking of what my mother and the matrons of Queens would make of Hot Sauce. Boy, was I ever ready to get on my high horse and fly away from Times Square! I felt so dizzy I had to sit down.

Rebecca crossed her arms and stared at me. "Santiago, honey, please don't be a party pooper and spoil my bon voyage revelry. Oh, before I forget. Let me go get it," she said leaving the room.

Now what, I thought. My life sentence?

Rebecca came back with a large plastic frame. "This is for that superb drawing Harry Hagin did of Mr. O'Donnell. Later we'll have to frame it right, but for tonight this will do, I'm afraid," she said, handing it to me. "We must have it prominently displayed in a place of honor. Now be an angel and start taking the goodies upstairs. As your cohostess I have to be ready when the first guest arrives. I wonder who will be the first person to arrive?" she said aloud, but it was obvious she was talking to herself.

My mother, of course, arrived first. And she didn't arrive with friends but with a wrapped cage that contained Simón Bolívar.

*"Ay, Dios mío, virgen santísima,"* Mother said as we met her at the door. "Those stairs are murderous. I have to sit down before I get chest pains. Rebecca, you look divine."

Using all the Spanish at her command, Rebecca said, *"Muchas gracias,* Lucy."

"Santiago, *mijito,* I left two bags downstairs. Please get them before the junkies steal them. I don't know how you can live in this neighborhood." Realizing that Rebecca too lived in the building, she added, "It does have its advantages, of course. It's so central and so close to Broadway."

Downstairs I found two large bags which I carried up the stairs. I found Rebecca and mother lounging on the couch.

"Sammy, the place looks wonderful; the flowers make a big difference," Mother commented.

Setting the bags down, I said, "Rebecca purchased everything."

"Thank you so much, Rebecca. You're too nice to Sammy. He needs a wife soon, now that you're going to be married."

"Keep your fingers crossed. He hasn't proposed yet."

"He will, he will, trust me. If I know everything about man, this trip means wedding," she said in her highly peculiar English.

"I hope you're right."

"I never mistaken about such things, my dear. Never. Always I'm right. Plus Francisco is so nice: nobody did my hair better than he did. And we are devouts to the same saints. You make good choice, Rebecca. Now you learn Spanish. Tell you this," she added, getting carried away, "to celebrate you wedding, Sammy and I will fly to Caracas for the church ceremony. And I can visit my sister

Aurora that I had not seen in many years. I will kill two birds with one rock."

"I would be so honored if you came down for my wedding. If you do, you have to promise me right now you'll be my maid of honor."

"Of course, I will be the maid of honor! Thank you for asking, my dear." Mother turned to me. "Well, Sammy, what are you doing standing there? Take the bags to the kitchen and start unpacking. And make me an *aguardiente*. Stiff. And one for Rebecca. And one for you if you want," she added grandly, as if I were her maid.

As I unpacked the victuals, I heard Mother and Rebecca giggling in the other room. Mother had brought half a gallon of *Aguardiente Cristal,* two pineapple flans, a large plastic container full of *fríjoles antioqueños* with pork, a large *jamón,* a five pound moist white Colombian cheese, guava paste, *arequipe,* stuffed figs, many odds and ends, and tapes of cumbias, *vallenatos,* and folkloric music of the Atlantic coast of Colombia.

I poured three generous shots of *aguardiente* and distributed them.

"I propose a toast to Mr. O'Donnell," Rebecca said.

Giving me a small smile, Mother said, "And not to forget your future marriage."

"Who's there?" a third voice said.

*"Dios mio, mi pobrecito,* Simón Bolívar," Mother said, setting down her drink to unwrap the cage, while Rebecca and I stood with our glasses raised.

With his nasty little eyes, Simón Bolívar glanced at me, then at Rebecca, and then he started looking around the room.

"You better, *cuchi cuchi?*" Mother asked.

*"Lorito real, lorito real,"* the hideous parrot cheered.

"Now we can finish our toasts," Mother said.

"To Mr. O'Donnell," I repeated.

We had finished downing our drinks when the bell rang.

"I can't stand the excitement," Rebecca said. "I haven't had so much fun in years. Who could it be?"

It was the entire Colombian Parnassus, the muses of Queens. Olga, the shortest, carried the flowers; Carmen Elvira, the tallest, carried two boxes—one containing a cake, the other one full of cookies; and Irma, the stockiest, carried two large Balducci's bags.

"Welcome," I said at the door. "What a nice surprise to see you."

I had to bend to receive Olga's kiss. "Please, Sammy," she said, handing me the flowers. "Put them in water before they wilt."

"I'll take care of the flowers," Rebecca offered. I handed her the bunches of roses and relieved Carmen Elvira of the boxes. None of the ladies had ever met Rebecca, but Carmen Elvira, in particular, couldn't hide her curiosity.

"This is Rebecca Allevant, my neighbor," I added, so there would be no misunderstandings.

Carmen Elvira, who undoubtedly had assumed Rebecca was a secret romantic attachment of mine, immediately lost interest. The women exchanged names and pleasantries as we wandered into the living room. Mother rushed to kiss her friends. Then they settled down on the couch.

"Sammy, where are your manners?" Mother said. "Aren't you going to offer your friends a drink?"

"Yes, of course, Mother," I said, irritated at her bossy manner. "There is *aguardiente,* and Coca—"

"*Aguardiente,*" they all cried out at once.

"Sammy, I have to go downstairs to get the vases for the flowers. I don't know if I have anything appropriate for such lovely flowers. I'll be right back," Rebecca said.

I went into the kitchen with the bags. While I was unpacking the viands, I heard Mother say, "If I had known you were going to arrive so early, I would have waited for you. I had to take a taxi all the way from Jackson Heights. There was no way I could carry the food and Simón Bolívar in the subway. We could have split the ride."

In her practical banker's style Irma commented, "It's called poor planning. How typically Colombian."

"*Sí, mijita,* but you forget we are professional women and housewives, too," I recognized Olga babbling. "I had to go home straight from work so I could take the pizza out of the fridge. Pizza and Coca Cola, that's what they'll have for dinner; the cook is on strike today."

I was surprised by the contents of the bag; I had expected *pasteles, arepas, buñuelos*. But the Balducci's bags actually contained Balducci's staples: pickled salmon, black caviar, soft French cheeses, quail eggs, artichoke hearts.

"If we hadn't just been invited this morning," Irma said, "we could have chipped in to cook a terrific Colombian meal. There's nothing like our own food."

"Well, *cariño,*" Mother said. "The cat just died last night, so we cannot to plan it in advance."

I poured the *aguardiente* in the cups and brought them out on the tray.

Crossing her legs and exposing her knees, and showing both rows of teeth, Olga said, "Thank you, handsome."

"Thanks, hon," Irma said in her laconic Wall Street manner.

Always the fake, Carmen Elvira said, "Thank you so much, Sammy. You're an adoration."

Rebecca arrived with four empty bottles that would serve as vases.

"Well, Sammy," Mother said. "Don't just stand there. Show my friends you know how to be a good host. Bring out the Colombian cheese. Nothing goes better with *aguardiente* than nice white cheese."

"I'm so hungry I could eat an entire suckling pig," Irma said.

"*Ay, mujer,* all you can think about is eating. That's what comes from having such a high pressure job," Olga said. "Look at me; I keep my doll figure because I eat *poquito, poquito* and I'm happy just being a secretary. While you look positively like a *Botero,*" Olga finished cattily.

The phone rang. I asked Rebecca, who was emerging out of the kitchen with the flower arrangements, to get it. "I have to get the cheese," I told her.

I was in the kitchen cutting the cheese into tiny pieces (Colombian style), when Rebecca arrived at a run. "Santiago, it's for you," she said, flinging her hands, her eyes dancing with excitement. "It's the *New York Post.*"

Carmen Elvira, who obviously had been eavesdropping, exclaimed from the other room, "The *New York Post!* Is it Suzy? Is it Page Six?"

"I don't know," I said, coming out of the kitchen and setting the cheese down. "Please, excuse me. I'll be right back."

"Hello," I said, sure that they were calling to sell me a subscription or that this was a mistake.

"Mr. Santiago Martínez?"

I noticed that Carmen Elvira had wandered into the room and was practically breathing in my ears. "This is he."

"We'd like to send a photographer to take your picture. Tomorrow we're running the story of how you helped the police to break into the ring of Colombian drug smugglers."

I was speechless.

"We're running a story about it and we'd like to illustrate it with your picture."

"Why?"

"You're a hero, Mr. Martínez. Is it okay if we send a photographer?"

"When?"

"Now. We need the picture tonight before the paper goes to press."

Carmen Elvira's nosiness was so intense that I was afraid she'd wrestle the receiver from me if I didn't hang up. "Okay," I said. I gave the man my address and hung up.

Carmen Elvira and I locked gazes. I lit a cigarette and walked back to the living room where the guests were as silent as if they were in church. Never in my life had there been so many people eagerly waiting to hear the next words out of my mouth. Relishing my moment of triumph, I cleared my throat. "The *New York Post* is sending a photographer to take my picture. Tonight," I added for more effect.

"Yes, but why?" Carmen Elvira demanded to know.

"The *New York Post!*" exclaimed Irma.

I chose my words carefully. "Well, yesterday, two men broke into the apartment. Gene and I were here and we caught them. It turns out the police had been after these criminals for a long time."

"I declare, Santiago," Rebecca said peevishly. "This all happened yesterday, under my very own roof, and I just find out about it by a mere fluke. Some friend you are."

"Sammy was saving surprise for us to celebrate," Mother interjected. "But I know about it. Gene tells everything to his grandma last night. Of course, I didn't believe him quite completely. That boy has such imaginative head."

"We'll have to run a big article about it in *Colombian Queens*," Irma said. "It will have to be the lead article in the upcoming issue."

"But, *mijita,* the material has already gone to the printers," Olga reminded her.

"We'll just have to can something, *cariño.* Maybe the poetry," Irma said.

"Not my 'Ode to My Mother'!" Olga said. "I promised *mami* her birthday poem would be coming out in the next issue."

Carmen Elvira pulled out her tape recorder. "Sammy, buttercup, a journalist's work is never done. You must answer a few questions for me before the guests arrive."

The bell rang.

"The *New York Post* is here," Rebecca screamed.

"Oh, *virgen santísima,*" Mother said, "is my hair all right?"

Trying to establish some semblance of order in the proceedings, I said, "It can't be the *Post;* it's too soon."

I was right. Ben Ami and Hot Sauce made their entrance. Ben leaned against the wall, heaving like a beached whale. He carried a large tray wrapped in aluminum foil.

"Here, Santiago, I brought a leg of wild boar," he said by way of greeting me.

I took the leg and moved aside to let him in—he was so wide he had to enter sideways. Hot Sauce walked in behind him, carrying two bottles of champagne. She wore a cotton skirt and blouse instead of her regular uniform, and her makeup was subdued, but she still looked like a Times Square hooker. I took a low bow to receive a peck on my cheek.

"*Chico,* I had forgotten about those stairs. Now I remember why I moved from here," Ben said inching forward into the living room. "*Doña Lucy, qué alegría,*" he shouted to my mother. "I'm so happy to see you."

"Ben, *querido,*" Mother said, getting up and rushing over. They exchanged kisses.

"Ben brought a leg of wild boar and champagne," I said.

"That's class for you," Mother editorialized to the other guests. Then she spotted Hot Sauce.

"Allow me to make the introductions," I said, standing with the leg of wild boar in my arms, "my old friend Ben Ami Burztyn and his . . . girlfriend Rosita Levine."

"I hate Rosita. I told her she could keep Hot Sauce," Ben corrected me.

*"Salsa picante,"* translated Olga, and mother and the Parnassus ladies started giggling. Hot Sauce looked nonplussed.

"Hi, Rebecca," Ben said, as she came out of the kitchen with a tray of hors d'oeuvres.

"Hi, Ben. I'll be in Caracas next week," she said, offering him a morsel.

"She's getting married," Mother informed him.

*"Felicitaciones,* Rebecca," Ben said, hugging her and the tray against his belly. "Hot Sauce," he said, letting go of Rebecca, "hand me those bottles. This calls for a toast. Champagne for everyone. This is," he shouted the name in French, "and it costs one thousand dollars per bottle," he boasted in typical nouveau riche Venezuelan manner.

Always the southern belle, Rebecca said to me, "But we don't have champagne glasses."

Hot Sauce came to my rescue. "Paper cups will do."

I set the leg of wild boar on the table and went into the kitchen to get the cups. The corks were popped, the champagne poured and all glasses were raised. "To Rebecca's happiness," Ben proposed.

"To Rebecca's happiness," we all chimed in.

"And I have an announcement to make," Ben said, passing the bottles around once more. "Hot Sauce and I got engaged tonight. Show them the ring, Hot Sauce."

Extending her arm, Hot Sauce flashed a diamond ring the size of a sugar cube.

"Oh, oh, ah, my, oh, ah," shrieked the ladies like excited teenyboppers.

We toasted their engagement.

The toasts finished, Ben asked me to carve the leg of wild boar. I was on my way to the kitchen when Carmen Elvira approached Ben.

"Your engagement is big news to the readers of *Colombian Queens*," she said. "I wonder if you'd be so kind as to answer a few questions for me."

When I came out of the kitchen, mother, Rebecca, Olga, Irma, and Hot Sauce were all snuggled on the couch in animated conversation. Ben and Carmen Elvira were seated at the table. As I began to serve the wild boar, Carmen Elvira, talking to her tape recorder, said, "Ben Ami Burztyn, the peripatetic scion of our sister Republic of Venezuela, has announced his engagement tonight at a reception given by his great pal, Colombia's poet laureate, Santiago Martínez Ardila."

The bell rang and, much to my disappointment, I had to stop eavesdropping to go meet the arriving guests.

"Yeah, I haven't been up these stairs since I was a young girl." I recognized the familiar basso voice of Mrs. O'Donnell coming up the stairs. And she was not alone! Mrs. O'Donnell's medusa head appeared at the landing of the third floor. I took two steps back. My God, I thought, she's coming with her sons and the cops to evict me.

I was about to run back into the apartment and shut the door, when I heard her boom, "Santiago, come down here and give me a hand."

I lurched forward. Mrs. O'Donnell was carrying a heavy tray. Behind her, I spotted Tim Colby. I felt my legs shake as I went down the stairs to meet them.

"Here," Mrs. O'Donnell said, handing me a heavy, warm tray. "It's chili con carne; I made it this afternoon. Sorry to hear about the cat."

It occurred to me that she had been the first person to offer her condolences. "Thank you," I mumbled, feeling my face blush. "It's nice to see you."

"Well, yeah. I know if Lucy hadn't called me about the wake, you'd never have invited me. Is she here?"

"Oh, yes. She'll be so glad to see you. Hi, Tim," I said to my agent.

Mrs. O'Donnell added, "I had to ask this nice gentleman to help me bring up the beer. Now move aside so I can get upstairs."

I smiled at Tim. Slowly, Mrs. O'Donnell made her way to the top of the landing. I waited until she had gone through the door before I let out a loud sigh.

"Tim, she gave me the scare of my life. I thought she was coming upstairs with eviction papers."

"Nah," Tim said. "She likes you. By the way, sorry to hear about," he whispered Mr. O'Donnell's name. "But cheer up. I have great news for you."

"What?" I said as I started walking up the stairs with the hot chili.

"The editor I told you about is crazy about the idea."

"What idea?"

"Writing a thriller about Christopher Columbus. She pointed out that 1992 is around the corner, so there'll be a big hoopla about it. We're talking big bucks, my friend."

We had arrived at the landing. "Well, I hope so," I said. "I'm tired of Eighth Avenue."

"You'll never have a better landlady," Tim said. "When I ran into her at the door she asked me if I was coming to the wake and then she asked me who I was. When I told her I was your agent she asked me if I could pay your back rent. I said, 'Don't worry. He's going to be rich soon.' And I told her the story of García Márquez and his landlady in Paris. She said, 'García who?' And I said, 'You know, the guy who wrote *One Hundred Years of Solitude*.' And she says to me, get a load of this Santiago, she says, 'If it hasn't been made into a miniseries, I don't know it. I'm too busy to read books.' " Tim broke up laughing. "Oh, man, that's a story for an anthology."

It was a mildly amusing story, I thought. But I wondered if he would have found it so funny if she had been his landlady. "I need an *aguardiente*," I said to Tim.

As I walked into the apartment, the phone rang. "Tim, please take the beer to the kitchen and make yourself at home. I have to answer the phone."

I set down the chili and picked up the receiver. "Hello," I said.

"Is this Santiago Martínez?" the unmistakable voice of the overseas operator asked.

"Speaking."

"A call from Caracas."

"Okay, go ahead."

*"Santiago, es Francisco."*

*"Hola, Francisco."*

"I'm sorry to hear about Mr. O'Donnell."

Between the long distance static and the raucous noises coming from the living room, I was having a lot of trouble hearing him. "It's very sweet of you to call," I screamed.

"I lit a candle for him," Francisco said.

"Thanks, Francisco," I said, sincerely touched.

"I loved that cat; he was so special. *Qué gato, chico. Qué gato.*"

This conversation was making me sad. "Rebecca is here. Would you like to talk to her?"

"Yes, please. If you don't mind."

I placed my hand on the receiver. "Rebecca," I shouted, "long distance from Caracas."

Like a drive-in waitress on roller skates, Rebecca sailed into the room with a tray heaped with delicacies. "Is it Francisco? Is it?" she asked.

"Do you know anybody else in Caracas, silly?"

"Francisco, Francisco, *mi amor,*" she cooed, dropping the tray on the desk and yanking the phone from me.

I grabbed Rebecca by the hand and led her into my bedroom, where I closed the door. I picked up the extension phone and we sat on the bed.

*"Palomita adorada,"* Francisco said. "I have great news," I interpreted. "My client has been elected Miss Venezuela."

*"Felicitaciones,"* I said, overstepping my boundaries as interpreter. I interpreted for Rebecca.

"I'm going to be very, very successful," Francisco said. "Now I can offer you the life you deserve, *mi reina.* Will you marry me?"

"I'm faint," Rebecca exclaimed, placing the receiver on her breasts and closing her eyes.

*"Rebecca, qué pasa?,"* asked Francisco.

"I think she's fainting," I said. "But I'm sure that means yes," I interpreted.

*"Sí, sí, sí, mi amor,"* Rebecca gushed, opening her eyes. Then she threw herself at me and started kissing me.

"She's kissing me," I informed Francisco.

"Oh, I'm not jealous, Santiago. Will you be our best man? *Chico*," he added, "you can move to Caracas and live with us."

The idea of being an interpreter indefinitely to the lovey-doves was not very enticing. "That's very kind of you," I said. "But I think you should learn a language in common first."

"Rebecca," Francisco said, ignoring my suggestion, "I'm counting the minutes till you arrive."

"Okay, I'd better go now," Francisco said. *"Adiós,* Santiago. Sorry to hear about Mr. O'Donnell. Bye, Rebecca my love."

*"Adiós,"* she sighed.

"Ciao," I threw in to break the linguistic monotony.

Rebecca leaped off her feet, took the tray and rushed in the direction of the living room. I trotted after her.

"He proposed," Rebecca screamed upon entering the room.

"See, I know everything about man," Mother screamed back, running over to kiss Rebecca.

The guests cheered and clapped and toasted. I noticed Carmen Elvira was still interviewing Ben, but had lost interest in him and was now eyeing Tim. "One last question," she said. "Are you still on friendly terms with Bianca Jagger?"

I was dying to hear Ben's answer, when Mother shouted, "Santiago, bring out the *aguardiente* bottle."

As I came out of the kitchen with the booze, Carmen Elvira approached me.

"Sammy, darling," she said in her most ingratiating manner. "I want you to know that everything is just hunky-dory." Now that she had flattered me she came out with what was really on her mind. "Will you please introduce me to your agent?" Seeing my resistance, she added, "I want to interview him for the magazine. Besides," she argued further, "now that we're about to publish our book of poems (with your translations, of course), we need representation. I hear it's very difficult to crack the American market without an agent."

"Sammy, the *aguardiente*," Mother called.

"Sure," I said, and walked over to where Ben and Tim were chatting. Ben made a face as he saw Carmen Elvira approach, but nonetheless I made the introduction and refreshed their drinks. I walked over to where Mother and Hot Sauce were merrily gabbing away. "Here, Mother," I said, handing her the *aguardiente* bottle. "You can keep the bottle by your side, okay?"

"Okeydokey," she said, and I could see she was completely sauced.

The bell rang. I went to the door to receive my guests. I heard Gene's thunderous steps coming up the stairs. Good, I thought, I have quite a few questions to ask him. Looking down, I saw Gene and behind him Wilbrajan and Stick Luster's golden curls. Behind Stick trudged Harry Hagin, carrying a wrapped package.

"Hi, Sammy," Gene greeted me. Giving me a crushing hug, he whispered in my ear, "I washed the coke down the drain. So be cool." Then he went through the living room door.

Much to my surprise, Wilbrajan looked radiant and happy. She offered me her cheek to kiss, though reticently, as if I had the flu, or worse.

"Hi, Sister," I said.

"Sammy, Sammy," Stick Luster said, giving me a bear hug. "I'm so happy to see you, my friend."

"Come, Stick," Wilbrajan said haughtily, taking Stick by his arm and dragging away my childhood friend before I could say anything to him.

"Man, do I have a surprise for you," said a beaming Harry Hagin as he reached the top of the stairs.

"Oh, yeah. What is it?"

"You got to wait, okay?"

Knowing that it would please him, I said, "I finally framed Mr. O'Donnell's drawing."

"You're catching on."

Two vaguely familiar women arrived at the landing downstairs.

"Who are those women?" I asked.

Harry gave them a quick inspection, and with his artist's intuition pronounced, "You know, they're . . . up to something." He went in and left me to deal with the strangers.

Are they old acquaintances of my mother I've forgotten? I wondered as they climbed the stairs.

"We fooled you," cried out Claudia, laughing and clapping her hands. She and Paulina were in disguise! They wore matching outfits: black skirts, white cotton blouses, and sneakers. Claudia hid behind black-rimmed glasses, a short brown wig, no makeup and no jewelry except for a modest gold chain with a cheap trinket.

Mother and daughter looked like Latin Jehovah's Witness missionaries. "Where's the Bible?" I kidded them.

"Man, I knew you'd get it," Claudia roared, slapping my shoulder. Her appearance had changed, but not her manner.

*"Mijito,* they're after us," Paulina whispered, looking behind her back. "We came because we know how much this means to you."

"We're getting the fuck out of this town tonight," Claudia elaborated. "You're welcome to come with us."

"I told Lucy that now that the cat's dead nothing is holding you here in New York. *Virgen del Carmen,* the joint is jumping. Come, Claudia, let's go in. *Muchacha,* don't get out of my sight for a minute. You hear me?"

Claudia winked and blew me a kiss as they went in. I closed the door behind them.

Mother's *cumbia* tapes were blaring, and Gene was lighting dozens of candles on the table. Ben and Tim chatted on the couch, and all the ladies surrounded Harry Hagin, who stood in front of Mr. O'Donnell's framed drawing which now hung in the living room.

"Here, have an *aguardiente,"* Rebecca said solicitously to Harry.

"Mr. Hagin, would you be so gracious as to answer just a few questions for the readers of our magazine?" asked Carmen Elvira.

Seeing Harry hesitate, Irma threw in, "We'll put you on the cover. We print fifty thousand copies of *Colombian Queens.* A profile in our magazine guarantees instant celebrity."

"I don't know if you're aware of the fact that there are many important Colombian art collectors," Olga said, referring no doubt to the coke kingpins who buy all the trendiest painters.

Paulina said, "Mr. Hagin, we just bought an apartment at Trump Tower. We already have a Salle, a Schnabel, a Keifer, and all the Italians, but we'd love to have a large painting of yours."

"I'll have to dip seriously into my savings," Mother said, "but I can pay a good price for a painting of Simón Bolívar."

"Thank you, Lucy. You can have my paintings for nothing. But I just don't paint parrots."

"Two thousand dollars," Mother insisted.

"Actually, I brought Santiago a present," Harry said.

"What? What is it?" asked Carmen Elvira.

"It's an oil painting. An homage to Mr. O'Donnell."

Everyone present looked in the direction of Mrs. O'Donnell. Her eyes widened thinking a portrait of her late husband was going to be unveiled. Then everyone looked at me.

"Ben, Tim, Gene," Rebecca called to break up the tension. "Harry is going to unveil his latest masterpiece."

"We have to toast to the unveiling," Mother said, pouring a big shot of *aguardiente* into Mrs. O'Donnell's glass.

"Watch it, Grandma," Gene said. "You're gonna get everybody shitfaced."

Harry finished unwrapping the painting. All the ladies, including Mrs. O'Donnell, looked at me with envious eyes.

"Oh, oh," Mother opined, "it's just beautiful."

"Pure Edgar Allan Poe," boomed Ben Ami.

"It's, like, so downtown," said Claudia.

"That's the baddest painting I've seen," Gene said.

"It's a masterpiece," sighed Paulina. "We want one just like that for Trump Tower." Maybe she realized I wasn't going to marry Claudia, and she thought perhaps this way she could get Harry to solve her problem.

"It's definitely appearing on our cover," said Olga. "We'll print seventy-five thousand copies."

The canvas was an expressionistic rendition of Mr. O'Donnell wearing some kind of crown, and with a real rat's skeleton glued to his mouth.

"What does the crown mean?" asked Mrs. O'Donnell.

"It's a halo," Harry explained. "The painting is called *Mr.*

*O'Donnell Enters Heaven.* I hope it'll always keep Sammy's memory green."

"But Harry," I demurred, "it must be very valuable."

"Someday it will hang in the Museum of Modern Art," Harry said.

Squealing and jumping up and down, Olga announced, "We have a tribute to Mr. O'Donnell, too."

"Irma will recite the elegy," Carmen Elvira said.

"How poetic," Mother mused aloud.

"Oh, God," I heard Wilbrajan snort.

"Colombians are most poetic people," Stick pronounced.

Harry put the painting on the table, leaning against the wall. Some of the guests sat down, Mother turned off the *cumbias,* and the rest of the audience stood with their backs against the walls.

Standing in the middle of the room, Irma began. "Ladies and gentlemen, this is the first collaborative effort of The Colombian Parnassus in Shakespeare's mother tongue. Also, please excuse my pronunciation." She closed her eyes, placed her hands on her Rubenesque breasts, and began:

> For we will honor Santiago's cat Mr. O'Donnell.
> For he was the best cat in Times Square.
> For he was from the alley but loved opera.
> For he was a foe to rats and mice.
> For he loved his owner and was loved in return.
> For his heart was too big.

"It has a familiar sound," I whispered to Tim, who was standing next to me.

"It's a rip-off of Christopher Smart's 'Rejoice in the Lamb,' " Tim informed me.

Fortunately, the elegy was shorter than Smart's original, and Irma was now bringing it to a conclusion with:

> For he's alive in Heaven.
> For God loves Mr. O'Donnell.
> For now he's been immortalized by Art.

The applause was thunderous. After receiving and giving zillions of kisses and hugs, Irma approached Tim. "What do you think, Mr. Colby?" she asked, obviously eager for his approval.

Always the gentleman and the diplomat, Tim said, "It's very appropriate. Congratulations."

"Tim loved it," Irma announced loudly to her fellow muses.

Rebecca was going around the room distributing printed matter. "This is a memento of the occasion," she said to me, handing me a sheet with an engraved photograph of Mr. O'Donnell. Under it were the dates Summer 1988 (when she had found him in the alley) and August 1990. Beneath the dates, in gothic calligraphy, was Albert Schweitzer's "A Prayer to Animals."

Rebecca asked for a moment of silence so she could read her farewell prayer to Mr. O'Donnell.

"Wait a minute," Mother said. "I always pray on my knees."

Gene gave her a hand and she kneeled, setting a lighted candle in front of her. Paulina and Mrs. O'Donnell joined her.

We all read: "Hear our humble prayer, O God, for our friends the animals." Rebecca read beautifully. We finished with, "Make us, ourselves, to be true friends to animals and so to share the blessings of the merciful."

A moment of silence followed. Still on her knees, Mother was the first to speak. "I can't get over we have a wake to Mr. O'Donnell and not to Bobby who died a few days past and now is like he never was alive. For my very own part," she went on, getting up, "I think it's a useless thing to try to impress a cat. I love my two cats because they killed mouses, and they in return put up with me because I open cans for them, I'm sure."

Striking a melodramatic pose, Wilbrajan stepped forward. Oh, my God, I thought, she's going to sing one of her gloomy tangos. Instead, she said, "Let's have a minute of silence for Bobby who can't be physically here, although he's with us in spirit." Even those who had never met Bobby bowed their heads. In the reigning silence I heard stifled sobs. I was about to raise my head and wipe the tears when the bell rang. "Who could it be?" I pondered aloud. "Everyone is here."

"It's the *Post*," Rebecca screamed.

"The *Post*," parroted Paulina, horrified, "Why?"

"For Sammy and Gene help to smash the ring of drugs," Mother told her.

"Claudia, *muchacha*," Paulina screamed. "We cannot have our pictures in the papers."

"I don't know what the big deal is," Wilbrajan sneered. "My picture has been in the *Post* and the *Daily News*."

I said to the Urrutias, "You can hide in my bedroom while they take the pictures. Just close the door and it will be fine."

Mother and daughter left the scene, and I opened the door. Two *New York Post* photographers shot their flashes at me.

"Please, come in," I said.

"You're Santiago Martínez, right?" a photographer queried. "Is your nephew here, too? We'd like to get a picture of the two of you if possible."

"Don't forget the cat," the other photographer added. "What's going on here anyway, a party?"

"The cat's dead; we're having a wake for him," I said.

"That's a real human interest story. Is that a Colombian custom? Wow! What a story." The man began to fiddle with his cameras.

Carmen Elvira handed two drinks to the men.

"What is it?" asked a photographer, taking his glass and examining the contents.

*"Aguardiente Cristal,"* Carmen Elvira told them.

"Firewater," uttered one photographer. "It's like tequila or something like that, right?" He wolfed down his drink. "Thanks, lady," he said to a flirtatious Carmen Elvira.

We entered the living room where silence reigned, and everyone was on their best behavior, with the exception of Wilbrajan, who somehow had managed to get everyone off the couch where she lounged seductively like one of Goya's *majas*.

"I'm Gene," my nephew introduced himself to the photographers. "I helped Sammy catch the drug smugglers. It was like this. I was here all alone . . . like really alone with the cat. You know what I mean?"

"I hear you. You were here alone," the man said. "Now please stand up against the wall," he ordered Gene and me. Then, noticing Harry's painting, he said, "What's that? A painting of the cat? Maybe you should hold the painting between the two of you."

"Great shot," agreed his partner.

"Watch it, man. Handle with care. That painting is still wet," Harry said.

"Is that the painter?" the photographer inquired.

"That's right," I said.

The photographers took a couple of photos of Harry and his painting.

"I wish my mom were still alive to see this," Harry commented.

Now the men turned to Gene and me. We positioned ourselves at either side of the painting.

"Be sure you like print my full name and everything," Gene told the men. "And like don't forget to say I'm an actor. Is that cool?"

When the picture was taken, the photographers were rewarded with another round of drinks. Ben commissioned the men to take a group photograph. Although Wilbrajan was quite miffed she had not been asked to pose for the men, she graciously consented to be part of the group composition. Saying they had to rush to have the pictures developed for the morning edition, the *Post* men exited.

As soon as the strangers left, Claudia and Paulina emerged from the bedroom and Mother began to play her *cumbia* tapes again, and the party went into full swing. Taking Simón Bolívar out of his cage, she perched him on a finger and, grabbing a lit candle with the other hand, she began circling the room, singing along with the tape, *"La cumbia cienaguera que se baila sabrosona."* Mother was totally lit but happy. Grabbing a candle (Colombian style), Gene became her partner and, bending his knees, he started circling around her like a rooster courting a hen. Paulina was the next guest to grab a candle, and she chose as her partner Mrs. O'Donnell, who, to my utter astonishment, needed no prodding to join in. Saying that he hadn't danced *cumbia* since he was a child, Stick took my reluctant sister by

the hand and they attached themselves to the end of the line that,
led by Mother and Gene, was heading toward the front of the
apartment. Ben Ami and Hot Sauce, Olga and Irma, Harry and
Rebecca, Tim Colby and Carmen Elvira eventually tagged in. Finally,
only Claudia and myself were left alone in the room.

I was standing with my back to the windows when Claudia
approached me. It occurred to me I should ask her to dance.

"No, man. *Cumbia* is so corny. I'd rather talk to you. What's out
there?" She pointed to the alley.

"The fire escape," I said. "Want to go out?"

"Yeah, let's do that."

I opened the gates and went out first; then I gave her my hand
to help her come through the window. We stood close together on
the platform of the fire escape, looking into the dark alley and a
patch of black-coated sky. The air reeked of the uncollected garbage
in the alley, but it was cooler than in the apartment where the lit
candles created a lot of heat. We sat down in silence and Claudia
rested her head on my shoulder. I was feeling a bit uncomfortable
with the closeness of this forced intimacy when Claudia said, "Hey,
look at that." She pointed to the building opposite the fire escape.
Reinhardt, wearing tiny red bikini underwear, stood in front of his
window waving at us.

"Do you know him?" she said.

"We've talked once."

"Oh, so you're friends."

"Not really. I told you: We spoke once. That's all."

"I knew you were kinky."

"Oh, come on, Claudia," I protested. "It's not at all what you're
thinking of."

"Anyway, Sammy. What are your plans now that the cat is
dead? Rebecca is going away. You just can't live above O'Donnell's
bar for the rest of your life," she said. "Now there's nothing standing
between you and me. Why don't you come with us to Europe?"

"Oh, thanks a lot . . . but just because Mr. O'Donnell is dead,
doesn't mean anything's changed."

"That's what you think. Nothing ever remains the same for

more than a minute. It's some law of physics or something. Yay!"
she cheered abruptly. A show of strobe lights and rock music went
on in Reinhardt's apartment as he danced seductively for us, with a
hand inside his bikini underwear.

"He's humpy," Claudia said, putting an arm around my shoulders. "Oh, what a turn-on, Santiago. I just feel like jumping your
bones and smoking."

Actually, out of her punk costume, I found her appealing, less
intimidating. I was pondering this when I saw her parted lips approaching my face. We kissed on the mouth, lips closed. Yet nothing
happened: it felt like when I used to kiss Mr. O'Donnell on his cold
nose. I turned to look inside the apartment—Carmen Elvira stood
behind the window smiling at us and scribbling furiously on her pad.

The last guest left well past midnight. I started to clean up right
away but was too exhausted. I sat on the couch by the window. I
looked across the valley. Reinhardt appeared at his window, completely naked and with a hard-on. He stood there without gesticulat-
ing, looking in my direction with great concentration. I got up, went
to the phone and dialed his number.

"Reinhardt, it's Santiago," I said, feeling a hot wave come over
me. "If you want to, you can come over tonight."

Something crawling across my chest woke me up. In my
half-awake state, I brushed it aside thinking it was Mr. O'Donnell.
Then I remembered Mr. O'Donnell was dead and I opened my
eyes completely: the lean and long body of Reinhardt lay next to
mine. He breathed gently, like a child. I moved my nose within
inches of his, to drink in the air he exhaled. It smelled sweet—
like rose water. The room was cool from the air-conditioning and
he was deep in his sleep. All of a sudden, seeing this stranger on
my bed, I wanted to run away and to be by myself. I covered his
body with a sheet, pressed my lips on his and went to the kitchen
where I put on the Mr. Coffee. While I was leaning against the
sink, waiting for the coffee, I spotted Mr. O'Donnell's china on
the floor and decided to put it away. I emptied the saucers in the
trash can and stacked the dishes in the sink. Next, I decided to

get rid of the contents of his litter box. I put the empty box in the bathtub so I could wash it later.

Sitting on the couch, I savored a couple of cups of coffee. In true August form, the weather had turned warm and sticky again. I didn't have any jobs lined up for the day, so I was free to go back to bed or to do anything I wanted. I wondered whether I should wake up Reinhardt or let him sleep for as long as he wanted; or whether I should go back and get in bed with him. This I wanted to do: to hold his warm body in mine, to exchange a kiss like the night before, which seemed to last for half an hour. It was the wildest and the tenderest act I had ever engaged in. Of course I had had sexual contacts off and on with anonymous men. But this was quite different. Reinhardt was my neighbor and, after teasing each other for a long time, I felt I knew him intimately—even though I didn't know the first thing about him. Did the fact that we had been to bed mean that he was now my boyfriend? Would we ever do it again? I didn't have a clue about any of these things. I wished Bobby were still alive and I could call him and ask him these questions. Rebecca was not homophobic, but did she know anything about gay men? What was very clear to me this morning was that after all the revelations of the past few days, my life was about to change. I didn't know what any of it meant; but for the first time ever, I felt grown up, ready to leave behind the shackles of the past.

A scratching noise distracted me from my galloping thoughts. I looked around the room but didn't see anything. I decided to remove the screens on the windows. Now that Mr. O'Donnell was dead, there was no need for them. As I approached a window, I thought I spotted something on the fire escape: a pigeon, a rat? I removed the screen to see what it was. A small, gray-and-white cat, looking very scared, stared at me with large, curious green eyes. We both froze. When I could breathe again, I said, very gently, "Hi, kitty. Come in. It's okay." His shyness disappeared and, in one motion, he jumped through the open window and landed on the couch. "Meow," he said. "Meow." It occurred to me that perhaps when Mr. O'Donnell had escaped in the spring he had mated with one of the cats in the alley, and this was part of the litter. I leaned forward and offered him my open palm. He sniffed the tips of my fingers and, smelling his father, tapped my hand with his paws before stepping onto it. Bringing the little furry purring machine to my face, I said, "Your name is . . . Christopher Columbus." Then I kissed his face. He purred and purred shamelessly, just like his father.